THREE WEDDINGS AND A BABY

FAUX LOVE BILLIONAIRES

CRYSTAL MONROE

BONUS NOVELLA

Get a spicy secret baby romance delivered to your inbox.

Grab your copy of Second Chance Daddy here!

https://BookHip.com/CDDJPXR

1

TRENT

I checked my Rolex as I stepped into the elevator. It was still early, so the office would be quiet. Good.

Dillon Tech wouldn't be what it was without my employees. But I preferred not to be around them if I could help it.

They called me a loner.

They called me a lot of things.

I didn't really give a shit.

I knew who I was and what I was doing. Validation from everyone else was the last thing I needed.

On the top floor, the elevator doors opened into the executive offices.

"Oh, my God. Seriously?"

Bella's voice rang through the hall as I exited the elevator. I rounded the corner to see my executive assistant bent over a filing cabinet in the reception area.

It was hard to miss her with that hourglass figure and blonde hair falling down her shoulders. Her black pencil skirt stretched tightly over the most perfect curves I'd ever seen.

She was struggling, her ass in the air as she desperately grabbed at something behind the cabinet frame. I stood there for a moment, quiet, my mind going places it shouldn't.

I would have given anything to see her bent over my bed, casually teasing me with a move like that, a playful invitation to grab her by the waist and pump into her as hard as I could—

Fuck.

My cock twitched in my pants. Why the hell was she able to do this to me when she wasn't even trying?

I'd hired Bella Williams because she was damn good at her job, not because of her tight, curvy little body or pouty lips that made me think of *filthy* things.

That had been a bonus.

One that you're not going to follow through on.

I adjusted myself, willing my cock to cool off. I couldn't get worked up by my EA.

I was her boss.

It would be wrong on so many levels.

Besides, Annabella Williams was the best EA I'd had since I started the company.

No way was I screwing that up over a fling.

"Yes! Got it!" Bella shouted as her heels made contact with the floor, now standing upright with a sheet of paper in her hand. "That's one point for Bella and zero points for you, filing cabinet—Oh! Mr. Dillon!"

Her face turned bright red and she flipped her long hair over her shoulder. "I didn't see you."

"Morning," I grunted.

"The weather out there is incredible, isn't it?" she asked.

"Yeah," I offered.

Bella was one of those happy sunshine-and-rainbows

types. Which was another reason to keep my distance. People like that made me grumpier than I already was.

I brushed past her to get to my office. I didn't need her distracting me any more today, and I was eager to get away before she noticed the tent in my pants.

In my private office, I exhaled. The sun poured in through the full-length windows. I crossed the space and sat behind my mahogany desk.

I'd barely powered up my laptop and opened my email when Bella knocked softly on the open door with a cup of coffee in her hand.

"Mr. Dillon?" She took a few steps toward my desk before setting the mug down in front of me. "I wanted to make sure you had your coffee first thing."

"Thank you, Bella," I said. "But what about the morning reports? And the mail?"

"Coffee first, Mr. Dillon," she confidently replied. "Then the rest. You know the drill."

My brow furrowed in frustration. "So, you're ignoring my request? Is this a mutiny, Ms. Williams?"

"Not a mutiny, Mr. Dillon." She shook her head. "I just know how you are. How you work most efficiently. You need coffee before you start the day."

I chuckled. "So, you think you know me?"

"No. I *know* that I know you, Mr. Dillon." She beamed. "And now, if you'll excuse me, I'm going to give you a few minutes before I bring in your mail and the morning reports."

She turned around, her head held high like she wasn't bothered by anything I said, like she was completely unaffected by my attitude.

That was something else that drove me crazy when it

came to Bella Williams. Nothing ever ruined her good mood.

She had such an upbeat spirit that it sometimes threatened to infect me. That was another reason to keep her far away from my general direction.

Optimism was poison in the boardroom. Poison in any kind of serious work, really.

I slowly sipped my coffee, my mind still too focused on Bella, even if I was mentally listing reasons to keep our relationship strictly professional. As I worked through my anti-Bella thoughts, her words floated back through my head.

I know that I know you, Mr. Dillon.

Ha. She couldn't have been more wrong about that.

If she really knew my preferences, she would be on top of me right now, that pencil skirt on my floor and my hands unbuttoning her blouse—

"Here you go. Here's your mail." Bella slid a stack of bound mail across my desk with a bright smile. "And I've got the morning reports here, too, whenever you're ready for me to go over them."

"Yep. Give me just a sec." I held up a finger as I quickly flipped through the mail.

It was mostly junk from wannabe employees and aspiring entrepreneurs, all hoping that kiss-ass handwritten letters would help them stand out from the crowd. I was ready to abandon the entire pile.

But then a familiar name on one of the envelopes caught my eye.

Grant Dillon.

My family sent everything to my office, rather than to my house. They figured I lived here.

They weren't wrong.

I tore it open to reveal a wedding invitation.

Another one.

This time from my brother.

This was the third wedding invitation I'd received from a family member in the last few weeks, the others coming from my sister and my cousin.

"What the fuck?" I said absent-mindedly.

"Is everything okay, Mr. Dillon?" There was concern in Bella's voice. "Can I help?"

"You can go over the morning reports," I snapped. "Have a seat. Let's get at it."

Unfazed, she took a seat in front of my desk, the reports held out across her lap. She read through the updates from each department manager.

I couldn't focus on a single word she said.

I was still lost in the deluge of upcoming weddings I'd be expected to attend.

Images of white dresses and tiered wedding cakes swirled in my head.

Was everyone getting married this summer except for me?

"So, marketing needs you to sign off on an elephant purchase."

"What?"

"Marketing needs you to sign off on an elephant purchase," she calmly repeated. "Or *potential* elephant purchase, I should say. No guarantee they'll be able to get one, but they still want to try."

A smile played around her lips, and she broke into laughter.

"Sorry, I couldn't resist," she said. "You were so distracted I figured I could say anything and get away with it."

"And the best you could do was ask for an elephant for

marketing?" I laughed now, too. "This would've been a perfect time to ask for a raise, Bella."

"Eh. The elephant would've been more fun. We could set it up in the break room and let everyone feed it peanuts during lunch."

"Why do I get the impression you've thought about this before?"

"You show me someone who hasn't considered a break room elephant, and I'll show you a liar." She chuckled again, then her expression turned serious. "Is everything okay, though, Mr. Dillon? Ever since I brought you the mail, you've been out of it. Do you want to talk about it?"

I looked at her, surprised. It wasn't her job to listen to my drama. I always talked to her about business—that was her job. But we never discussed personal shit.

Her big hazel eyes were trained on my face, her expression sympathetic. She waited for me to make the call.

"Do you have a big family, Bella?" I asked.

She shook her head slowly. "No. I have some distant relatives in other states. But here in LA, it's just me."

I nodded, feeling a pang of guilt I didn't know that detail about her. But why should I? She was my employee, not my girlfriend.

I swallowed. *Definitely* not my girlfriend.

"Well, I have a *huge* family," I said. "They're very pushy and very loud. And apparently, they're all getting married at the same time."

"What do you mean?" Bella asked. Amusement danced in her eyes.

"This summer I've been invited to three weddings. *Three.* My cousin Patrick's getting married in Vegas, then my sister Anya in Colorado, and then my brother Grant in Napa Valley."

"Destination weddings all around?"

"Yes," I harrumphed. "Which only makes it worse."

"I love going to weddings," she said with a dreamy smile.

I shook my head. "It's not my scene."

"Oh, come on. You get to dress up, you get free food and a fun reception. If you're lucky, there's a bit of drama. And it's not your responsibility to make sure things run smoothly. What's not to love?"

"The fact that it's *my* family," I deadpanned. "There's a *lot* of drama, and I can't get out of it because I'm related to them. I'll never hear the end of it if I don't go."

Bella smiled, but she tried hard not to. "I guess that could make things complicated."

I sighed. "You have no idea." I glanced at her, trying to decide how much to tell her. "The thing is, my family is full of matchmakers."

"Yeah?" Her eyes sparkled. "That sounds interesting."

"Not when I'm the target." I bristled. "If I don't have a date, my mom will arrange one for me."

Her eyes still danced with amusement, but she had the good sense not to laugh.

The more I thought about the weddings, the more it pissed me off. My family really got my hackles up.

"Really? That sounds—"

"Don't tell me it sounds sweet," I cut her off. "It's not. The last two family weddings I attended were disasters."

"Why?" she asked, clearly trying to hide her smile.

"Because my mom set me up with dates I didn't want. She could at least run these women by me first." I drove a hand through my hair. "And when anyone in my family gets married, it's a huge production. It's much more than a ceremony and a reception."

"It is?"

"Yes. They make it a multi-day thing with dinners and parties. It gobbles up your whole weekend. And I get stuck making small talk for three days with some girl my mom picked out."

"No offense, Mr. Dillon, but I'm not really seeing the problem here."

"What do you mean?"

"If you need to bring a date, just ask one of the women falling all over themselves to be with you," she said. "One of your... *friends*."

I bristled at that.

I might have played the field for a few months after my last serious relationship ended. But not lately.

I'd gotten sick of waking up to another nameless face in my bed. Maybe it was because I was getting older—I was forty now. These days, one-night stands didn't do it for me.

"Or ask whoever you're seeing right now," Bella continued. "Even if it's a casual relationship, it's still better than a random person you don't know."

"I don't do casual," I said, correcting her assumption. "And when was the last time I had you order flowers for anyone?"

Bella's brows pulled together as she thought about it. Fuck, she could be so cute.

"When I started working here, two years ago..." Bella's words trailed off as she replied. "Wait. You're not saying it's been two years since you were serious with anyone—"

Her mouth snapped shut, and she shook her head. "You know what? It's none of my business."

"I appreciate the restraint."

"Still. This wedding date thing is not a problem, if you ask me." Bella beamed again.

"Oh? And why is that?"

"Because you're a very rich man," she started. "And a very rich man can always *Pretty Woman* the whole thing if he needs to."

"What?"

"You know, hire an escort to pretend to be a woman you're dating. You've never seen *Pretty Woman*?"

Her mouth fell open with shock as I shook my head.

"Just don't fall in love with her, and you should be fine," she said. "Or wait. Maybe *do* fall in love with her? I don't want to spoil the ending of the movie, but you'll see what I'm talking about when you watch it—"

"I'll take that under consideration."

"Which part? Watching the movie? Or hiring an escort?"

"That'll be all, Bella. That'll be all."

2

TRENT

*W*ith a nod, she stood and walked to the door. I caught myself staring at her ass.

Again.

Fuck, Bella had me mesmerized. I'd always found her attractive, but these days something about her drove me crazy.

I didn't know what it was. She was still the same person, and so was I.

But I couldn't stop staring at her. Couldn't tear my eyes from her face. Or her body.

And the way she stood up to me when everyone else backed away... It was icing on the cake.

As the hours ticked by, I tried to focus on work. I threw myself into business meetings in the morning and worked on reports through the afternoon. I blazed through emails and phone calls—whatever it took to keep my mind off the weddings.

And Bella.

Her words echoed in my mind, no matter how hard I tried to block them out.

You could hire an escort.

Maybe it was a good idea. Not quite in the way she'd meant it, but that didn't matter.

I was a businessman, and if there was one thing I did well, it was business.

The more I thought about it, the more it made sense.

This was the only way I could endure the three weddings. There was no way in hell I'd risk a blind date with some random woman my mom picked out for me. Let alone three of them.

And now that my sister and my brother had invited me to their weddings, I *had* to go. As irritated as my family made me, I couldn't just not show up.

By six o'clock, I knew what I had to do.

I always worked late, and today I waited until I knew most of the employees had left. Bella would still be at her desk—she stayed as long as I needed her.

"Bella, come see me," I said, pressing the button on my phone that accessed a direct line to her desk.

A moment later, she opened my door.

"Have a seat," I said.

Bella nodded and walked to the chair she'd occupied this morning, sitting down. She crossed her legs at the ankle —finishing school perfect—and waited patiently.

"I want you to be my date for the three weddings this summer," I said. "If you agree, you'll have to pretend to be my girlfriend around my family. It's the only way to keep them off my back."

Bella's eyes widened. "What?"

"You heard me," I said. "It's a business deal, not a favor. I'll pay you for your time, just like you suggested."

"I didn't suggest you take *me*!" she cried out.

"I know. But I'm not interested in hiring a stranger to be

my date. You already work for me, and we have an under-standing. We can keep things professional."

She gasped, looking for the right words.

I took the opportunity of her stunned silence to finish my offer.

"I'm thinking three hundred thousand dollars for the three weddings. I'm paying for your discretion, as well as your acting skills."

I knew Bella could play a role. Anyone who could stay composed and professional when I was on a rampage was a born actor.

She blinked at me. "Three hundred..." Her voice trailed off, and she mouthed *thousand dollars,* as if she was afraid to say it.

"Yes. I'll cover all the travel expenses as well. And this is an independent arrangement. If you say no, it won't affect your job."

"And if I say yes?" she asked in a breathy voice.

Her eyes were still wide. I wasn't sure how to read her reaction.

Was it a good thing that she looked so stunned? Or a bad thing?

"Then you'll keep it a secret from the rest of the office," I said. "You understand my reasoning, I'm sure."

Bella swallowed hard and nodded. I watched her care-fully. A part of me was suddenly nervous she would say no.

It's just a work contract. It means nothing either way.

"Can I take some time to think about it?" Bella asked.

It wasn't the response I'd expected. I wanted an answer now, but I couldn't blame her for needing some time. I'd just sprung this on her.

Besides, it wasn't a hard no, and that was saying some-thing. I could work with that.

"Let me know tomorrow morning," I said.

"Okay," Bella said. She looked uncomfortable, and her hands fidgeted in her lap. "Is there anything else?"

I shook my head. "I'm about to wrap up here, and then I'm done for the day. You can head out."

She nodded and stood. "Goodnight, Mr. Dillon."

"Goodnight, Bella."

She turned and walked out of the office, closing the door quietly behind her. I let out a breath I hadn't realized I'd been holding and tilted my head back against my chair.

God, I had to wait the whole night for an answer.

Why was I so tense? Why did I care so much if she said yes?

If she said no, it would be a kick to the balls.

I'd told her she could say no, that it wouldn't affect her job. I was planning to follow through on that.

If she declined, I could still hire an escort. But I didn't like the idea of taking a random woman to my family's weddings. Bella and I knew each other. That meant something to me.

I couldn't imagine myself with a stranger on my arm, introducing an escort to my family.

She had to agree. It would spare me my dignity and save me from my matchmaking, meddling family.

But if I was being honest, there was something that excited me about spending time with Bella outside the office. I didn't expect anything physical from her, but the thought of spending three weekends with my EA made my pulse race.

I just hoped she'd say yes.

3

BELLA

*O*h, my *God.*

When Trent asked me to pretend to be his girl-friend for the weddings, I had the good grace to keep a straight face.

After more than two years working for Trent Dillon, I had one hell of a poker face.

Trent was known around the office as *Diablo*—a fitting name for the devil he resembled when he was in a bad mood.

As his executive assistant, I'd learned to hide my emotions.

What kind of emotions?

Well, the frustration that I had with him for being an ass sometimes, for starters.

And, if I was being *totally* honest, the physical attraction I'd felt since I walked into his office the very first time.

He was, after all, a gift from the gods. An Adonis among us mere mortals. Physically, at least. Even on the days he was a total jackass to his employees.

Trent was the kind of man women forgave because he

had the charm that made knees go weak and hearts flutter, that made logical thoughts leave the brain.

With dark brown hair and baby-blue eyes, he could do everything wrong, and with one puppy-dog look, a flex of his bicep and an arrogant grin, he was right back on top.

Just where I would want him to be, too.

Stop it, I scolded myself as I shut his office door behind me.

As soon as I was out of sight, I leaned against the wall and let out the breath I'd been holding.

What. The. Fuck.

"Hey," Angie said, walking toward me as she stepped off the elevator.

"Hey," I said with a smile.

"Ready to get out of here?" she asked.

"Yes." I nodded enthusiastically as I headed toward my desk to grab my things.

Angie was my friend and roommate—we'd shared an apartment for several years. We also both worked at Dillon Tech.

She'd been in human resources for ages, and when it was announced that Trent Dillon needed an EA, she'd told me about the opening. It was partly thanks to her I got this job.

"What's up?" Angie asked with a frown. "You look like you've seen a ghost."

I swallowed, pausing. "I'm fine. It's just... Trent's assigning me a tough project. I just heard about it."

"Let's go already." Angie ran her hand through her dark brown hair, pulling it back into a ponytail. "I could use a drink."

"Me too," I breathed.

I was still reeling. Trent Dillon wanted me to be his *girlfriend*.

Okay, no.

He wanted me to *pretend* to be his girlfriend.

But judging by the way he kept everyone at arm's length, that was pretty much the same thing.

And either way... there was good money involved in this, and I could certainly use it. In a city as expensive as LA, I was just scraping by, despite my generous salary.

"Hello? Earth to Bella," Angie teased as we rode the elevator down to the lobby. I was in a daze, and I suddenly realized I hadn't heard a word she'd said. "You're not even listening."

"Sorry, Angie," I said. "I'm a little distracted."

Angie rolled her eyes as the doors opened into the lobby. We left the building together and got in her car in the parking lot. We took turns driving to work, and this week it was her turn.

I concentrated on her story about her argument with her manager as she drove us to our apartment building and parked. Instead of going inside the building, we walked toward our favorite bar, The Grove.

It was only two blocks away, which suited me just fine. We were never tempted to take stupid risks like driving after a few drinks.

The Grove was a dive bar with a laid-back atmosphere. It featured an amateur hour for musicians to cut their teeth and—our favorite—drink specials on Wednesdays that were so cheap they had to be a loss for the owner.

I loved it here.

We walked in and nodded at Charlie, the bartender on duty tonight.

"What will it be, ladies?" Charlie asked when we sat

down in our usual booth toward the back of the bar. Sitting at the bar itself felt too exposed to talk about personal things, which we usually did when we came to drink here.

"I'll have a vodka tonic," I said.

"Keto mojito. You know me, Charlie. Always watching my waist."

Angie was reed-thin and lived on low-carb food and drinks. Her model-like figure was beautiful, but she was so different from me. When I met her in college, I'd been intimidated by her looks and her constant focus on them, but I'd learned to love my curves since then.

Charlie grinned and nodded. "Coming right up."

He turned to leave and Angie looked at me, her eyes narrowing.

"So, tell me."

"Tell you what?"

"What's going on with you? You're *never* this distracted about work, so it must be something else."

I laughed. "You know me too well."

"We *live* together," Angie pointed out. "If I don't know you by now, I'm not paying attention very well, am I?"

I chuckled and shook my head.

"It's this thing with Trent... it's not exactly a work project, per se."

"Then what is it?"

"Can you keep a secret?" I asked.

Angie lifted an eyebrow. "You know I can."

I took a deep breath. "He has to go to three weddings this summer for family members who are getting married."

"And?" Angie prompted impatiently.

"He wants *me* to go with him. As... his fake girlfriend," I whispered, as if I was afraid to say the words.

"Are you serious?"

"Very."

I watched Angie's shocked expression as I told her the whole story.

"So you'd travel to three different cities with him?" she asked.

"Yep."

"And pretend to be his girlfriend in front of his family?" Her eyebrows rose. "*Diablo's* girlfriend?"

"That's the deal. If I agree to do it."

She shuddered. "Do you really think you could pull it off? No one is *that* good of an actress."

"I don't know. Maybe I could do it for the money he's offering. I'm supposed to give him an answer tomorrow morning."

"Sleeping on it isn't much time at all," Angie mused. "It's a big decision."

"It is," I agreed.

Angie shook her head. "I can't imagine it. You and Diablo, sitting in a tree! First comes love, then comes marriage... Bella, you could be Diablo's *bride*!"

I cut her off. "Hold it right there. The illusion won't go that far, trust me. I won't let it."

"It's still insane. You'd have to act like you *like* Diablo." She stuck out her tongue. "Three hundred grand, though? Not bad."

Charlie arrived with our drinks, and I gladly took my cocktail.

"Charlie, would you pay someone to date you?" Angie asked him.

I nudged her with my foot under the table. She ignored me.

"What?" Charlie asked, confused. "Do you think I'd

need to *pay* someone? I like to think I'm a nice enough guy that someone would actually *want* to be with me."

"You're great," I said to him. "Don't listen to her. After her mojito, she'll talk more sense."

Charlie chuckled. "I'll never understand women," he said as he walked away.

I gave Angie a sharp look. "You're not supposed to tell anyone," I pointed out. "I'm telling you this in confidence. You know what that means, right?"

"Oh, come on. I didn't tell Charlie anything. I just asked an innocent question. He'll never guess."

I sighed. Half the population of Los Angeles knew who Trent Dillon was. He was a self-made billionaire with an empire he'd built from the ground up. The last thing I needed was for rumors to start circulating before I even said yes to him.

"So, you're going to do it, then?" Angie asked.

"I think so," I said.

"But... it's Trent *Diablo* Dillon we're talking about here."

"I need the money," I admitted. "You know how things are. Despite my good salary, it's a struggle to make my student loan payments each month. Our rent and utilities are so high, I can barely keep my car running. If the clunker breaks down one more time, I'm screwed. If I do this, I could buy a new car, get out of debt... This could change everything." My eyes lit up. "I could maybe even make a down payment on a house."

"I thought you liked being roommates," Angie pouted.

"I love being roommates," I said. "But I'm twenty-eight now. I didn't think at this age I'd still be trying to find my feet, you know? It's not like it's an immoral way to make money, anyway. I'm sure we'll sign a contract and everything."

God, talking about it like this made it seem so *clinical*.

Wasn't that what Trent had in mind, though? It was a business agreement, after all. There was nothing personal about it, aside from my *personal* feelings for him.

My feelings were beside the point, though.

"Do you think you'll be able to handle the close proximity?" Angie asked.

"Yeah, why wouldn't I?" I answered almost too quickly. "Trust me, the last thing on my mind is sleeping with Diablo."

Actually, that had been one of the *first* things on my mind.

But I was wise enough to know sleeping with him would be dumb.

I took a sip of my vodka tonic. "I have more sense than that."

Angie's eyebrows rose over the rim of her glass as she sipped her mojito.

"Honey, I was talking about his grumpy mood swings," she said. "I didn't mean sex."

I flushed. *Oh.*

"Are you attracted to him?" Angie asked, her lips curling into a smile.

"No." I took another long sip of my drink.

"You are!" Angie cried out, her eyes sparkling, an incredulous smile growing. "Oh, my God, why didn't you tell me you had a crush on Diablo?"

"Because I don't," I said hotly.

Angie laughed with glee. "Don't try to deny it, Bella Williams. I know you too well—you said so yourself!"

I shook my head, my cheeks warm.

I'd been attracted to Trent since I started working for him. Not the teenager kind of crush where I tripped over my feet and doodled his name on a notepad—I was an adult. I could keep my feelings in check. But that didn't mean I didn't feel attracted to the guy. As insane as it was.

"Seriously, though, if that's the case..." Angie studied my face. "It might be hard to resist him, if you're spending all that time with the guy. What if you do something you'll regret?"

I rolled my eyes. "I've spent every workday for two years with Trent without doing anything I regret. I see him every day and keep it professional."

"Right," Angie said skeptically. She didn't believe me.

"I'm serious," I said. "I can handle it. It's just another work project."

I was more than capable of taking care of myself and not falling for Trent Dillon. He was a pain in my ass on a *good* day.

He was also my boss, so I'd been very careful with my feelings around him. It didn't matter that he was scorching hot, drop-dead gorgeous, and the idea of being with him made me melt into a puddle of need.

This was strictly business.

"So, you've decided?" she asked.

I nodded. "I'm doing it. And *only* for what that money can do for my future."

"Well, then," Angie said, slapping the table. "We should have shots."

"That's a bad idea on a weeknight," I said.

"Come on, live a little," Angie laughed. "We're grown-ups. We can do what we want." She waved at Charlie and ordered two tequilas.

I groaned.

"We have to celebrate your windfall," Angie said, leaning over and squeezing my hand.

"I'm not sure I want to celebrate," I said.

But Angie was incorrigible, and she waved my protests away.

I sighed and sat back, preparing myself for a night that wouldn't end soon. It was okay. I liked hanging out with Angie, and maybe a bit of alcohol was a good thing to take off the edge.

Because suddenly, I was nervous.

I was, after all, going to pretend to be Trent Dillon's girlfriend.

If there was ever a tall order, this was it.

Diablo's bride, Angie had teased, but I shook off the thought. She was being dramatic, as usual.

I wouldn't let it go that far. Obviously.

4

BELLA

When I stepped out of the elevator onto the top floor of Dillon Tech the next morning, my stomach turned.

I didn't know if it was nerves or the aftermath of last night's drinking—maybe a bit of both.

Trent arrived soon after me—I heard him entering his private office as I made his coffee at the machine in the staff kitchen.

With a deep breath, I walked to his office, knocking on the door before letting myself in.

This was all routine. Going through the motions should have grounded me. Instead, it just made me more nervous.

"Good morning, Mr. Dillon," I said brightly.

Trent sat up, his face open and eager. "You're here." He didn't usually look this interested to see me. My stomach twisted again.

"Where else would I be?" I asked with a nervous chuckle.

I set his coffee on his desk and sat down in the chair I

always occupied for our morning meetings, but I didn't say anything.

Instead, an awkward silence grew between us.

"So?" Trent asked. "Did you give it some thought?"

"I did," I said.

I gave it *a lot* of thought, in fact. After the shots, I'd had some doubts. I'd started to worry I would get in over my head if I said yes.

It had kept me up half the night—I'd tossed and turned until the early hours of the morning. In the end, though, I knew I couldn't turn down so much money.

"And?" he asked.

His face was carefully curated, as his expressions usually were—I'd seen him in enough business meetings to know what that mask looked like.

But there was something different in his eyes.

Was he... hopeful?

"I've decided to take your offer," I said diplomatically.

A smile spread across his face. "Good."

"I have a few conditions, though."

"Oh?" He settled back in his chair, resting his arms on the armrests.

I knew this faux-casual attitude he took when he was negotiating. It made me that much more nervous to realize I was negotiating with Trent Dillon.

"No sex, and no sharing a bed," I said.

Trent blinked at me, then scoffed. "That's not a problem." A smile played around his lips. "I'll be sure to *restrain* myself."

"Good," I said. "Then we're on the same page."

"These weddings won't be easy, you know," he said. "You'll have to be a damn good actress and play the part of my committed girlfriend to make it convincing."

"I can put on a face," I said. "Trust me."

"Great. And I have a rule of my own," he said.

"Sure."

"No getting emotionally attached."

It was my turn to blink at him. It was all I could do to keep from bursting out laughing.

"We have to continue our professional working relationship in the office," he said. "And after the third wedding, we'll carry on like none of this ever happened."

I nodded, composing myself. "That won't be a problem."

"No?" Trent said as he flashed a charming smile at me.

"Not at all," I said tightly, looking him dead in the eye.

He chuckled, and the sound was like velvet. My body tightened in all the right places.

I harbored a lot of lust for Trent Dillon, that was for sure. But love? No way.

I wouldn't fall for him. He was grumpy and difficult, and getting attached hadn't even crossed my mind.

"Good," he said, echoing my earlier response.

"If that will be all, Mr. Dillon, we can get started on the morning reports—"

"Trent," he interrupted me. "I mean, as long as we're alone, you might as well get used to calling me that. You can't call me Mr. Dillon around my family."

I nodded. "Trent."

He tilted his head a little, his eyes darkening when I used his first name. He cleared his throat.

"Forget the morning reports for now. I need you to get started on the travel arrangements," he said. "We'll need flight plans and accommodations for Las Vegas, Colorado, and Napa Valley."

I nodded, making mental notes.

"Here are the wedding invitations with the location information and dates."

He handed me the three invitations from their spot on his desk. I looked down at the sleek envelopes, my heart picking up speed.

"The first wedding in Vegas is two weeks away. Let my pilot know we'll fly around 5:00 p.m. on Friday."

I nodded, trying not to look stunned. I'd never get used to the fact that Trent had private jets.

"We'll share a suite at my cousin's hotel to make it look real, but you can book one with two bedrooms."

The tension that had coiled in my stomach when he talked about sharing a suite unwound a little.

"Oh, good," I said. "I was just thinking how much you'd hate sleeping on the couch."

Trent chuckled, his eyes sparkling. "Who says I'd be the one to sleep on the couch?"

"If you were any kind of gentleman at all, you'd never consider making me give up the bed."

Trent offered a mischievous smile. His expression was teasing—he was enjoying this.

Something told me he wouldn't *ever* make me take the couch.

And the fact that he actually was a gentleman irritated me.

"Here," he said and reached into his pocket. He took out his wallet and handed me a black credit card.

"What's this for?" I asked, confused. Whenever I made a booking for Trent, it was automatically charged to his account.

"That's for you to go buy some items for the trip." He gave me a quick look up and down. It felt scandalous, but oddly delicious. "Clothes, shoes, bags. Whatever you need."

Right. Because I didn't dress like someone in his *circles* would?

I was almost offended, but I couldn't deny that I didn't exactly have a designer-label budget. I wore off-brand clothes, some of which I'd thrifted. My wardrobe wouldn't fly with Trent's family, I had to assume.

"We'll spend a weekend in each destination, so make sure you have enough to wear for the weddings, daytime outings, and evening dinners."

I hesitated before I took the card.

"The card has no limit," Trent said.

"I won't go crazy."

Trent shrugged and turned his attention to his computer, dismissing me.

I turned and left the office, my heart racing, blood rushing in my ears.

A hot date—even if it was just pretend—and an unlimited credit card? This felt like a movie.

~

"I can't believe Diablo's paying for your shopping spree!" Angie cried out as we headed toward my car on Saturday morning. Trent's credit card was in my purse.

It was two days after I'd agreed to the arrangement, and now it was time to shop.

"It's not that big of a deal," I said.

"What? You're kidding, right? It's a *huge* deal! And it's the best way to get revenge on Diablo, if you ask me. I'd clean him out."

I rolled my eyes. "That's not the point of all this, you know. I'm not trying to take advantage of him."

Angie shook her head. "You're too nice, Bella. He's a dick, and he deserves someone to show him what's what."

"You really don't like him, do you?"

"The guy is an ass," she said as she sat in the passenger seat.

"You never work with him!"

"I don't have to work with him to know what people say about him. What *you* say about him."

I sighed. "So, he's a grumpy SOB sometimes, but that doesn't make him a bad guy. He's just rough around the edges, but there's good inside everyone."

"Not Diablo," Angie said confidently.

I shrugged it off and started the car. She didn't work with him, and she wasn't going to be directly involved in any of this.

"Well, thanks for going shopping with me." I turned my car, clanking and rumbling, into the road. "I need your help picking stuff out."

"Of course! Where are we going, anyway?"

"I'm not sure," I admitted. "Somewhere downtown?"

"Oh, my God. We *have to* go to Rodeo Drive!"

I shook my head. "I can't do that. Everything's way too expensive there."

"That's where you're going to find the clothes he wants you to show up in. Everyone who's rich and stylish shops there, and you want to look the part, don't you? I bet his family goes there, too."

I didn't know if that was true, but Angie had a good point. If I wanted to pull this off, I had to go all out, and Rodeo Drive was the best place to do that.

I headed toward Beverly Hills, and Angie switched on the radio. It was a hot day and we rolled down our windows, singing to the radio as the warm wind blew through the windows.

Rodeo Drive was just how they showed it in the movies —extravagant, exciting, riddled with people who had tons of money to spend. I'd only driven past the fancy stores before, wishing I had enough money to shop there. I'd never actually gone inside one.

I was overwhelmed as soon as we parked and approached the shopping area. Angie, however, seemed to know exactly where to go and what to look for.

"How do you know so much about this stuff?" I asked as she guided us toward an intimidating-looking store. "The last time we went shopping together, we both got jeans from Target."

Angie giggled. "Just because I don't have the budget to look stunning doesn't mean I don't know what stunning is."

I rolled my eyes. "You always look stunning, no matter what you wear."

"Thanks," she said, shimmying her shoulders before we walked into the first boutique.

Everything from cocktail dresses to ballgowns hung on the racks—and they were all incredible.

A sales assistant walked over to us, dressed to the nines herself. When I glanced at her feet, I saw she wore four-inch stiletto heels. How did she walk around on those all day?

"How can I help you, ladies?" she asked.

I half expected her to turn up her nose since we didn't dress like the other customers, but she was perfectly sweet and helpful. When Angie told her what we needed, the assistant's eyes sparkled.

"I think I have just what you're looking for," she said as she led me to a fitting room.

She brought me a series of dresses to try on. Some of them were meant to be more casual for a daytime event, others were for a fancy dinner or a cocktail event. Angie helped me pick colors that worked with my fair skin and blonde hair.

I was lucky to have her along. Angie had great taste in fashion, and she knew everything about color schemes.

After three fashion boutiques, I was armed with several gorgeous dresses for the weddings, rehearsal dinners, and casual events. I had to admit, the clothes were fabulous.

Next, we browsed a few shoe stores. Angie helped me choose stilettos, strappy heels, and ballerina flats, matching them all to different outfits.

After we took the purchases to the car, I thought I was finished. But Angie reminded me that my duffel bag and roller carry-on with the broken wheels would likely embarrass Trent—and me. She was right.

So I bought a new carry-on and a suitcase from the least expensive line in the store. Then a couple purses—one for daytime and one for night. Both would go with anything I wore.

Then Angie pushed me into a jewelry store. I thought jewelry would be much too extravagant, but Angie encouraged me to buy a few necklaces, earrings, and bracelets so I'd fit in with Trent's family.

I tried to go for the least expensive items so Trent wouldn't be in shock at his credit card bill.

Angie insisted on one more store after that, where we looked at blouses, pants, shorts and sneakers.

"Just in case you need something *really* casual," she said.

"I don't think I'm going to need this much," I said as she picked out another outfit for me.

"It's three weekends with rich people, honey. You're going to want to stock up. Trust me."

I giggled and shook my head. Angie was in her element.

Although shopping wasn't quite my thing and I'd never followed high fashion, it was a lot of fun shopping in these high-end stores. I never wore clothes this expensive, and the luxury fabrics felt heavenly against my skin.

I looked different when I saw myself in the mirror—not the girl with the financial troubles, with no family to speak of.

I looked... *sophisticated*. I barely recognized myself.

As I reached for Trent's credit card to pay at the last store and glanced at the total, I nearly fainted.

I'd been very careful not to take advantage of Trent—I'd gotten only what I needed to play the part. Still, it was more than I'd spent on clothes in my entire adult life.

My phone pinged with a text. I fished it out of my purse and saw Trent's name on the screen.

Having fun? You're holding back. I thought you'd spend more.

Really? He'd expected me to spend *more*? I'd already spent a ton.

I replied, **Got everything I need.**

I waited, but there was no reply from him. Still, his message had set me at ease.

"Let's go get something to eat," Angie said. "I'm starving. Shopping is hard work."

I laughed. We dropped off my latest purchases in the car, then we found a restaurant not too far off.

When we stepped in, the restaurant was as chic as everything else we'd seen today, and we sat down at a table. Angie ordered a salad, as she always did. I ordered a gourmet sandwich.

"He's going to die when he sees you in those outfits,"

Angie said, sipping the sparkling water the server had brought us.

"I'm hoping they will help me fit in with his family. That's the main goal." Secretly, I hoped Angie was right— that Trent would like what he saw.

"He'll die and go to... hell. Where he belongs," Angie said, laughing at her own joke.

I gave her a weak smile and bit into my sandwich.

"Get it? Hell? Diablo?"

"I get it," I said.

Angie shook her head, irritated. "Come on, that's funny."

"He really isn't that bad, you know."

She blinked. "Since when do you defend your boss?"

I shrugged. "I don't know."

I had no idea why, but suddenly I didn't want to hear Angie making fun of Trent. Nothing had changed, other than the fact that I had agreed to his proposal.

He'd looked so hopeful when he was waiting for my answer that day in his office. Something in his eyes made me think this was more serious to him than he let on.

Trent had a sweet, almost vulnerable side to him about the whole thing, and I didn't want to poke at it.

The first wedding in Las Vegas was two weeks away. It wasn't a lot of time at all. I'd booked the flight and the hotel suite, but things in the office had returned to business as usual.

Except it wasn't *quite* like it used to be.

The next two days after Trent and I decided to do this, I felt awkward at the office. How was I supposed to act around him?

Logically, acting normal was the way to go—it wasn't like anything had changed between us. We weren't *actually* dating.

Trent treated me differently, though. Not so much that he wasn't himself. He still had moments where he looked like a thunderstorm and he barked orders at everyone. He still had moments where he treated me like I didn't know exactly what I was doing, even though I'd done it all for two years.

He wasn't as grumpy as he usually was with me, though. Sometimes, when he looked like he would explode, he softened instead and changed his tone.

He also started sharing tidbits about his life with me.

My parents are retired, with a perfectly happy marriage. So my mom gets in her kids' business because she has no drama of her own.

Trent was the oldest of five kids, and he'd grown up in a happy family with people who'd always been close to each other. It sounded like a picture-perfect childhood, with everyone caring and being there for each other.

When he told me that, a pang shot through my chest.

My own childhood had been lonely. I was an only child. My parents were always broke, and I spent a lot of time alone as they juggled multiple jobs.

Then I'd lost both my parents, and my world collapsed.

My cousin Patrick, and brother Grant and I used to be so tight. We called ourselves the Three Musketeers.

When I'd asked him if that would make him D'Artagnan, he only scoffed at me.

I wished I had a close-knit family like that.

But Trent seemed irritated by his family, like he didn't want to spend time with them. He told me that he'd started growing apart from them a couple of years ago.

"Why?" I asked when he told me.

He shrugged. "Things change."

"I don't know... if I had people that close to me, I would do what I could to never lose them."

Trent only grunted in response before he eyed me carefully.

"You don't have family like that?"

I shook my head. "My dad passed away when I was seventeen, and my mother when I was twenty. I was an only child. Besides a few distant relatives I've never met, I don't have any other family. My parents met in foster care, so I don't even have grandparents."

"Oh, fuck," Trent said, his lips pursed into a thin line. "I'm so sorry, Bella."

I looked at him. I'd never seen him look like this. Or speak to me in a gentle tone of voice.

It was *shocking*.

"That must be so hard," he said.

"It's not as hard as it used to be," I admitted. "Pain gets better eventually, right?"

"I don't think it gets better," Trent said softly. "You just get used to it."

I didn't know what to say to that, so I nodded.

"Well, I better get back to work," I said after a moment of silence.

With a lump in my throat, I left his office and went back to my desk.

I tried not to focus on how soft his eyes had been. I never knew Trent Dillon could be so sweet.

Why was he being nice to me?

It made me nervous. I'd thought I could handle this because I knew just who Trent Dillon was. I could handle him because he was a grump, and I'd become a pro at grump-wrangling.

This side of him, though, was new. I wasn't sure what to make of it.

It's because he's relieved he has a date to save his ass from embarrassment.

That was what it *had* to be, I decided. He wasn't really being nice. He was just grateful he didn't have to spend a ton of money on an escort he'd never see again.

This didn't mean anything.

But it didn't *feel* like it meant nothing.

It felt good.

5

BELLA

*F*inally, the time for the first wedding came.

It felt like it was on top of me immediately —two weeks had flown by. Yet at the same time, it felt like I'd waited for this in anxious anticipation forever.

We flew to Vegas on one of Trent's private jets. Yeah, *one* of them, because he had more.

"What do you use the others for if you're just one person?" I asked when we boarded. "It's like having more than one car, too. You can only use one at a time."

"It depends on what I need to do," Trent said. "Sometimes, when I have a lot of guests, I use the bigger ones. Sometimes, I want to fly solo and then I don't need anything more than the six-seater."

"You have your pilot's license?" I asked.

"Of course," Trent said. "Didn't you know that?"

I shook my head. Trent hadn't been very forthcoming about his personal life with me until two weeks ago. It felt like I was getting to see a whole new side of him.

No, scratch that—I was seeing a whole new *person*.

"For the record," Trent said with a chuckle when he buckled himself in, "I have a lot of cars, too."

I rolled my eyes and buckled myself into the cream leather seat, ready for takeoff.

The flight was quick, and I enjoyed the royal treatment from the attendant. I drank champagne and sampled a fruit and cheese tray while looking out the window at the scenery below.

This fancy billionaire life was something I could get used to.

The casino and hotel that his cousin owned was only a short drive from the airfield. We got in a sleek black car and were driven through Las Vegas. I gawked at everything with wide eyes.

Trent chuckled. "First time in Vegas?"

I nodded. "Yes. It's even fancier than it looks on TV."

"Wait till you see Patrick's hotel. It's one of the best in Vegas."

When we arrived and Trent announced who we were, the concierge took care of us personally. He fussed about getting everything just right, fawning over Trent. When he said, "Only the best for you, Mr. Dillon," Trent rolled his eyes at me. I hid my smile behind my hand.

The suite was incredible. It was, indeed, decked out with only the best, most luxurious items. The large living area was outfitted with leather couches, oil paintings, and plush carpets. A wet bar opened up onto a balcony that looked out over the Las Vegas Strip.

The two bedrooms were each bigger than my entire apartment, with poster beds and more leather couches arranged around fireplaces in intimate circles, even though we were in the middle of the desert.

"Oh, my God!" I shrieked as I stood in the bathroom.

Trent ran up behind me. "Are you okay?"

I nodded. "It's this bathroom. I didn't know they made bathrooms this huge."

He laughed as I gaped at the room. It was the size of my living room back home, with a jet bath, a waterfall shower, and heated lamps that warmed up the bathroom when the water went on.

"Are the accommodations to your liking?" Trent asked me.

"They're amazing," I said.

Trent chuckled. "Good. Patrick fucks up a lot, but he sure knows how to do business."

"It must run in the family," I said.

Trent nodded curtly.

"We should get ready for dinner," he said. "It's go time in an hour."

"Okay," I said as he closed himself in his room.

I did the same, unzipping the luggage the bellhops had brought up to my room.

I went through the dresses, trying to decide which would be most appropriate for tonight, and settled on an emerald-green dress that Angie had said made me look like a goddess. I chose the strappy heels that went with it and laid out the black clutch I'd bought.

In the bathroom, I curled my hair with a curling iron so that it hung down my back in waves, and I put on makeup the way I'd taught myself from videos online. Black smoky eyes, a nude lip, and light contouring.

I put the dress and heels on and fastened a faux diamond necklace around my neck.

I looked at myself in the mirror.

I barely recognized myself, dressed to the nines like this. I usually lounged in leggings and a loose top when I wasn't at work. It felt strange, but I had to admit it felt good to get dressed up like this.

The last time I'd remotely dressed up was for senior prom. Mom had still been alive then. Dad had just passed weeks before, and I'd been an emotional mess—we both were. Mom had made sure I had everything I needed to feel like the princess my dad always believed I was, and the night had been incredible.

I ran my hands down my stomach and onto my thighs, feeling the smooth fabric beneath my fingers. It was light and thin, and the color brought out the green specks in my hazel eyes. I loved it.

My stomach twisted. The dress looked gorgeous to me, but would the Dillons approve? Would Trent?

I was nervous about meeting his family. Not only would I be rubbing elbows with a different tier of society now, I had to act like his date.

Could I pull it off? Maybe they would see right through me.

Suddenly, panic rose in my stomach.

Why had I agreed to this?

What was I thinking, telling Trent I could pretend to be his girlfriend?

I shook off the doubts. It was too late to turn back now— I had to go through with it.

I'd act like I belonged here. Like I really was Trent's girlfriend.

When I stepped out of my room, Trent stood in the living room with his back to me, studying a large oil painting on the wall. He wore a black suit, his dark hair stylishly messy.

"We should go if we don't want to be late," I said.

"Yeah," Trent said and turned to face me. "I—"

He cut himself off and stared at me. His eyes slid down my body, and it felt almost like a physical touch. I shivered.

"You look beautiful," Trent said, his voice low, and another shiver ran down my spine. His eyes were deep like the ocean. If I didn't know any better, I would have sworn he was sincere.

Did I know better?

We left the suite together and stepped into the elevator that would take us down to the dining room that had been reserved in one of the fancy restaurants the casino hosted.

When the doors slid open, Trent smiled at me. "Ready?"

I nodded and swallowed hard. *Ready as I'll ever be.*

He slid his hand into mine, interlinking our fingers.

My heart beat in my throat and I felt flushed.

It's just for show, I reminded myself, but God, it felt good for Trent to hold my hand. He led me through the restaurant like a prize on his arm and eyes fell on us before patrons leaned toward each other and whispered. They all looked excited, dazzled to see us.

That made butterflies erupt in my stomach.

It's just for show.

When we walked into the private dining room, it was filled with people. My steps faltered just for a moment. It was hard to think that all these people together, laughing and talking, were Trent's family.

"There they are!" someone called, and all attention turned to us. I watched Trent as he plastered his usual business smile on his face.

Everyone stood up and surrounded us as we approached the table. I could tell they were excited to meet me, and apparently they hadn't seen Trent in a long time.

An older woman with short blonde hair and red lips met

us first. She wore a golden blouse that shimmered when she moved, and she flashed us a smile.

"You must be Bella," she said as she opened her arms to hug me. "I'm Trent's mother, Joni."

I hugged her back, then smiled at her warmly. "It's nice to meet you, Joni."

"I can't believe you decided to grace us with your presence," an older man with a receding hairline and Trent's eyes said. His voice was loud and booming, and he clapped Trent on the back. "I'm glad you made it, son."

"We thought you dropped off the face of the earth," another guy said who was a spitting image of Trent. This one looked close to Trent's age.

Now that I looked at them, they all looked like versions of him. Slimmer, wider, a little shorter, hair a little lighter, eyes a little darker—but all of them looked like him. It wasn't hard to see the family resemblance everywhere.

Trent introduced me to them one by one, and I could tell they'd all been curious about me.

Grant was Trent's brother, the second oldest after Trent. He was getting married later in the summer. His fiancée, Megan, greeted me warmly, and I learned they lived in LA, too.

Anya was next in line, the only blonde of the five siblings. She looked exactly like Joni, with a broad smile and a polished air about her.

"Welcome to the family," she said and hugged me. "We're not as scary as we look." Her smile was genuine, and I liked her instantly.

She was getting married soon, too, and I met her fiancé, Kevin, who looked like a cowboy, complete with the hat and boots—albeit a rich cowboy. I learned that he was a cattle rancher in Colorado, and it all made sense.

Patrick was Trent's cousin and the owner of the hotel. He was getting married to Jessica this weekend.

"She's a dancer," Joni said to me.

"Oh," I said with a smile, though I wasn't sure exactly what that meant.

"A professional dancer," Jessica added. "A showgirl, not a stripper like everyone assumes."

"You can strip for me anytime, baby," Patrick murmured close to her ear, and Jessica blushed and giggled.

"Get a room!" a young guy called out.

Trent introduced him as his brother Isaac, and the young woman next to Isaac as their sister, Claire.

"Are you two twins?" I asked. They looked so alike it was uncanny.

"God, no," Isaac said. "I'm not attached to this one. She wants to be as cool as I am, but it's not happening."

"You're just salty that you're two years older than me, but I'm already more successful," Claire said with a laugh. She turned to me and gave me a hug. "I love your dress. You're brave to join us like this, meeting everyone in one go." She glanced at Trent. "Why haven't we heard about Bella before?"

"I like to keep her under wraps. She's too special to share with the whole world." Trent winked at me and I blushed despite myself. I had to keep it together with him. He was more charming than usual. Plus, his family was loud and crazy, and it made for a giddy atmosphere. I loved them immediately.

"This is Enid, Ray's mother," Joni said, introducing me to Trent's grandmother. She was a short, gray-haired woman with dark eyes and a lot of spunk.

"I'm so glad Trent brought you," Enid said to me. "The more the merrier, eh? And you're gorgeous!"

I blushed. "Oh, thank you. I—"

"Trent has had women in his life before, but we were all a little worried about his taste."

"Gram, come on," Trent said, looking embarrassed now.

"Yeah, yeah, they were all pretty on the inside, we know," Enid said. "But Bella here is beautiful on the outside too, isn't that right?" She nudged Joni, who laughed.

"Don't mind her, she loves making people feel uncomfortable," Joni said with a hand on my shoulder.

I smiled. "I can take it."

"Oh, that sounds like a challenge to me," Enid said, but she smiled at me and squeezed my hand.

Next I met the parents of the bride and groom. Everyone greeted me warmly.

We finally took our seats at the table, and the night was underway. The family joked and bantered back and forth, lobbing insults at each other across the table like a volleyball and trading information about their lives like playing cards. They had a lot of money, there was no doubt about that, but they seemed down-to-earth, taking the banter, the insults, the prying questions, all in stride.

"So, how long have you and Trent been together?" Anya asked.

"Oh, not long," I said and glanced at Trent.

"It hasn't been official until recently," Trent said smoothly. "But we've known each other over two years now."

"You work together?" Joni asked.

"Yes," I said. "I'm his executive assistant."

"How romantic," Anya said. "Just like the movies."

I nodded. "We're around each other every day. You know what they say about familiarity."

"It breeds contempt," Grant joked. Everyone laughed.

I blushed. "Well, there are times Trent makes me want to pull my hair out, but he's got a heart of gold under all that."

Trent stared at me, surprised. "You think so?"

I reached for him and squeezed his hand. "You're growing on me."

Everyone burst out laughing again, and the topic of conversation changed when Isaac started talking about a woman at his work he was dating.

I was relieved—we seemed to be pulling this off.

I'd been so nervous to meet the Dillons, but they immediately put me at ease. They were amazing, all of them.

It shot another pang through my heart. I missed my parents so much.

What would my mom have said about Trent? What would she have thought about our arrangement?

She might not have liked it. She'd always been so serious about being a straight shooter, about doing the right thing. Here I was, swindling a whole clan of people.

It wouldn't be a permanent thing, though, I reminded myself.

Even though I could see myself being with these people long-term. Hell, maybe I could even imagine myself on Trent's arm long-term.

Stop it, I scolded myself, not for the first time since we'd started this farce. I had to keep my head in the game.

"Have you been in serious relationships before?" Enid asked, turning to me.

"Oh, not really," I said, feeling uncomfortable again.

"What was it that lacked about the men you saw?" Enid asked.

"Gram, seriously," Trent said, clearly irritated. "You're getting pretty nosy. This isn't exactly dinnertime conversation."

"Well, it's the first time we've seen you in forever, and the first time we've seen you with a woman in ages," Enid said. "I figured we better ask while we can, before you crawl under your rock and it's years before we see you again."

I glanced at Trent, who clenched his jaw. He wasn't happy.

Why hadn't they seen him in so long? I loved his family —even their nosiness. They were open and conversational and caring. If I had a family like this, I'd spend as much time with them as I could.

They weren't overbearing, no matter what Trent had said to me when he asked me to do all this in the first place.

The dinner was a five-course meal. Every course was something different that I'd never tasted before, and it was incredible. Every course was also paired with another kind of wine, and they were all so good. I always drank cheap wine with Angie, but there was nothing cheap about the wine on this table.

After this, I wasn't going to be able to go back to the screw-top wine we loved so much.

My head felt light and airy, and my skin was on fire. When I glanced at Trent, he was drinking more and more, too.

The courses were all interrupted by toasts to Patrick and Jessica, the bride and groom, and with each toast came champagne. The bubbles fizzed in my veins and made me giggly.

I hadn't had a time like this in... well, ever.

The more we drank and the more comfortable we got, the more Trent opened up and eased into the evening. I felt less nervous, too. He took my hand more often. He planted kisses on my knuckles after a toast, held onto me when we drank to the happy couple. When we waited for our plates to be cleared, he put his arm around me.

I knew at the back of my mind that we were just pretending, but it was so convincing, I had to keep reminding myself that this was an act.

It didn't *feel* like an act. It felt wonderful.

It was the wine, I told myself. The wine and champagne and the good conversation that made me so giddy.

Finally, when dessert was over and it was time to go to our rooms, I was wobbly on my legs. I nearly lost my balance, but Trent snaked his arm around my waist.

"Careful," he murmured, his lips against my ear. "I've got you."

Shivers ran down my spine, and his hot breath on my neck gave me goosebumps.

Trent led me to the elevators, arm still around my waist, and I leaned into him. I drank in his warmth, and when the doors slid shut, he didn't let go.

We didn't have to pretend anymore.

6

TRENT

*B*ella was a little unsteady on her heels, so I held onto her until we were inside the suite. It wasn't the only reason I was holding onto her, though. She was hot as fuck in that dress.

Since the day Bella started working for me, I'd thought she was beautiful. She had a quiet confidence about her, like someone who'd been through a lot and that had strengthened them, but tonight I saw a different side of her.

The way she held her own with my family, the way she leaned against me at dinner. And in this dress, she shimmered. She was like a vision. I couldn't stop staring.

When we stepped into the suite, Bella let out a sigh. I let my hand linger on her lower back a little longer—her dress had a low back and I touched her bare skin. The feel of her was soft and delicious under my fingers and I was reluctant to let go.

"Can I make you something to drink?" I asked, walking to the bar.

"Oh, no, I think I've had enough. I feel buzzed, but not

drunk, and I want to keep it that way so I don't feel like crap tomorrow morning."

I grinned at her, took off my blazer and folded it over the back of a chair before I poured myself two fingers of whiskey. I could still drink a hell of a lot more before I felt anything other than a little tipsy.

Around my family, I usually got smashed just to cope with their chaos and nosiness. But tonight, I'd paced myself. A lot of that had been because of Bella. Her presence had strangely set me at ease.

I was *never* at ease around my family.

"So, how did I do?" Bella asked, sitting down on one of the leather couches.

"You were great," I said. "They loved you."

She blushed. "Good. That's what we were going for. They seemed to buy it."

They more than bought it, and it wasn't just because I'd told them I was bringing a plus one. Bella had played the role perfectly. She'd been attentive and caring toward me, letting me take her hand, brushing her arm against mine or intertwining our fingers. She'd been gracious when asked about our relationship, and she'd picked up the rhythm of my family's banter well.

"I think they like you better than they like me," I said and walked to the couch, sitting down next to her.

"Never," she said. "Family doesn't work that way."

"Oh, you don't know my family," I said, a flicker of the irritation I felt about them coming back despite how good tonight had been.

"You seem to have a strained relationship with them," Bella said carefully. "What happened?"

"Oh, you know how it is sometimes," I said. I didn't want

to go into it after tonight had been such a success. I hadn't been this comfortable around my family in a long time. Bella didn't know it, but she'd protected me from a lot of questions and comments with the way she'd joined in with the joking, clapping back where it was needed and deflecting the attention away from me.

I appreciated that—the reason I hadn't seen my family in a long time was because they always insisted on reminding me of a past I was desperate to forget.

"Are all your family events like this?" Bella asked. She leaned slightly toward me.

"Do you mean loud and invasive? Then yes."

Bella giggled. "I loved it. There are so many of them."

"And they're *all* up in each other's business. Trust me, you don't want that on the daily."

Bella shrugged. "I don't know... it seems to me that you should cherish what you have while you have it. One day, it could be all gone and then it'll be too late." She glanced up at me and her hazel eyes were serious. "I'd give anything to have family like that. You don't know how lucky you are."

"I'm lucky because you're here in this with me," I said softly and lifted my hand to tuck a strand of hair behind her ear. It was a cliché line, but I actually felt that way. Maybe I was a little more buzzed than I realized, baring my soul like this when I usually never put my feelings to words.

Either way, I wanted her badly.

I'd *been* wanting her for two years.

Her eyes were large and her lips slightly parted, and she was the most beautiful thing I'd ever seen. I couldn't decipher the expression on her face, but when her gaze slid to my lips, I knew what she was thinking.

I'd been thinking it the whole night, too.

I leaned forward and kissed her.

Bella stiffened for just a moment before she gave in and kissed me back. I slid my tongue into her mouth, and she tasted like wine and peppermint and something completely Bella. The combination was more intoxicating than the alcohol had been, and I put my hand behind her neck, fingers in her hair.

She slid an arm around my neck and moaned softly into my mouth, and the sound made a direct line to my cock. It punched up in my pants, and I wanted her.

No sex, and no sharing a bedroom.

Those were the rules she'd given me.

I broke the kiss.

"We shouldn't do this," I said.

"I know."

We were caught in the moment, staring at each other. The sexual tension grew between us, the atmosphere turning thick, and she was like a magnet, pulling me closer.

I closed the distance and kissed her again.

Fuck the rules.

When we kissed this time, it was urgent. She threw her arms around my neck. I wrapped my arms around her waist, pulling her against me.

Our bodies took over, and it was like a wildfire igniting. Bella fiddled with my buttons, undoing them one by one. She slid her hand onto my bare chest as she pushed my shirt open. Her hand was hot, branding me as she traced my pecs and curled her fingers through the patch of dark hair on my chest.

I found the zipper of her dress behind her back and slowly, teasingly, I pulled it down. The dress peeled away from her body and it was like unwrapping an exotic gift. I pulled the dress off her shoulders. It had built-in bra cups, and when she wriggled out of the dress, she was naked except for her G-string.

Holy *fuck*. She was incredibly hot.

I kissed her again, pushing her back on the couch, and I crawled on top of her. My cock was rock-hard in my pants and I positioned myself between her open legs, grinding my erection against her so that she moaned and gasped. I nibbled on her bottom lip, probed her mouth, and traced her naked body with one hand while I held myself up with the other.

I slid my hand down her side, over her small ribcage, following the dip of her waist and the curve of her hip. Her skin was smooth and blemish-free, a pure treat.

When I slid my hand up her body again, I cupped her breast and she whimpered as she kissed me.

I massaged her breast, tweaking her erect nipple. She moaned a little louder. She liked what I was doing and I took that as a sign to keep going.

I kissed my way down her neck and onto her chest. I cupped both breasts and pushed them together, licking and sucking her nipples, kneading and massaging. She breathed hard, arching her back so that she pushed her breasts closer to my face. I planted kisses all over her chest before I moved further down her body.

She was warm and sweet, and I wanted to lick and taste every inch of her body.

I drew a line down her abdomen with my tongue, circling her belly button, and her breath hitched. I nibbled a line down her hip bone, and she gasped, pushing her hand into my hair.

When I pulled her panties over her thighs, she moved her legs together while I pulled them off, letting them drop to the floor.

She opened her legs for me again, offering herself up to me, and I dove in.

I closed my mouth around her pussy, and she cried out when I flicked my tongue over her clit.

Fuck, she tasted incredible.

Sweet like honeydew, and her scent drove me crazy.

I lapped at her pussy as she squirmed on the couch. She tugged at my hair and bucked her hips against my mouth, and judging by the way her moans and whimpers turned into cries of pleasure, she was getting closer and closer.

My cock throbbed, aching to take her when she sounded like that, but I wasn't going to give in to my urges just yet.

I wanted her to come. I wanted to hear her cry out, to watch the way the pleasure rippled over her body and see her face, riddled with ecstasy. I wanted to reduce her to a puddle of pure pleasure.

She writhed on the couch, creeping closer and closer to the edge as I sucked on her. Her breathing was shallow and erratic and her muscles contracted involuntarily as the pleasure built in her body.

When I pushed two fingers into her, she cried out and I felt her pussy tighten around them. It was enough to make a man come in his pants.

Her walls felt like silk, hot and demanding. Her body begged for a release as I sucked on her clit and pumped my fingers in and out of her.

"Trent!" she gasped, and the way she said my name was hypnotizing.

She cried out, bucking her hips and curling her body as the orgasm crashed into her. She squirmed and writhed, letting out gasps and moans of pure ecstasy as the orgasm rolled over her in waves.

My fingers were still buried inside of her, but I lifted my

head and watched as her muscles tightened. Her nipples were erect and her face was riddled with pure sexual bliss.

The orgasm took her breath away, and she was caught in a world of pleasure.

Finally, she gasped for air and panted, her body relaxing on the couch. I retrieved my fingers and grinned at her when she glanced down her body at me.

I stood and kicked off my pants, setting my cock free. I wanted her as hard and fast as I could get her.

As soon as I was naked, I found a condom and ripped the foil, rolling it over my cock. Bella pushed herself up from the couch.

"Where are you going? I'm not done with you yet," I said in a thick voice.

"I was hoping that was the case," she said, her voice husky.

She stood in front of me and I kissed her. My cock pushed up against her stomach.

I spun Bella around so that her back was against my chest. I kissed her over her shoulder, cupping her breast around her tight little body. I held onto her hip and pushed her forward with a hand on her back, and she braced herself on the back of the couch.

Her back was beautiful. Her blonde hair fell over her shoulders and I guided my cock to her entrance. Her ass was delectable—round and perfectly sculpted. I grabbed it and she shivered, and when I pushed into her, she let out a long moan as my cock slid home.

She trembled around my cock, her pussy tight after her orgasm. She felt like a wet dream. I held onto her hip and ran my other hand up and down her back, feeling her.

Slowly, I slid out of her, and almost slower, I pushed back in.

She felt incredible, and I did it again, in and out, painstakingly slow.

"Trent, you're driving me crazy," she moaned. I was teasing her, but teasing her meant I was teasing me, too, and I was driving myself just as crazy.

I picked up the pace, and Bella's moans turned into cries as I fucked her from behind. I pounded into her, fucking her harder and harder. Her ass looked incredible as I slapped my hips against it and her breasts jiggled. I reached around and fondled them, bending my body over hers. She was petite—Bella had such a strong personality that I didn't always realize how small she was.

She was getting closer and closer to another orgasm, and I bit back my own release. I wanted to drag this out for as long as I could.

Her cries had been in the rhythm of our fucking, but they became more and more erratic as she got closer and closer.

When she came a second time, her body tightened around my cock and I felt the orgasm roll through her, tightening her core and pulsating all around me.

It took everything I had not to fuck her as hard as I could and come, too.

I wasn't ready for that yet. I didn't want it to be over and I didn't want to end things like this.

I suddenly had the urge to look her in the eye, to be closer to her than this fucking from behind. It was usually how I did it—it kept things impersonal—but with Bella, I wanted it to be up close and personal. I wanted to be right there with her.

I waited until her orgasm subsided before I slipped out of her. She collapsed onto the couch.

I climbed onto it with her, and her legs fell open for me

again. Her eyes were hooded and she smiled at me. A red flush had spread across her breasts and her cheeks were pink with the effort, too. Her breath still came in gasps.

I lay on top of her and my cock pressed up against her entrance again. I kissed her, and she held her breath in anticipation. When I slid into her, she let out a breathy moan, her lips pressed against mine.

When I started bucking my hips, I broke the kiss and looked into her eyes. Her hazel eyes had green flecks in them—I'd never noticed them before. I'd never been this close to her before.

I cupped a breast and bucked my hips, pounding into her again. Bella cried out, eyes rolling shut, and I watched her face as pleasure took over once more. She held onto my shoulders as if I was her anchor, as if she would float away if she didn't, and her nails dug into my skin. I gritted my teeth and groaned in pure pleasure. The small jolt of pain only added to the erotic moment and I pounded harder and harder.

I was getting closer to an orgasm. My balls tightened and my cock was harder than before, growing bigger it seemed. Or maybe Bella had just become incredibly tight after her two orgasms. Whatever it was, the feel of her clamping down around me was enough to bring me to the verge of an orgasm in no time at all.

I kissed her again, and Bella moaned into my mouth as I pounded into her. She cried out a moment later and her body tightened again, her third orgasm. God, if that wasn't an ego boost, I didn't know what was.

It was enough to push me over the edge, too. With a sharp cry, I pushed into her as deep as I could, and my cock twitched and jerked as I released inside of her.

We trembled and moaned and gasped, riding out the

wave of pleasure together. There was something incredibly intimate about coming together. I hadn't had that many times in my life, where I was that in sync with the woman I was fucking.

Then again, Bella wasn't like any other woman I'd met before. The better I got to know her, especially now, outside of work, the more I realized how true it was.

Finally, when we came down from our climax, Bella gasped for air and I slid out of her. I collapsed on top of her for just a second before I pushed up.

"That was incredible," she breathed.

Oh, hell yeah, it was. I'd been dreaming about fucking Bella like this for two years. I couldn't believe I'd actually done it.

What if it was a mistake? Maybe we should never have crossed this line...

I pushed the thoughts away. I wasn't going to let my brain ruin the moment.

"Come," I said and took Bella's hand.

"Where?" she asked.

"To the bedroom."

She hesitated. I pulled her up and kissed her.

"I'm not nearly done with you, sweetheart," I said.

My cock needed a minute to recover, but if I worshipped Bella's body a little more, it would stand right at attention and be ready for round two.

I wanted her. I wanted as much as I could get of her.

She was incredible, and I felt like I'd been wandering in the desert my whole life, only to finally have a sip of water from her. I wanted to drink until I burst.

"We shouldn't," she said.

"Babe, we already did."

She nodded, giving in. I was right. I kissed her again and

led her to my room so that I could kiss her and taste her and then fuck her again and again until neither of us could walk anymore.

This might be the only night I could have her. I had to make the most of it.

7

BELLA

The first thing I noticed when I woke up the next morning was the sharp pain that throbbed between my temples.

So much for trying not to drink too much. Wine gave a whole different kind of headache, even the good stuff, apparently.

The second thing I noticed was Trent, sprawled out on the bed, one arm casually slung over me and his majestic cock out for the world to see. Not only that, he was clearly in the morning glory phase. His cock was impressive, to say the least.

I realized I was staring and I blushed, looking away.

Shit. Reality started to dawn on me.

I'd slept with Trent. My boss. The guy I was pretending to date.

The guy I'd vowed I wouldn't sleep with.

Shit.

The sex had been *incredible*. I'd lost count of the number of orgasms I'd had after we'd had at it one round after the other.

What the hell had I done? How could I have given in to my urges so easily? Sure, I'd had a crush on the guy since day one, but actually going through with sleeping with him? After I'd been so determined to make a rule that it *wouldn't* happen?

I had to get out of here. I had to get away from him so I could get my head straight. I carefully lifted his arm off me so I could make my escape. When I was free of his embrace, I slipped out from underneath the sheets that were half-covering my body.

"Morning," Trent said when my back was to him and I'd just put my feet on the plush carpet in the bedroom.

In *his* bedroom.

I tucked the sheets against my chest, covering up my nakedness, and looked over my shoulder.

"Morning," I said softly.

Trent cleared his throat and covered himself with a pillow. It was supposed to make him more decent but for some reason it just made him that much hotter—his perfectly chiseled abs showed and I knew exactly what was under that pillow. It made me shiver, and a new spark of lust ignited at my core.

I squashed it. This was *not* the time.

"Did you sleep okay?"

"Not a lot," I answered. "But not bad." That was a lie. I'd slept like a baby. The sex had tired me out so much that even though it hadn't been a long sleep, it had been so good just to rest. Not only that, but to have Trent's arms wrapped around me...

"How's your head?" Trent asked.

I groaned. "I shouldn't have drunk all that wine."

"Yeah, I'm feeling it, too."

The vibe between us was awkward. Trent obviously

regretted what we'd done, and that just made it so much worse.

"Look, about last night," Trent started. "We probably shouldn't have done that."

"No," I said. I agreed with him, but it stung for him to say those words. "It was just a lapse in judgment."

"Yeah," Trent agreed. "Alcohol makes people do stupid things."

"I know, right?" I said. My stomach twisted. "It won't happen again."

"It can't," Trent agreed. "We have to keep things the way they were before this."

"We will," I said.

Trent looked visibly relieved. It only made me feel sick. It really had been a mistake, but for something so wrong, it had felt so *good*.

"We should get ready," he said. "We have brunch. Then they're going to want to do some activity together today."

"Okay. I'm going to shower," I said.

Trent nodded and got out of bed, turning his back to me. I took the opportunity for privacy he gave me to leave his room and walk to my own.

I turned on the water in the shower and stepped underneath it when it was hot. The smell of our sex filled the room as the hot water ran over my body, and I relived last night. The way he'd held me, the way he'd kissed me.

The way he'd fucked me. Different positions, different angles. Tender, sweet, caring.

Loving. But that had just been in my head, because Trent didn't do *loving*. He was Diablo, for crying out loud! The office grump that no one could stand. Except, he hadn't been like that with me last night.

I forced the thoughts away. I had to stay positive about

this. We were going to pretend nothing had happened between us and keep up the act that we were together for his family.

That was all. How hard could it be?

Still, just thinking about Trent and how he'd ridden me last night... heat washed over my body again and pooled between my legs. I was still raw from our sex, throbbing. I could still feel him inside of me, but holy shit, I wanted more. I wanted *another* round. It hadn't been just sex with some stranger, the kind I'd had before, and no doubt, he'd had, too. It had felt like so much more...

Too bad. It won't happen again.

It had been nothing but sex, giving in to urges. It hadn't meant anything.

It was nothing more than a one-time mistake, and we would leave it where it was and move on.

It was a pity.

But it had to be done.

I dressed in the day clothes Angie had helped me pick out. A pair of striped linen shorts that were so loose they looked almost like a skirt, and a white tank top to go with them. I strapped on brown gladiator-type sandals, and I pulled my hair back in a ponytail.

When I stepped out of the room, Trent was already waiting for me. He wore khakis and a blue collared shirt that made his eyes look like the clear sky.

"Ready?" he asked, just as he had last night.

"Ready," I said.

This time, he didn't compliment me on my looks, but the way his eyes lingered suggested he thought about it, anyway.

I blushed, but fought it, and we left the suite together.

We had brunch with his family. Meeting everyone last

night meant that I was more comfortable around them this morning. They all looked a little worse for wear.

"How do you do it?" Anya asked me as she sipped a mimosa.

"Do what?" I asked.

"You look so fresh and put-together. You can't tell me you don't feel like crap after drinking, too."

"I feel horrible," I said with a laugh.

"You don't look it at all," Anya said. "Here." She handed me a mimosa. "Hair of the dog that bit you."

I laughed and took the drink, sipping it.

Strangely, drinking more alcohol did help a bit, but I wasn't going to go overboard.

After brunch, Patrick and Jessica announced that we were going to have a day filled with fun activities. We were given a list of possible adventures, and I looked at the options.

"Let Bella decide what we're doing," Joni said after the girls had all argued about what they did and didn't want to do.

"Me?" I asked.

"Of course, you're the guest of honor," Joni said with a smile.

"I would think the bride might be," I said, blushing.

"Honey, they're used to me. You're a hot commodity around here." She nudged me with a wink. "Go on, you can choose."

It made me feel a little on the spot, and I studied the list of options. Finally, I settled on indoor sky-diving—since Jessica seemed to secretly favor that one—followed by a spa day that would work for all the women.

The men were headed off to play golf and race cars.

Trent walked over to me as the guys were getting ready to leave. "Have fun."

He planted a kiss on my lips that made my toes curl, and I had to remind myself it was just for show. We couldn't sleep together again, but in front of everyone, we still had a ruse to keep up.

"I'll see you later," I said in a breathy voice.

He smiled at me, his eyes holding something I couldn't decipher before he left with the guys.

"You guys are beautiful together," Anya said with a smile. "He really cares about you. I haven't seen him like this before."

I smiled. He just *acted* like he cared about me, I reminded myself. This was an act. None of it was real. Even when it *felt* real.

We walked to the indoor skydiving arena together.

"You're from LA, right?" I asked Megan. She was engaged to Trent's brother Grant, and she looked as excited about the whole wedding atmosphere as the bride-to-be, Jessica. "What do you do?"

"I own an interior decorating business," Megan said. "It was touch-and-go for a while, but it's working well right now."

"You started it yourself?" I asked.

"Yeah," Megan said. "I had to do something to keep my head above water. I lost my mom when I was pretty young, and my dad is on disability after a car accident, so no one was bringing cash into the house aside from state assistance. I had to do *something.*"

"I admire you for that," I said. "I know what it's like to lose family."

"Yeah?"

I nodded and told Megan about my dad, who passed

away when I was seventeen in an accident at his construction job.

"It was just my mom and me, and for a while, I thought she would grieve herself to death."

"It's tough, losing someone you love like that. I never truly understood the pain my dad had to go through until I met Grant. I can't imagine carrying on without him if something had to happen."

"Right. It was hard for my mom. And then I lost her, too, three years later."

Megan's eyes went round.

"To breast cancer," I added.

"Oh, my God. I'm so sorry," she said. She put her hand on my arm and squeezed. "You and I have a lot in common."

I nodded, feeling like I'd found a kindred spirit. I bonded with Megan immediately. She was so much like me, and we'd had similar pain in our lives, even if we didn't discuss the details. I felt like she understood me.

We chatted a bit about our parents, but then switched to her design business—neither of us wanted to keep dredging up painful memories at the moment.

The conversation shifted to last night and how hungover we felt. Megan laughed.

"I love wine. Sometimes a little too much. Then I regret it in the morning, but I do love the stuff. I'm fascinated by the whole wine-making process, actually."

"That's why you're getting married in a vineyard?" I asked.

"Exactly," Megan giggled. "So cliché, but what is love if it's not cliché? It's the best when it's like a fairytale. Of course, you know that."

I smiled and nodded. What Trent and I had wasn't exactly a fairytale, but it was a hell of a story. Of course, I wasn't going to tell anyone that. It was a secret Trent and I shared.

It was better that way, anyway. I was embarrassed that I'd let things go as far as they had with Trent last night.

I wouldn't have wanted anyone to know, although I wished I could tell Megan the truth. She might have been able to give me some advice about the feelings that swirled in my chest.

"Finding the right guy is already most of the fairytale," Anya interjected. "The location, the wedding, the details... that's just an added bonus. And, of course, getting more sisters!"

"That has to be one of the best parts," Megan agreed, and she and Anya high-fived each other.

I watched their interaction with a pang of envy. Trent had grown up in a large family, and with each one of his siblings marrying off, they were adding more members to their family—more siblings they could spend time with, turn to and confide in. I'd never had that.

Sure, I had friends. Angie was always there for me, although she didn't always support me or agree with the way I looked at life. It was different when it was blood, though. Or in Megan's and Jessica's cases, people marrying into the family. It created a whole different level of bonding that I'd never had.

I didn't understand why Trent wanted to keep his family at arm's length. I would have given anything to have a family like his. With both my parents gone, it was just me, and that could get lonely sometimes.

The rest of the afternoon, I enjoyed my time with all the women from the wedding party. Joni and Enid had a great relationship, and although they didn't hang out with the younger women all the time, the atmosphere was never uncomfortable. Megan and Jessica were never excluded from the Dillon family. And Anya and Claire were comfortable enough to talk about seemingly any topic under the sun in front of their mother. I would never have talked about sex in front of my mom.

But everyone here was so laid-back and open. I loved it. Anyone could be themselves and still find acceptance.

"Do you have a big family?" I asked Megan.

"I have a sister, and a few cousins, but my family is nothing like this." She sighed contentedly. "It's nice to be a part of something bigger, you know?"

I nodded. "I would love to be a part of this family."

The words had tumbled out of my mouth before I was able to stop them.

"I mean—" I started, hoping to do damage control, but Enid had heard me and she turned her eyes to me.

"You should tie Trent up and drag him to the altar before he slips away, dear," she said.

I giggled and blushed. Hard.

"I don't think it's just up to me," I said with a grin.

Enid snorted. "Waiting for the man to make the move is an archaic convention. Back in my day, we stayed at home until a man came to carry us off into the sunset, but times have changed."

I laughed and glanced at Megan and Anya, who both nodded.

"I still don't think—"

"Trent has trouble committing, obviously," Enid said with a wave of her hand.

"What?" I asked, blinking.

"Waverly didn't make it through his obstacles," Enid said.

"His ex?" I asked.

"We don't need to talk about this," Joni cut in. "It's not exactly the time or place." She gave her mother-in-law a pointed look.

I swallowed hard and glanced at Anya, who didn't make eye contact with me. I knew Trent and Waverly had been together a long time ago, but they'd broken up just after I started working for Trent. I didn't know much about their relationship at all.

Judging by the way Joni had shushed her mother-in-law, I got the idea the break-up had been more painful than Trent had let on.

"Well, whatever the case is," I said brightly, "I guess we'll see where it goes, right?"

"Right," Megan said. "There's still plenty of time."

I nodded. Plenty of time... until these weddings were over and we went back to our separate lives, forgetting the ruse had ever existed in the first place.

The idea made me feel sick, but I forced myself not to think about it. There wasn't much that could be done about a contract that would inevitably come to an end.

Trent had made a rule about getting attached, anyway, and I was planning on sticking to it.

8

TRENT

"Fuck," I said when I crossed the finish line second.

I pulled my helmet off, dumped it on the seat next to me, and climbed out of the car through the window.

"Maybe next time, cuz," Patrick said, coming to me with a winning grin. "I thought you were going to take me on that last turn for sure, but you're not as good as you keep bragging you are."

I snorted. "I just let you win because you're getting married."

Patrick laughed. "All I hear are excuses!"

Grant, Kevin and Isaac walked over to us from where they'd been cheering on the sidelines.

"Man, that was fucking good," Grant said, clapping Patrick on the back.

"Yeah," Isaac agreed. "I thought he was going to take you in that last turn, but—"

"I'm just letting the groom shine," I sniffed.

Kevin laughed and shook his head. "Or maybe your

mind is somewhere else. A girl will do that to ya, huh?" He winked at me.

I hated that he was right.

The whole day, I'd been thinking about Bella.

I shouldn't have slept with her. But the thing was, it hadn't been a conscious decision. It had just happened.

Being with Bella was so easy. I felt comfortable when she was around. She made it bearable to be with my family. And last night, one thing had led to another...

Alcohol makes people do stupid things.

The thing was, it hadn't felt stupid. It had felt *good*. Being with Bella had been natural, and no matter how many times I told myself it had been a mistake, it just didn't feel like one.

What if I decided to date her? What if, after this contract ended, I told her I wanted her for real? No pretenses, no money, just me and her, together.

Until something goes wrong again.

If I fucked it up, or she did—it would happen either way —then it would go sour between us and I would lose her. Not only as a woman in my life, one who might get close to my heart, but as an executive assistant, too.

I could deal with heartbreak. I'd been there, done that, gotten the fucking T-shirt. I was an old pro at picking myself up and putting myself back together again.

I also knew what it was like to headhunt for a new EA. It wasn't easy to find someone as good as Bella.

I didn't want to lose her as an employee, which meant there was no way in hell I was ever going to date her and risk that.

The fact that I valued her as an employee over what my heart said about her was more than enough of an indication that I shouldn't do this.

I just wasn't the type of guy who found true love, happily

ever after, and all the other bullshit that my family bought into.

I didn't doubt what they had was real. It just wasn't in the cards for me. It was better to accept that now before I did something stupid.

Like losing my assistant.

"Uh, hello? Earth to Trent?" Grant asked.

I hadn't listened to the conversation at all. My mind had been all over Bella and our fantastic sex.

Again.

"What?" I asked.

"Come on, man," Patrick said. "Stop thinking about work while you're here."

"Okay, okay," I said. If they thought I was distracted by work, that was fine by me.

"We were asking about you doing a speech at the wedding," Grant said, bringing me up to speed on what I'd missed.

"Oh," I said. "Do I really have to?"

"Fuck, man, are you kidding?" Patrick asked. "Of course you have to. You're family. The head of it, in fact."

I snorted. "Dad's the head of it."

"Yeah, yeah," Grant said. "He's the head but you're the oldest of our generation. Come on, say a few words."

"But don't embarrass me," Patrick added.

"Oh, you do that all by yourself," Isaac chipped in.

Patrick punched Isaac in the shoulder. Isaac pushed him playfully, then Patrick wrestled him into a headlock until Isaac tapped out.

"I thought so," Patrick said and let go.

I glanced at Kevin, my soon-to-be brother-in-law, who laughed at the whole thing. He was so laid-back.

If we didn't know who he was and how much money he

had, he would have come across like any other rancher. That was what I liked about him and why he was good for my sister Anya.

He was down-to-earth. Solid. Anya needed that. She needed someone who would be there for her, no matter what. Thick or thin, rich or poor, all that jazz.

Bella was that kind of person. She would be there no matter what.

Get her out of your damn head.

"Bella is nice," Kevin said to me, as if he could read my mind.

"Oh," I said. "Thank you."

Kevin laughed. "You respond like you're surprised."

I shook my head. "It's not that. I just don't usually introduce women to the family."

"You don't even spend time with the family yourself," Grant pointed out.

I rolled my eyes. "You're never going to drop that, huh?"

"Not until *you* drop it," Grant challenged, but he was grinning.

"He's just being full of shit," Patrick said. "We like that you're here and that you brought her. She fits in with us, which isn't easy."

"It's not easy," I agreed. Bella had really outdone herself last night, and I could imagine how she was getting along with the girls. She was really good at what she did—no matter what it was.

Even in bed...

"Tell us more about her," Grant said.

"What's there to tell?" I asked.

"Like, how it all happened?" Patrick chipped in. "Come on, don't hold back. Let's hear it."

"We already told you last night," I said with a chuckle. "We work together. Over time, it turned into more."

Grant groaned. "That has to be the most boring way to meet your future wife ever."

I stiffened at the mention of a future wife.

"Not everyone has crazy love stories, you know," Kevin chimed in, and I was grateful he took over. "Sometimes, it's a slow burn that creeps up on you when you don't expect it. Not everything can be turned into a movie."

Grant sighed. "Yeah, I guess so."

"Since when are you such a hopeless romantic?" I asked.

"Love does shit to you, bro," Grant said. "I bet you're starting to realize that, too, huh?"

I shrugged. I wasn't going to give them something to run with. My family loved teasing more than they loved gossip. And they *loved* gossip.

"Well, I think you guys make a good couple," Kevin said. "She's a good one. Best hold onto her. They don't come along every day."

He was right. Women like Bella were a once-in-a-life-time deal.

"So, are you going to make sure she sticks around?" Isaac asked. "You know... give us a fourth wedding this summer?"

"You just want more free booze," I answered, avoiding an actual answer.

"Yeah, well, I love going to weddings," Isaac said simply. "They're fun, and I don't have to deal with the headache of being involved."

"Until it's your turn," Grant joked.

"That won't be this summer," Isaac said. "I'm not even thirty yet. Plenty of time to sow wild oats."

"Yeah, not like this old fart," Grant said, slapping me on the back. I laughed in spite of myself.

Soon, we left the racetrack, the banter moving into a safer direction—away from all the wedding talk.

I was sticking to my story of how Bella and I ended up together, but my family pried and probed as a hobby. It was tough to avoid the difficult questions.

So far, I was doing a good enough job to keep up the charade.

Now I just needed to keep my head straight with Bella, too.

9

BELLA

*T*he day with Trent's family was great. They were all so kind and drew me in. It was amazing how quickly they felt like family to me.

I'd been stupid to mention that I wanted to be a *part* of that family, though. Although it had been true, it had been a dangerous thing to say.

Trent and I would never be something more than what we were now. No matter how natural it felt to be with him, and how good it felt to sleep together, this was all it would ever amount to. To say something like that to his family... I'd put ideas into their heads that would never come to fruition.

I didn't want any of them to get hurt. This ruse was for Trent's sake, but now that I'd started to get to know his family, lying to them felt wrong.

Of course, telling them the truth would hurt Trent, and that was the last thing I wanted to do. So I'd have to continue to pretend.

When I returned to the suite after the day's activities, Trent hadn't returned yet. He was probably still with the guys, and I was glad I had some time alone.

My mind was filled with his family and how great they were, but I had to remind myself that this wasn't going to last forever.

That was the problem with things like this—it was so easy to get lost in the fantasy. I hadn't considered what it would be like with the rest of his family. I'd braced myself for a pseudo-relationship with Trent and guarding my heart, but I hadn't considered that I might love his family.

"Keep it together, Bella," I told myself. "This is just an act. None of it is real, and you should remember who you are and where you belong."

It was just so easy to feel like I belonged when I was with Trent's sisters and soon-to-be sisters-in-law.

I chose a dress for the rehearsal dinner tonight, and silently thanked Angie again for the shopping trip she'd been on with me. I'd been so set on not spending a lot of Trent's money, I would have been grossly unprepared for most of the events on this trip if I hadn't listened to her. Now, I felt more confident with these fancy clothes, like I fit in.

I wasn't from their circles, after all. Now I was swimming with the big fish.

The dress I chose was a red one, with layers and layers of sheer fabric falling around my legs so that it gave the illusion of being see-through while covering me fully. The bodice was a corset that laced up across my back, and it made me look elegant and edgy at the same time.

I pinned my hair up into a bun, pulling out bits of hair so that it framed my face.

I put on silver shoes and grabbed a silver clutch, and another set of jewelry that Angie had insisted I buy.

I would have been happy to wear the same jewelry every night.

Those people would never do something like that, Angie had said. *They probably only wear a piece of jewelry once, ever, and then get rid of it. You should get different sets for every outfit if you want to fit in.*

I'd complained that she was just trying to get as much out of the shopping trip as she could since we had Trent's limitless credit card. But now, I was so glad she'd suggested it.

When I looked in the mirror, I again barely recognized myself. I looked like a vision, a classy woman who had every right to be among the very rich.

A knock sounded on my bedroom door just as I tucked my phone and lipstick into my clutch.

"Bella?" Trent's deep voice sounded on the other side of the door and goosebumps ran over my arms.

"Yeah?"

"Are you ready?"

I walked to the door and opened it.

Trent straightened from the door where he'd probably hunched over to hear my replies. He was already dressed in a tuxedo.

"I didn't hear you come in," I said.

His eyes slid down my body, taking in the dress. Heat pooled between my legs.

"I didn't want to bother you," he said, his eyes meeting mine again.

I nodded. "Well, I'm ready."

Trent smiled. "Good. Let's go."

He didn't say anything about my outfit. It was probably better that way—tonight I had to behave myself. I didn't mention that he looked handsome as hell in that suit, either. Everything he wore this weekend was worth drooling over.

Behave, I reminded myself again as I led the way to the hotel suite door.

When we joined the others in the restaurant, it was a lot more comfortable than it had been last night. Now that I knew the women better, I felt more at ease. And although I didn't know the guys all that well yet, I didn't feel like I had to put on as much of an act.

After all, they were already convinced we were a couple, right?

The conversation flowed as freely as the wine did, but I checked myself and didn't drink more than two glasses.

I joined in the conversation as the women chatted about the skydiving and the spa day. Then the men bragged about the racecar driving.

But tonight, Trent seemed a lot more distracted than he had last night.

I glanced at him. He was quiet and withdrawn, barely commenting on the conversations and only taking his brothers' and cousin's bait for banter now and then.

What was wrong?

I tried to catch his eye, but he didn't look at me.

I considered reaching out to him to draw him in. I almost reached for his hand and interlinked our fingers, but I didn't want him to misinterpret what I was trying to do.

After what had happened between us last night... Maybe that was why he was so closed off and withdrawn. Was he trying to keep me at arm's length?

After dinner was over, the men and women split up again. It was time for the bachelor and bachelorette parties.

Trent turned to me and put his hand on my hip. I was very aware of his touch—his skin branded me through the dress.

"Have fun tonight," he said. His eyes pierced my soul.

"You too," I said.

For a moment, the rest of the world fell away, and we were in a bubble of our own, just me and Trent. He looked like he wanted to say something. His eyes slid to my lips for just a second before he looked me in the eyes again, and the atmosphere shifted between us.

"Come on, man!" Patrick called. "The night isn't getting any younger!"

"I'll see you later," Trent said with a slight smile, but the spell had been broken.

"Yeah," I breathed.

He let go of me and walked away, but the feel of his hand on my hip still lingered. I wished we didn't have to split up right now.

"Ready?" Megan said, coming up to me with a glint in her eye.

"Ready," I said and pushed the thought of Trent away completely.

10

TRENT

*W*alking away from her was the hardest—and the best—thing I could do right now.

Fuck, I'd much rather have left the parties behind and taken her back up to the room, getting her naked and horizontal underneath me again.

But that wasn't going to happen. Patrick wouldn't tolerate me missing the bachelor party.

It was better this way, anyway.

The more emotional distance I could put between me and Bella, the better.

I really had to get myself in check because I was starting to look at her in ways I wasn't supposed to be looking at my executive assistant.

"You okay?" Kevin asked, falling into step next to me.

"Sure," I said.

"You were quiet at dinner."

"Patrick talks so damn much, it's hard to get a word in edgewise," I said with a grin, making light of it.

Kevin laughed. "He's on a high because he's getting married. Your turn will come."

I groaned. "Yeah, I don't know about that. I'm not as eager to run to the altar as the rest of you."

Kevin snorted. "You're trying to be the tough guy but I see what's underneath your mask, you know. I know what you're up to."

I stiffened. "What are you talking about?" Shit, did he know? Had he figured it out?

"You're as smitten as the rest of us, if not more."

I blinked at Kevin.

"Don't think I didn't see you stealing glances at Bella tonight."

I let out a breath of relief. Okay, so he didn't know. He *thought* he knew, but he had no idea.

He was right, though. I'd been unable to stop staring at Bella, no matter how hard I tried.

She looked like a dream in that red dress, with her blonde hair up so I could see the elegant line of her neck. She was stunning. Incredible.

Fuckable.

No.

It was so hard to behave while I was around her. It was even harder to forget about her while we weren't together, because everyone in my family seemed to think she was wonderful. They were right, of course.

Every time I talked to my mom or my grandmother, they sang Bella's praises, and the guys wouldn't stop hounding me about being head over heels in love.

Which I wasn't.

It didn't do much to ease the pressure I'd hoped to get away from by bringing Bella in the first place. In fact, it was worse than I'd expected it to be, with everyone suggesting I ask her to marry me right here, right now.

I wished I could just tell them to back the fuck off.

That would ruin the whole illusion, though, and we had to keep up the act for two more weddings after this one.

I took a deep breath and let it out slowly as we walked to the limos that would take us to the party.

Patrick wasn't the kind of guy to go all out at his bachelor party. We ended up in a club with go-go girls dancing on stage, and the lighting was sensual and moody. My brothers were set on getting Patrick as drunk as they possibly could, which he fought every step of the way.

"Come on, man," Grant complained. "You're not even *trying*."

"I'm trying *not* to get wasted," Patrick countered with a laugh. "I'll feel—and look—like shit tomorrow. Jess deserves better than that, you know."

"Since when are you Prince Fucking Charming?" Isaac asked, and the guys all burst out laughing.

I stood to the side, grinning, enjoying their bullshit. I was more comfortable here on the outside of their antics, looking in.

After all, that was what my life had always been with my family.

My dad came to stand next to me.

"They're having a hell of a time," he said.

"Yeah."

"Not drinking with them?"

"I don't want to look hungover in the photos tomorrow, either," I said.

Dad snorted. "You've changed a lot."

I shrugged. Everyone changed—wasn't that normal? After what had happened with Waverly, how could I stay the same?

"As long as they're having fun," Dad said.

"What about you?" I asked, looking down at his glass of

water. When he was younger, he was never without his scotch.

Dad laughed and shook his head. "Son, at my age you don't drink yourself into a stupor anymore. If you think recovering in your thirties and forties is hard, you should try it in your sixties."

I laughed. "I'll keep that in mind when I get there."

"Hey, honey," one of the dancers said, sidling up to me, the glitter on her skin shimmering in the low lighting. "What do you say? I'll give you a dance."

I shook my head. "No, thank you."

"It will be worth your while," she said. "I promise."

"I'm okay, really."

"If I don't keep my promise, I'll have to give you a do-over, how's that? You could get two for the price of one, just by complaining the right way." She smiled coyly at me, but I shook my head.

"I'm serious. I'm not interested."

She looked dejected.

"Try the other guys, maybe they'll want something," Dad suggested, but we both knew it wasn't going to happen, except for Isaac, who was single. The Dillon clan could be a handful, but we were faithful to a fucking fault.

"Good on you, son," Dad said with a grin and he lifted his water glass in a salute. "It's nice that you're staying faithful. You're a good man."

I didn't lift my glass to clink it against his. Instead, I downed my drink and walked away from the party and my dad. My ears rang and my heart hammered in my chest. The alcohol didn't help.

Why the fuck had my dad said that?

It had been a long time coming that my dad would admit I was a good man.

How long had it been that they'd all thought I was the one to fuck up in my relationship, and not Waverly?

I didn't need this shit.

I didn't want to be reminded of a time when I thought I'd found my woman, only to discover that I'd only been one of her *many* men. Plural.

Whatever. This was the reason I didn't date. I was pissed off at my dad, but maybe it was a good thing that he reminded me of the true nature of love.

If I kept that thought front and center, it would be easier to keep my feet on the ground and not entertain this fantasy about being with Bella.

After all, I wasn't going to give my heart to anyone, not even her. It was too dangerous, and it was safer to pretend than let in the real deal.

11

TRENT

I hated weddings.

The whole fuss was for the women, who loved planning a fairytale event. It always cost a shit ton of money, and the couple's friends and family had to get dressed up for a big show.

A show that meant nothing.

I woke up grumpy as hell, and despite my intent to not drink myself into a stupor, I was still hungover.

It only served to blacken my mood even more as I showered and dressed for my cousin's wedding.

Bella, of course, looked like an angel when she emerged from her room.

She wore a mint-green dress with lace over her waist that trailed down the skirt, and the shimmery satin came alive when she moved.

Her hair hung over her shoulder in soft waves and whatever she'd done with her makeup, she looked divine.

Divine and completely forbidden.

I insisted on taking a car for just the two of us to the

chapel for the ceremony. I wasn't in the mood to deal with my family any more than I had to today.

As we took our seats in the chapel, Bella looked around.

"This is beautiful," she said in a breathy voice. Her cheeks were flushed with excitement. "When you think about Vegas weddings, it always brings to mind Elvis suits and tacky dresses, bad decisions and drunken nights, you know? This is completely different."

It *was* very different from all that. The wedding had cost a fortune, but it was also between two people who really loved each other and had planned this day for a long time.

The idea of true love, of finally being together as husband and wife, just pissed me off more.

"Are you okay?" Bella asked.

"Just hungover," I grumbled. I couldn't explain to her what the real problem was.

"That's a bummer," she said.

She didn't look hungover at all, and I wondered what the girls had gotten up to. Had there been male dancers? Had they gotten Jessica as drunk as my brothers had managed to get Patrick?

The idea of a male dancer all over Bella made me cringe. Jealousy flared up in my chest.

What was wrong with me today? This was nothing like me—I didn't usually give a shit about things like that, because... well, I didn't give a shit. Period.

With Bella, everything was different.

"How was the party last night?" I asked, trying not to sound like I was prying. I didn't want to ask at all, but my curiosity—and jealousy—was getting the better of me. "You don't look very hungover."

"Makeup does wonders," she said with a giggle. "I feel like crap."

"So... it was a good party?"

She nodded. "It was pretty fun. I think Jess loved it, and that's the main thing, right?"

"Right."

I sighed. She hadn't given me anything to work with at all. It was a small consolation that at least I wasn't the only one nursing a hangover.

Of course, she would have had fun with my family. She fit in so well with them, and it annoyed me even more.

I didn't know exactly why that bugged me. The whole point of her being here was to set them at ease, and she had gone above and beyond, throwing herself into the act so well they were all convinced.

I wanted to get her away from them.

"I can't wait to see her dress!" Bella said in a lowered voice, her excitement palpable. "That's the important part, you know."

"So I hear," I said with a scowl.

Bella frowned. "You're pretty worked up, huh?"

"I'm fine," I said.

She nodded, pursing her lips, and she turned her face forward and her attention away from me.

That only made her seem more distant. I didn't feel very connected to her today. I hadn't since that first night in my bed.

That's a good thing. If we weren't connected to each other, then we wouldn't get attached to each other. Which was exactly what I wanted.

The doors opened and everyone stood, turning to face the bride. She beamed at us all before her eyes fell on Patrick. As her father walked her down the aisle, she didn't look at anyone else.

He only had eyes for her, too, and the love they both exuded for each other was beautiful.

It was the kind of love I would never have.

Fuck, I would be glad when the ceremony was over. Then I only had to endure the reception before we could leave Vegas. At least there would be drinks at the reception.

I sure could use one. Or three.

One, to drown the bitterness that I would never have the kind of love everyone in my family was finding.

Two, to get rid of this shitty hangover.

And three, to stop thinking about Bella and how fucking perfect she was.

12

BELLA

*W*hen we arrived back in LA, it was late Sunday night. Trent gave me Monday off to recover after the weekend.

It would have been sweet of him if he wasn't in such a foul mood. Instead of coming across as a favor, it felt like he didn't want me in the office.

Of course, that was all in my head. It *had* to be. We'd just spent a weekend in Vegas pretending to be a couple. And he himself said I'd done a great job.

Why would he want to get rid of me?

It felt like a rejection. He had his driver drop me off at my apartment, and I refused Trent's offer to carry my luggage. I wanted to be alone.

I walked in the front door with my tail between my legs.

"So?" Angie asked, emerging from her bedroom as I shut the door behind me. "How was it?"

I shrugged. "It was a wedding. Aren't they all the same?"

Angie's jaw dropped. "Not when you're spending time with one of the wealthiest families in America. Come on, it couldn't have been like any other wedding you've been to. I want to know *everything*."

I dreaded telling her what had happened between Trent and me. Then I realized she meant the details about the wedding itself. The dress, the décor, the prices of it all.

That was easier to do.

Taking a seat on the couch, I told her about Jessica's dress and how perfect the mermaid style had been for her figure. I described the bouquet of lilies and the decorations at the reception. I answered her questions about what everyone had worn at all the events, the activities we did and the food we ate.

Angie's eyes sparkled all the way through the conversation.

"What was Trent like?" she finally asked.

I shrugged, trying to look nonchalant. "He was just himself, you know?"

"A total jackass," Angie said, nodding. "I knew it."

I smiled at her, glad that it was settled.

"Did you manage to handle him, then?" she asked.

"I did," I said.

Angie looked satisfied and offered to make us a cup of tea. I agreed, relieved she hadn't pressed for more information about Trent.

Sure, he'd been his grumpy self, but at times, he'd been different. Like when he held my hand at dinner the first night. The way he'd treated me in bed.

Those times, he'd been kind and caring and affectionate, a side of him I'd never seen before.

That was the part that messed me up so much—Trent had been a great guy. At least, for the first part of the weekend. After that, he'd turned into his grumpy self again.

I had no idea what to make of it.

Thank God I didn't have to tell Angie about any of that. Especially not about the sex.

I was afraid she'd be able to read it on my face, but luckily she didn't. I wasn't in the mood to deal with her teasing me over it.

It had been a terrible idea to sleep with him, and I regretted it every time I thought of it.

Except that the sex had been *incredible* and I wished we could do it again and again.

What was wrong with me?

I scrubbed my hands over my face and walked to my room to unpack while Angie puttered around the kitchen.

While I unpacked, I thought about how cold Trent had been at the wedding and reception today. The icy flight back to LA on his jet, when he hardly spoke to me.

In the chapel, he'd asked me about the bachelorette party. Had he been jealous?

Of course not. He'd have to care about you for that.

What if he was jealous, though? What if he worried I'd done something with another guy, and that was why he was upset?

No. That couldn't be right. Aside from the fact that I hadn't actually done anything—I'd barely glanced at the male strippers—it wasn't any of his business if I was attracted to anyone else. As long as I kept to our agreement and played the part of his faithful girlfriend, what did he care?

We were just pretending, right?

After what he was like with me today, I was pretty sure all hell would break loose in the office on Tuesday.

He would be Diablo on a whole new level, and that was going to make things interesting to say the least.

13

BELLA

*O*f course, I was right. I hated that I was, but Trent was a huge ass in the office on Tuesday.

His mood was worse than usual, and he was snappy as hell with me, even though I did everything the way I always did.

He worked late, pushing hard to keep his contracts going, and he was driven to close a deal that he'd started just before we left. He was trying to secure the IT security accounts of a regional department store chain. He threw himself into his work and expected only the best from everyone around him.

The tension in the office was so thick, I could almost run my fingers through it, and it wasn't the good kind of tension.

"I don't know what's going on with him," Becky, the receptionist on the top floor, said to me on Wednesday when I arrived. She lowered her voice so Trent wouldn't hear her from his office, even though we were out of earshot. "He's been here before I arrive every morning this week, and I always come in at seven. He's working like a demon, and he's so full of shit, it's not even funny. He nearly had my head because I directed a call to him from someone he didn't feel like talking to."

I shook my head with a sigh. "He's in the worst mood I've ever seen him in."

"I wish he would just get laid or something," Becky said. "It might help him ease some of that tension. I would volunteer myself, but I'm worried I wouldn't get out of it alive."

She giggled, and I forced a smile to hide my reaction.

The problem was Trent *had* gotten laid. I had a feeling that was the problem, and I didn't know how to feel about it.

Had sex with me made him grumpier than normal?

It was hard not to be offended by that.

When Trent called me from the door to his office, his voice was clipped and rough.

"I don't pay you to gossip," he barked down the hall.

I sighed. "That's my cue."

"Good luck," Becky mouthed.

I walked to Trent's office where he glared at me and barked out orders.

That continued for the rest of the day.

I'd thought that Trent's bad mood would come to a head and then even out, but I was wrong.

By Friday, he was a hot mess on wheels, snapping at everyone. His employees walked on eggshells around him and shuddered when he spoke to them, terrified that he would do something drastic like fire them. Trent wouldn't do that, of course. He could be a prick, but he wasn't unfair when it came to his employees.

He was just a royal pain in all our asses right now.

When it was lunchtime, I brought him the sandwich he asked for from the new store that had opened on the other side of town. I'd fought a hell of a lot of traffic to get it for him, furious that he'd wanted food from there rather than the deli just down the road, but I hadn't said a word.

Right now, I was trying to pick my battles.

"What the fuck is this?" Trent snapped when he opened the wrapper around his gourmet sandwich.

"What's *what*?" I asked, struggling to swallow my irritation.

"There are pickles on this. I fucking *hate* pickles."

I knew that, of course. I'd noticed the pickles on the menu description when I ordered, but I'd forgotten to ask them not to add them to the sandwich.

Maybe a part of me had been so irritated that I hadn't tried to do the right thing.

"Do I have to do everything myself?" Trent muttered, opening the sandwich and scraping the pickles into the trash. "I have people working for me so that I *don't* have to run a one-man show. But if I want something done right, it looks like I have to do it myself."

I blinked at him, shocked at his words and the tantrum he was having.

For a moment, everything seemed to stand still, and it was so damn comical, I burst out laughing.

Trent stared at me when I laughed. He hadn't expected me to react that way. Hell, *I* hadn't expected to react that way, but it was just so funny.

Trent's face got redder for a moment, his eyes becoming fiery, but then he shook his head, embarrassment taking over. He started laughing, too.

"Yeah, fuck," he said, setting his sandwich on his desk and wiping his hands on a napkin. "I guess that was pretty damn pathetic."

"I'll say," I said, still giggling. "What the hell, Trent?"

He shook his head. "Sorry."

"Yeah, me too... about the pickles."

"It's fine," Trent said. "It's not the end of the world."

"Seemed like it almost was," I pointed out.

Trent shrugged and bit into the sandwich. "I was just... pissed off."

"No kidding," I said.

He glanced at me, chewing. The laughter had broken the tension between us, and for the first time this week, Trent looked at me like a normal person again.

"I have a couple of things to take care of," I said, excusing myself from the office.

Trent nodded, and although whatever was wrong hadn't been resolved yet, the rest of the day was better.

That counted for something, at least.

I sat down at my desk as a text from Megan popped up on my phone. It was an invitation to join her and her two friends, Shelby and Paige, for drinks that evening.

Happy to hear from her, I typed a response.

Hey! I'd love to come but I already have plans with a girlfriend of mine.

I hated having to say no. I loved Megan and I wanted to hang out with her and her friends.

Bring her along! Megan replied almost right away.

I hesitated. I wanted to see Megan again, but Angie knew that it was all a lie, and if she spilled the beans, it would be a disaster.

Angie would keep my secret, though. She was my best friend.

Okay, sounds good! I typed in response. Then I rode the elevator to HR to talk to Angie about the change of plans for tonight.

"So, I'm going to meet some of the Dillons?" Angie asked, excited.

"Well, no. Megan is Grant Dillon's fiancée, so she's not a Dillon yet. Technically."

"Who cares about technicality?" Angie asked. "It's going to be great."

"You have to promise me you'll keep our secret though, okay?" I said. "No one can know what Trent and I are doing."

"Who would I tell?" Angie asked.

I gave her a pointed look.

"I promise," she said. "I don't want to ruin things for you, I just want to get a glimpse of what you've got going on!"

That was enough for me.

A few hours later, after work, Angie and I walked into a cocktail bar in downtown LA. I spotted Megan at a booth in the back, and she excitedly waved us over.

Megan grabbed me and hugged me like I was a long-lost friend.

"It's so good to see you!" she said. "It's a little weird, too, outside the confines of the Vegas hotel."

I laughed. "Yeah, but I like this. Thanks for inviting us. This is my roommate and best friend, Angie."

Angie greeted Megan and the other girls, and we sat down in the booth.

"Tonight, they have half-price cocktails, so I hope you know we're going all out," Megan said, scanning the menu. "I hope Trent doesn't mind you getting wasted tonight."

I giggled. "He doesn't mind."

He wouldn't know either way, but I didn't say that. It was true that he didn't care, though. Why would he, if we were nothing to each other?

The thought shot a strange pang into my chest, but I didn't have time to decipher it.

When we ordered our cocktails, Megan held hers up in the air.

"To new friends!"

"Cheers," I said, and we clinked our glasses together.

"To good men," Angie added and glanced at me. I knew she was laying it on thick just to tease me. She didn't think Trent was a good man at all.

"You can say *that* again," Megan said with a grin and we sipped our cocktails.

Angie gave me a dubious look, but I ignored her.

Shelby's phone pinged and she picked it up, enthralled by whatever message thread she had going on. Angie and Paige fell into deep conversation almost right away, and Megan leaned back in her seat with a contented sigh.

"So, you've been working on a big project?" I asked Megan.

"Yeah, huge. I'm a little nervous I can't pull it off, but I've done big things I was scared of before, so I'm just going to close my eyes and jump."

"That's the only way to do it," I said and held up my glass again.

Megan giggled and clinked hers against mine.

"I feel like that with Trent," I said. "I was so unsure about him at first, but I closed my eyes and jumped, too."

"Did it pay off?" Megan asked.

I nodded.

It was paying off financially, of course, in a big way. He'd already written me a check for the full amount of three hundred thousand dollars, per our agreement. It was more money than I'd ever had in my life, and I was going to use it wisely.

The highlight of my week was paying off my student loan debt in full.

I was finally free of debt, which was wonderful. Soon, I planned to buy a new car and invest the rest. For the first time in my life, I'd have a decent retirement fund.

Was it paying off emotionally, though? I was still confused as hell.

After how he'd acted this week, I had no idea where we stood. I just knew we had to keep up the ruse for two more weddings.

But tonight, I wanted to forget that and have fun with my new friends.

"Hey, Shelby, get off your phone and join the conversation!" Megan cried out when Shelby was still messaging back and forth, keeping herself out of the loop.

"It's my next modeling assignment," Shelby said with a sniff.

"It's Friday night," Megan pointed out.

"It's important. You know how these things are. I can't just blow them off. They might need me urgently."

"For what?" Paige snorted. "You're doing a shoot for a discount clothing store. Unless they need you for a Friday night pajama party, I don't see why you can't get to it tomorrow."

Shelby rolled her eyes when she was called out, but she put her phone down and joined the conversation, a little tightly at first.

I loved Megan, and her friends were great. Shelby was the only one I didn't click with right away, but it was great to meet Megan's friends. Angie fit in well, too.

The rest of the night was fun. We drank so many cocktails I lost count, and we talked about everything from guys and sex to shopping and work. Megan and her friends weren't from the uber-rich circles the Dillons moved in, and I didn't feel shy about my working-class background.

When we finally left, I could barely balance on my heels. Angie looked like she'd had a good time, too.

"Did you like them?" I asked her in the cab on the way back to the apartment.

"They're pretty great," Angie admitted.

"Right?" I said with a sigh. "I'm excited about seeing Megan at the next wedding. And then I'll get to see her get married to Trent's brother."

"It sounds like one big happy family," Angie said.

I nodded. "Yeah, it really is. It's nothing like what I used to have, you know?"

"I know." Angie nodded, then looked out the window. "It's cool, I guess. You spending time with them."

"You guess?" I asked.

"Well, yeah. I mean, it's weird to hear everyone talking about you and Diablo like you're a thing. I had to keep reminding myself I'm not in the Twilight Zone."

I looked at her. "Is it really that weird to imagine us together?"

"Yes. Obviously. Trent is a total dick."

"He's not," I said in his defense. "He's grumpy, sure, but he has a lot to deal with."

Angie raised her eyebrows at me. "Are you serious?"

"What?" I asked.

"I didn't think you'd stick up for him. Is that part of the act, too?"

I rolled my eyes and turned my head to look out of the window, trying to breathe through the nausea that was starting to creep in after how much we drank.

Thankfully, Angie dropped the subject. I didn't want to

keep talking about him, especially if she was talking shit about him.

It hit me like a ton of bricks that I would defend him no matter what Angie said. I was starting to see the good in Trent behind the mask he wore, underneath all the grump.

What was going on with me?

I crawled into bed that night wondering what Trent was up to.

~

On Monday morning, Angie and I stepped into the elevator on the ground floor of Dillon Tech.

"God, I'm never drinking that much again," Angie said. "It took the whole weekend to recover from Friday night. I could have been out doing something."

"It was totally worth it," I giggled.

The elevator doors opened on the first floor, and Trent stepped in.

Angie and I collectively tensed, and the doors slid shut. His cologne wrapped around me.

"So, Wednesday should be fun," Angie said to me. "I'm glad Megan invited us out again."

"Yeah, I'm looking forward to it," I said.

"She really is as great as you said," Angie added.

I felt Trent's eyes on me. When I glanced at him, his jaw was tight, his eyes fiery.

What was *that* about?

The doors opened at HR, and Angie stepped out after offering me and Trent a small wave.

The two of us rode toward the top floor in strained silence.

When the doors slid open, Trent let me walk out first.

"I'll see you in my office," he said in a clipped tone.

He marched on, and I swallowed hard.

What the hell was going on with him?

I walked to the kitchen to make his coffee, and while I waited for the pot to brew, my stomach twisted into a knot of nerves.

Why did I feel like I'd done something wrong—again?

14

TRENT

*W*hat the fuck did Bella think she was doing?

I didn't want her hanging out with my family. I didn't want Bella's roommate—another employee of mine—hanging out with my family, either.

Even though Megan hadn't officially married into the family yet, it still irritated me.

Bella was the only person on my side. She was the only one who stuck up for me. If she integrated with my clan, that would be over.

She knocked on the door and stepped in.

"Close the door," I ordered.

Unfazed by my cool reception, she shut it and brought my cup of coffee to the desk, setting it down without a word.

She sat down, folding her legs at the ankle, the reports and mail in her lap. She looked at me with her head held high, waiting patiently.

I hesitated a moment before I spoke.

"My parents invited us to dinner tomorrow night," I said.

Bella blinked at me, surprised.

"Really?"

"Yeah," I said. "Of course, we don't have to go. I'll tell them we're—"

"I'd love to see Joni and Ray again," Bella said with a smile.

"What?" I asked.

"They're really great. Will Enid join us, too?"

"I don't know," I said tightly.

"Do they want us to bring something? I could make a salad. If I—"

"You're not making a fucking salad," I said, cutting her off.

Bella frowned. "Excuse me?"

I took a deep breath, trying to keep my anger under control. The more excited she got about seeing my family, the more it pissed me off.

"I'm paying you to pretend to be my girlfriend," I snapped. "Not to become best friends with my family."

She was taken aback, and it took her a beat to answer. I saw the confused emotions on her face—anger, frustration and shock fighting for first place. "Why did you mention the invitation at all?" she asked, irritated. Anger had won out. "It sounds like you don't want me to see your family."

I shook my head. "I'm not saying I won't go."

I sounded like a spoiled child. I knew that. I just didn't know how to handle Bella getting chummy with my family. It made me *very* uncomfortable.

"I don't know why the fuck they keep inviting me," I admitted. "I've declined every invitation to go to their house for dinner in the last two years, but they don't get the hint. They still send the damn invites."

Bella frowned. "They're your parents, Trent. They're not going to give up on you."

"Well, I wish they would," I snapped.

I was as surprised at my words as Bella was.

"I don't think you understand what you're saying," Bella said.

I snorted. "And you do?"

Bella pursed her lips.

"So you and Angie went out with Megan?" I asked, my jaw clenched.

"Yes, Friday night. It was just Megan and two of her friends. She invited us."

"Does Angie know about our... arrangement?"

"Yes."

"For fuck's sake, Bella," I cried out.

"It's okay, she won't say anything. I *had* to tell her. She's my roommate, Trent. I couldn't just fly out to three of your family's destination weddings this summer without her getting suspicious. She's taken a vow of secrecy, and she can keep a secret. Don't worry about her."

I sighed. "Fine. But Megan doesn't know, does she?"

"Not at all. She thinks we're... in love."

I sighed and leaned back in my chair, closing my eyes for a moment.

"Look, if you're game, and willing to play along for an extra bonus, we'll go tomorrow night," I finally said, looking at her. "I'll endure one of these family dinners now that I have you to accompany me."

"You make it sound so fun."

I ignored that.

"But you better remember where your loyalties lie," I said, leaning in closer. "I *pay* you for them."

Bella stiffened. "Of course. I won't forget this is a job, and that it doesn't mean anything. You keep reminding me."

I looked at her.

She stood. "Is that all?" she asked tightly.

I nodded once, and she turned and stormed out of my office, furious at me for being... well, for being me.

As she closed the door a little too hard behind her, I slumped in my chair and let out a sigh.

Fuck, I was such a son of a bitch to her. Maybe I'd laid it on a bit too thick.

Still, it was better if she hated me. It would make it easier to keep her at arm's length if she didn't get any ideas about something happening between us.

Again.

I closed my eyes and thought back to the night we'd shared. I flashed on her naked body writhing beneath me, her hair spread out over my chest when she was on top of me, her curvy body pushed up against mine...

My cock punched up in my pants.

Keeping my distance wasn't that easy when I ached for her every minute of the day.

I wanted her right now. I wanted to bend her over my desk and push up that pencil skirt that made her legs look edible—

Fuck.

I had to calm down. I had a damn erection at my desk now.

How had I gone from fighting with her to wanting to fuck her?

The truth was I *always* wanted to fuck her. Although *fucking* was a little too dirty, too emotionless.

The alternative, though... I wasn't going to think about it.

Whatever I felt for her, it wasn't *that*. It couldn't be.

I pushed all thoughts of Bella Williams from my mind and focused on my work. I had a metric shit ton of paperwork to get through if I wanted to close my next contract.

I couldn't afford a distraction. And lately, she had become a big one.

By the end of the day, I pressed the intercom on my phone and called Bella back to my office. She walked in, poker face on.

"Yes, Mr. Dillon?" she said in a faux-cordial voice.

I gestured for her to sit down. When she did, perched on the edge of the chair as if she was ready to leave again, I took a deep breath and let it out slowly.

"Let's try this again," I said. "My parents have invited us to dinner tomorrow night. Will you accompany me?"

That was more gentlemanly, wasn't it?

She hesitated, then nodded.

"Okay. I don't have any plans."

"As I mentioned, I'll pay you extra for the outing, since it's not a part of our agreement," I said.

I wanted to keep things businesslike. Not just for her sake—I had to remember what she was to me.

An employee.

"That won't be necessary," Bella said tightly. "I'll gladly spend time with your family. *That* I'll do for free."

I bristled, her words riling me up again. Wasn't *I* worth spending time with?

"But if you want to buy another round of loyalty," she added, "feel free."

I stared at her. Clearly, I'd hurt her by saying that.

Fuck, I hated that I had.

But I wasn't paying for her feelings. We'd both agreed on that from the start.

We'd agreed to not get attached. We hadn't agreed that hurting each other was part of the game.

Fuck, I wasn't going to overthink it. I refused to be drawn

into a tangled web of emotions. That sounded *way* too close to a relationship.

This was business. Emotions shouldn't matter.

"We'll drive from the office to their house tomorrow night, so bring the appropriate clothing to work with you. My house is on the way, so we can leave your car at my place. I'll drive us the rest of the way."

"Got it," Bella said stiffly and got up. "If that's all, I'd like to call it a day."

"That's all," I said.

Bella nodded and left my office without another word, leaving me to wonder what I'd gotten myself into.

15

BELLA

*T*rent was an ass. There, I said it.

I mean, we all knew it. Since the day I started working with him, I'd known he was an ass.

He was always grumpy, he had no tact, and he was never afraid to call anyone out.

Later, as I worked with him and got to know him better, I'd realized he wasn't as bad as I'd thought. But now, he'd turned up the heat in a new way.

The worst part? I'd let myself get hurt by him.

Why the hell did his icy manner hurt me? I'd known this whole thing was just a farce, and I'd known who he was. So why did it bother me that he treated me without regard for my feelings?

That just pissed me off more.

None of this made sense. He was upset that I was getting closer to his family, but wasn't that the point of this whole act? He was paying me to act like I was his girlfriend, so I'd thought he would be happy about it.

Instead, he was furious.

The next day at the office, I only spoke to him when

absolutely necessary. If he asked me a question, I answered. If I had to tell him something work-related, I did that.

Otherwise, I gave him the silent treatment—not because I was trying to be petty, but because I didn't know how to behave around him.

Anything I said could push him over the edge and wake Diablo. And I had to pretend to like him tonight when we visited his parents.

The problem wasn't that I disliked Trent, though. It was that I *did* like him.

Part of me was pissed off at his shitty attitude.

But a bigger part of me liked him. And that wasn't supposed to happen.

Not that it mattered. He didn't want that. The sex had been amazing—better than anything I'd had with anyone before—but that didn't mean anything when he pushed me away like this.

Keep it together, Bella.

I had to remember what this all was. It was a job.

These feelings I harbored for Trent were nothing but trouble.

After work, I followed him in my car to his house.

No, his *mansion*.

It was huge and gorgeous, and I didn't even go inside.

I parked my car out front and got in his Aston Martin.

The drive out of town to the Dillons' beach house was strained. Trent put on the radio and we focused on the road, the scenery, and everything and anything that would allow us not to focus on each other.

The tension in the car was palpable, and yet, I was painfully aware of how close he sat to me, the smell of his cologne, his large hand that rested on his thigh.

I wore black leggings and a loose blouse with fashionable boots and feather earrings. It was an outfit Angie had helped me put together last night, and I felt good in it.

Trent, of course, hadn't mentioned anything about how I looked, but I hadn't dressed up for him, so that was fine.

"There you are!" Joni called out when we parked the car in the driveway and got out. She hurried to me and wrapped me in a hug. "Oh, you look beautiful!"

I smiled and thanked her. This was who I'd dressed up for.

Ray came and hugged me after shaking Trent's hand, and they ushered us inside.

The house was huge and ornate, with marble floors and tall ceilings. I tried not to gawk as they led us through the massive foyer and to the dining room.

I had a moment of nervousness as I remembered just how out of my league these people were, but their warmth soon set me at ease.

The dinner table was set with fine china and a chandelier hung overhead. Large oil paintings hung on the wall— no doubt all originals—and everything in the house was classy, just like Joni and Ray.

I'd almost expected Grant and Megan to be here, but it was just the four of us. That was fine with me. It would give me a chance to get to know Joni and Ray a little better.

As we sat down at the table, Trent looked sullen and tense.

The staff—two women in fancy uniforms—brought out the first course. It was a cold cucumber and mint soup, and it tasted divine.

"How did you decide to become an executive assistant?" Joni asked while we ate.

"Oh, I sort of fell into it," I said. "I studied marketing and communications in college. I didn't plan on becoming an EA, but it turns out my studies help with my job."

"You're quite versatile," Ray said. "Just like Trent. You make such a good match."

I glanced at Trent, who ate his soup stoically. I shifted in my chair, a little uncomfortable. Everyone kept telling us that we were such a great couple, but if they knew the truth about how strained we were, they wouldn't feel the same way.

"I think it works well to be a jack-of-all-trades," I offered. "It allows us to do different things in life, right?"

"I've always known what I wanted to do," Trent said.

"Make money," Ray said with a grin.

Trent rolled his eyes. "Don't make me sound two-dimensional or anything, Dad."

Ray just kept laughing despite Trent's response. Maybe they were used to his grumpy attitude. Neither of his parents seemed to think anything of his sarcastic remarks.

They knew who he was on the inside, of course. They knew him the way I was getting to know him—underneath all the grump and sarcasm, Trent was a good man.

He had a great work ethic, a good heart, and although he had a pretty crappy way of showing it sometimes, he did care about the people around him.

Even Angie had to admit that he treated his employees well. He paid us generously, with great benefits, and made sure we had a good working environment—except for his occasional outbursts.

Plus, it said a lot that he was making this effort with his family. I still didn't understand what he had against them, but he clearly held a grudge. Despite that, he was going to the weddings and now to this family dinner.

Even though he kept telling me he didn't want to.

That counted for something.

"You've always been three-dimensional, honey," Joni said with a smile and winked at me. "You've always been versatile, too. Bella, did you know that when Trent was eight, he played a tree in the school play?"

"Really?" I asked with a giggle.

"Someone had to do it," Trent grumbled. "There's nothing else to say about it."

"You must have looked adorable," I said.

"Oh, I have a picture," Joni said.

"Mom, don't." Trent's voice was stern, but she laughed. She didn't get up to show me the photo, although I wouldn't have complained.

"He was such a good tree, too," Joni said. Her eyes sparkled when she talked. "He took it very seriously, the way he stood on stage without moving a muscle."

Ray nodded in agreement, smiling at the memory.

Trent groaned. "She tells this to everyone, and it's silly."

I giggled. "I think it's very cute."

"You would," Trent grumbled.

That only made me laugh more. "It's nice to imagine you as a little boy. And to know you have a softer side." I grinned at Trent, but he wasn't amused.

Still, despite his obvious irritation, a smile tugged at the corner of his mouth when he lifted his spoon to take another bite.

"He sounds like he was a great kid," I said.

"Oh, he was," Joni said. She looked at Trent. "You've always been special, honey."

"Thanks, Mom. It's sweet of you to share embarrassing childhood memories with people who had some form of respect for me before all this."

I burst out laughing. Trent was so grumpy, and Joni and

Ray seemed to love giving him a hard time for it. I couldn't help but like them even more.

"Well, I think it's great," I said. "It's so nice to see all of you together for these weddings, too. It's not every day a family comes together for a big celebration."

"Oh, Patrick's wasn't Trent's first wedding appearance," Ray said. "Remember when Sandra got married?" he asked Joni. "Trent and Grant were little kids then. Weren't you pregnant with Anya at that point?"

"Yes, I was," Joni said, smiling. To me, she said, "Sandra is Ray's younger sister. It was a huge wedding."

I glanced at Trent. His eyes were fixed on his almost-finished soup. He was trying very hard to ignore me.

"And Trent was the ring bearer," Ray continued. "He was only about four years old."

"Guys, come on," Trent said, dropping his spoon loudly. "Please, stop."

"Don't stop," I said. "I want to hear this."

Trent snorted and shook his head. "This is ridiculous."

"He was pretty nervous because of the huge crowd," Ray said.

"When it was his turn to walk down the aisle," Joni continued, "he saw Ray and me in the front row, and he waved at us. In his excitement, he dropped the ring cushion, and the rings rolled underneath the pews. Everyone had to crawl around on the floor to find the rings."

"Oh, goodness!" I cried out.

"It was a disaster, but so funny at the same time," Joni said with a laugh. "When we finally found the rings, we tied them back on the pillow, more securely this time. We handed it back to Trent to go the last bit of the way down the aisle. Just before he got there, he tripped over his shoelaces. He just sat down in the middle of the aisle and cried. He refused to keep going, no matter how much we tried to encourage him. He was done."

Trent stewed silently next to me.

"You poor thing," I said and squeezed his hand. "What happened then?"

"Dad picked me up and carried me and the rings," Trent said in a grouchy tone.

"We got some really cute photos, though. He was the sweetest little thing, and no one minded the little disruption."

"I mind now," Trent said.

Joni and Ray glanced at each other and burst out laughing. Trent rolled his eyes.

I loved them. They were so great.

I couldn't figure out why Trent was so set on pulling away from them.

The staff brought out the main course, which was duck à l'orange on a bed of wild rice and roasted vegetables. Everything was delicious. Trent steered the conversation away from himself, prompting Ray to talk about his golf game.

Dessert consisted of chocolate and spun sugar sculptures that apparently had taken two days to put together.

"You didn't have to go through all that trouble, Mom," Trent said when Joni mentioned it.

"Oh, but I did!" Joni cried out. "It's not every day I get to host you for dinner, you know."

I felt a twinge of sadness in Joni's words. I was aware of just how much they had missed seeing Trent.

What was his problem?

When the evening concluded, and we got into the car to head back home, I waited until we had driven out of the neighborhood before I started talking.

"That was pleasant," I said.

"Yeah."

Trent gripped his steering wheel with both hands and stared at the road. I watched the lights of oncoming cars pass.

"Why don't you see them more often?"

Trent only shrugged.

"It's really unfair to them, you know," I said. "They're so nice, and they really make an effort. They want to have a real relationship, and you're set on pushing them away."

Trent glared at me, his eyes dark in the dim light in the car.

"It's none of your business," he said.

"I don't think that's true," I pointed out. "You're paying for it to be my business, remember?"

Trent rolled his eyes.

"Come on, what can be so bad about having a relationship with your parents? You won't realize what you have until it's gone, but when it's actually gone, you'll miss it. Trust me, I know."

Trent shook his head. "I don't want to talk about it."

"Why do you hold this grudge against them?" I pushed. "They really care about you, and—"

"Do they really?" Trent snapped. "Do you know that for a fact?"

"Why do you think they don't?" I asked.

"They might care, but only when whatever I do is on their terms."

"What are you talking about?" I asked.

Trent sighed. "Waverly cheated on me."

I stared at him. "What?"

"My ex-girlfriend. All my family loved Waverly. It was always, 'when are you going to propose to Waverly?' They thought she could do no wrong. And she didn't, until she cheated on me."

"Oh, my God," I murmured.

"Yeah, she confessed to me and everything. I guess the guilt was too much for her."

"That's awful," I said. "But what does that have to do with your family?"

"I broke up with her, and they were upset she was gone. Since my family likes to control everything, they decided I'd broken up with her for selfish reasons, that I had issues with committing. They wanted me to fix things with her." He shook his head in anger. "They didn't fucking believe me, Bella. They didn't believe that Waverly had cheated on me. They took her side, and they said it was my fault."

I shook my head. "Wow. I had no idea."

"Why would you?" Trent snapped. "They won't ever tell you shit like that. They'll put their best foot forward for you, like they do for everyone who isn't family. They're the Dillons, always gracious and kind. But behind the scenes, it's not that simple."

"I can't believe they didn't believe you."

"Yeah, well, shit happens, right?"

"So they still think it was your fault?" I thought back to what Enid had said about Trent's commitment issues, that I should drag him to the altar as quickly as possible.

"Yes," Trent grumbled. "And now they're pushing me to move on. Work on my so-called issues. Find someone new. That's why Mom's always trying to play matchmaker." He scowled. "I'm sick and tired of their demands. They want me to date, they want me to be perfect, and when it all falls apart, they want me to move on like my heart isn't on the line."

I didn't know what to say. I'd thought he was wrong to

act the way he did toward them, but there were always two sides to a story, weren't there? How could his family not believe him about Waverly?

"I'm done. I can't play their games anymore. The only reason I'm going to these weddings is that I don't want to let my siblings and Patrick down. I'm still pissed at them, too, but I'm not ready to cut them all out of my life completely."

"I'm sorry," I said.

"For what?" Trent asked.

"Laying into you when I didn't know the whole story."

Trent shook his head. "It's fine. It's just not that simple."

"I'm starting to see that," I said.

We drove in silence for a while. Finally, Trent pulled into his driveway and parked his car next to mine.

"For what it's worth," I said, "I know what heartbreak feels like. I know what it's like not to have anyone in your corner, and I hate that you went through that."

"You didn't have your family in your corner?" Trent asked.

I shook my head. "I did, until I lost my parents. I guess it's similar to being disbelieved. You're alone in the end, and that sucks."

Trent's eyes slid over my face, studying my expression. He looked open and caring, nothing like the grump he was at the office.

He lifted his hand and cupped my cheek. He stroked his thumb over my cheekbone, and his eyes bored into my soul. He was so handsome, and his expression was so vulnerable, my heart constricted.

When Trent leaned forward and kissed me, I didn't pull away. I didn't stop him.

I wanted this, no matter how wrong it was.

"Come upstairs," he said in a hoarse voice when he broke the kiss.

"We shouldn't do this," I whispered.

"I know," he answered.

He kissed me again, and I couldn't say no to him. I didn't want to.

We climbed out of the car and he took my hand, leading me to the front door, which he unlocked. He led me inside and shut the door behind us. He didn't let go of my hand.

His house was incredible, but I was more focused on him.

I only had a moment to take it all in before Trent pushed me against the wall next to the door and kissed me. He ran his hands down my body and back up again. He cupped my breasts and ground his hard cock against me.

He wanted me as much as I wanted him, and there was no stopping where this was going.

I undid the buttons on Trent's shirt and slid my hands over his naked chest. I planted kisses on his chest, working my way down to his abs.

I wanted more. I wanted to taste every inch of him.

I grabbed his shirt and turned us around, so that he was against the wall. He leaned against it and looked at me with eyes filled with hunger.

I kissed him down his chest again, to his abs, and while I did, I fiddled with his belt buckle.

When I undid his pants, I worked them down his legs so that his cock sprang free. I dropped to my knees and licked the head. It was as large and delicious as I remembered. He groaned and sucked his breath through his teeth as I took him in my mouth.

I bobbed my head, sliding him in and out of my mouth.

The feel of him on my tongue and pushing against the back of my throat was erotic as fuck.

I cupped his balls, massaging him as I moved faster.

"Bella," Trent said in a hoarse voice. I slowed down, moving my eyes up to his. "I want to finish inside of you." His eyes were dilated with need.

I stood and Trent pulled my top over my head without ceremony.

"You're wearing too many clothes," he said as he kissed me again.

We stumbled through his house, undressing each other as we went along, leaving a trail of clothes in our wake. At the stairs, I was only in my underwear, and he was in his boxers.

He lifted me into his arms and carried me to the second floor. In his bedroom, he laid me on the bed.

I reached up and tugged his boxers down, his cock already poking out of them. Trent pulled down my panties and tossed them over his shoulder. He looked at me hungrily.

Trent was so fucking hot, it was hard to think straight. All I knew was that I wanted him inside of me.

I pushed him onto his back and straddled his hips.

"Wait," Trent said, his breath coming in ragged gasps. He rolled over underneath me so that my body tilted, and he rummaged in the nightstand drawer, retrieving a condom. He made quick work of rolling it over his cock, and when he lay back, ready for me, I guided his cock to my entrance and sank down on him.

I moaned when his cock pushed into me, my body stretching to accommodate him.

He groaned when he was buried to the hilt, deep inside

of me, filling me up to bursting. I paused, getting used to the feel of him.

I braced my hands on his chest and rocked my hips back and forth, sliding him in and out of me.

Trent gripped my hips. He pulled me forward and pushed me back so that he went deeper with every stroke.

My clit rubbed against his pubic bone as I rode him, and pleasure spread through my body, building at my core as I crept closer and closer to orgasm.

Trent clenched his jaw and his brows knitted together as he stared at me, taking it all in.

I rocked harder and faster, fucking him until my orgasm erupted inside of me. It spread through my body with searing heat. The pleasure took my breath away. I collapsed on Trent's chest, and he bucked his hips underneath me, fucking me while I was unable to do it myself.

I cried out as the movement enhanced my orgasm, making it more intense.

"Trent," I moaned.

"Fuck, Bella," Trent bit out through gritted teeth as if he was struggling to hold back.

He rolled me over, holding onto me, completely in charge and in control.

I was suddenly underneath him, panting in the aftermath of my orgasm. My body was on fire, humming with need.

He bucked his hips against mine, pounding into me. My breaths came in shallow gasps, in rhythm with Trent's fucking.

He moved faster as he neared his orgasm, his strokes shortening. I knew he was close, and I held on for dear life as pleasure hummed through me.

When Trent thrust into me, burying himself as deep as

he would go, he let out a sharp cry and I felt him release inside of me. The sensation pushed me into the next orgasm, and a flood of warmth coursed through my body.

The pleasure seemed to swallow us whole as we lay there, connected and gasping.

He planted kisses on my lips, my cheeks, my forehead.

Finally, when the pleasure subsided, he rolled off me, slipping out. We lay side by side, trying to catch our breath.

Trent glanced at me, then pulled me closer to him. I snuggled against his body, my head on his firm, muscled chest.

I wasn't supposed to be here. We weren't supposed to be doing this at all.

But being together felt like the most natural thing in the world, and I didn't want to go.

Not yet.

I closed my eyes as Trent's heart beat against my cheek. His breathing deepened and slowed down as he drifted off to sleep.

I was suddenly exhausted, and although I knew I should get up and leave, I just couldn't bring myself to do it.

Instead, I fell asleep on his chest where it was warm and safe.

Where it felt like home.

When I blinked my eyes open the next morning, the light had a silver quality to it. It was just after dawn, still very early.

Trent was tangled in the sheets, his arm thrown over my body.

I watched his perfectly chiseled face, and my heart constricted. He was great in so many ways... but we shouldn't have done this.

I shouldn't have done this. I was putting my heart in danger when obviously, this was never going to last.

This arrangement was going to come to an end, and where would that leave me?

Carefully, even slower than the last time I'd done this, I crawled out from underneath his arm and the covers, getting off the bed. I froze and watched, but Trent was still asleep, breathing deeply.

I let out a breath of relief and moved around the room quietly, finding my underwear and putting it on. Downstairs, I found my clothes where he'd tossed each item. I got dressed, located my phone and purse, and quietly let myself out.

It was a shitty thing for me to do, leaving like this before he woke up, but I didn't want the morning-after conversation.

I didn't want him to tell me this was a mistake. I didn't want to have to agree.

It was better for me to just go.

I got into my car and drove to my apartment. Angie's door was shut, and I moved quietly through the space.

I showered and got ready for work, trying not to think about Trent. Trying not to *feel* anything for Trent.

16

TRENT

*M*y bed was empty.

The sheets were a tangled mess, proof of what had happened last night, but Bella was nowhere to be found.

Not in my bed or the bathroom, the shower or the kitchen.

She'd left without saying goodbye.

Shit.

What the fuck had happened between us last night?

Damn it, I shouldn't have slept with her. I should have just sent her home.

She'd been so sweet and understanding, and it had been a long time since someone saw my side when it came to my family.

Not to mention the fact that Bella was incredible in every way. She'd been so gracious with my parents, playing along just like I'd asked her to, even though she could have been a total jerk after I hurt her.

She could have been spiteful and made the night hell for me, but she wasn't that person.

It made me like her that much more. And last night, I hadn't been able to resist her.

I got into the shower. When the hot water ran over my body, the memory of Bella's touch on my skin returned to me.

She was so fucking hot, and the way we came together when we had sex was pure magic. Everything about her was gorgeous, and I couldn't stay away from her.

Clearly, she didn't feel the same. If she did, she wouldn't have snuck out like that.

I got dressed, made coffee in the kitchen, and finally left the house to go to work.

Bella would probably call in sick today. If she wanted to avoid me this morning, being in the office wasn't going to help. I would have to wait until tomorrow to talk to her.

Was that something I was willing to do? A part of me wanted to call her right now and find out what was going on. A part of me was feverish about where we stood.

Damn it, I was starting to fall for her.

That wasn't the plan. Hell, I'd told *her* not to get attached, and now I was doing exactly that.

Maybe it was better if she wasn't in the office today. It would give me a chance to clear my head, to think straight again.

At work, I rode the elevator to the top floor, walked to my office, and sat at my desk. A moment later, a knock sounded on my door.

Bella walked in, holding my cup of coffee and the reports the way she did every morning. As if nothing had happened.

I stared at her as she crossed the office and put my coffee down in front of me.

She didn't look like she'd slept well. Her hair was a mess,

pulled back into a ponytail with flyaway strands around her face, and despite wearing makeup, she had light circles under her eyes. Her face was guarded.

I felt like shit. I'd done that to her.

Bella sat down and opened the report file.

"Can we talk?" I asked.

Bella glanced at me and closed the file again. She knew what I meant—I didn't want to talk about work.

"I was surprised you were gone when I woke," I said.

She paused, biting her lip. "I guess I figured you'd want it that way."

"I don't, though," I said. "I *don't* want it that way. Do you?"

She studied me. "No. I wanted to stay in your arms, to be honest."

I exhaled. So she felt this connection between us, too.

"I can't keep pretending this isn't happening," I said.

"What?"

"You and me. And I'm not just talking about the contract. Tell me you feel it, too."

Bella pursed her lips, but she nodded. "Yeah, I do."

Something inside me uncoiled. I realized I'd worried that she didn't feel the same way about me, but if last night had been anything to go by...

"What are we going to do?" I asked. "This wasn't supposed to happen."

"We broke my rule," she said with a small smile.

I chuckled. "Yeah, well, I've never been good at sticking to rules."

Bella smiled, but it faded again. "I don't want to fight it. I can't."

"I don't want to, either," I admitted. "It's dangerous,

though. We work together, and that can cause all kinds of shit..."

"It's a bit late for that now," Bella said, and she was right. I shouldn't have slept with her the first time if I wanted to avoid complications in the office. Who was I kidding? Even the contract with her pretending to be my girlfriend had caused complications, I was just too stubborn and proud to admit to that.

"Maybe we should just see where this goes," I suggested.

"Ride it out until it burns out," Bella added.

"Right," I said. I was hoping it *wouldn't* burn out, but it was a fair suggestion.

"Okay," Bella said, agreeing.

I smiled, feeling on top of the world.

But then an alarm bell went off inside. Was I getting too close to her?

I needed to add a caveat before things got out of control.

"I'm not trying to date you," I said quickly. "It's not a relationship, by any means. It's just—"

"Sex," Bella finished for me. "I get it. We'll stop trying to fight the physical attraction. We'll get what we need from each other, but keep it no strings attached."

"And you're okay with that?"

"Yeah, it works for me," Bella said.

"No strings attached," I said, although I was already starting to feel the metaphorical strings. Still, if I could channel that energy into sex with her, it would be fine.

"Of course," Bella said. "We'll still keep it under wraps, too."

"Yeah," I said. The last thing I wanted was for everyone to know that not only were Bella and I pretending to date, we were also sleeping together. I appreciated the discretion.

"Okay, good," I said, glad that we'd cleared that up. "It should make things easier for both of us."

"I think so," Bella said.

I nodded.

"Do you want to go through the reports?" Bella asked, bringing us back to business.

I nodded. There was nothing else to talk about, and business was a better focus right now. My body still hummed with the aftermath of our sex, and if I had my way, I'd be all over her again. I couldn't stop thinking about the way she rode me last night, her breasts jiggling, her face contorted with pure pleasure as my cock pounded into her.

I shifted in my chair and tugged at my belt to adjust my pants as my cock got hard again.

Behave.

I'd already gotten what I needed from her.

I just wanted it again. Bella was intoxicating, addictive, and I wanted more.

She opened the file and started reading off the numbers. I forced myself to stop picturing her naked and listen to the facts she was reading out to me, but it was hard to focus. Still, now that we'd agreed to sleep together, I could have her more often. I didn't have to fight my clear attraction to her anymore.

We'll keep our fake relationship and our sex separate from the office.

Yeah, right. That was going to be a hell of a lot harder than I thought, since she worked with me and everything she did was mesmerizing. Her voice was soothing as she read out the report, and I stared at her mouth. I wanted to kiss her. Her lips were perfect—I could conjure the taste of her in my mind. I wanted another taste.

I'd been dreaming about her for two years, and somehow the reality was *so* much better than the dream.

It was rarely like that, but with Bella everything was different than the norm.

I was one lucky son of a bitch that I had her here. This thing wouldn't last forever, I knew that, but I wasn't going to think about any of that. All I would do was focus on right here, right now.

On Bella.

17

BELLA

*T*he next couple of weeks passed in a blur. We worked together. We fucked—regularly.

Everything about Trent was incredible and the more comfortable we got around each other, the more it unlocked who he really was. I'd thought our sex the first time had been amazing, but now that neither of us held back, it was better than ever.

In the office, we were on our best behavior, but it was impossible not to be drawn to him. The tension between us when we were alone was so thick, I felt like I could choke on it. I wanted to grab him and kiss him, and I wanted him to fuck me on his desk all the time.

Of course, we behaved. I wasn't going to do anything stupid at the office that would blow our cover—we had way too many nosy people working with us. The moment someone caught wind of what we were doing, the gossip would run through the office like wildfire. I still had a reputation to protect, and so did Trent.

Aside from the sex, I was starting to get to know Trent better as a person, too. Our sessions always ended with us collapsing in a puddle of sweat next to each other. The first few times, we'd gotten dressed and gone back to our separate lives, but as time went on, we started talking.

I'd come to love our pillow-talk sessions.

I told him more about my parents, opening up about how I'd lost them, and how I'd dealt with it. It felt so good to be able to talk to someone about it, and when we talked, Trent really *listened*. I told him about the student loans I took to get myself through college, and that my life hadn't turned out the way I'd hoped it would.

He told me about Waverly and the way her cheating had crushed him. Trent always seemed very careful not to open up too much, but Waverly had been someone he'd trusted with his heart and she'd stepped on it, ripping it to pieces and giving it back to him barely recognizable.

I felt for Trent. He'd been through so much, and I started to understand his grumpy attitude and his approach to life now that I knew who he was under that invincible mask of his.

Talking to Trent was easy. Surprisingly, he cared. He saw things about me, who I really was. I cared about things more than most people knew about, and Trent was starting to see that about me. He was starting to understand me, and that made our working relationship that much easier, too.

The Tuesday before the Denver wedding—a couple of weeks after Trent and I decided to start seeing each other informally—I started feeling strange.

I woke up sick.

My stomach twisted and rolled and when I got up from bed, I was dizzy. When my stomach lurched, I ran to the bathroom and hunched over the toilet bowl. I retched until the little contents I still had in my stomach were out.

I sat back and wiped my mouth with toilet paper. I

pressed my hand against my head, but I couldn't feel it if I had a fever.

Had I eaten something wrong? It wasn't food poisoning, I was pretty sure of that.

I got up and steadied myself on the sink before I brushed my teeth and washed my hands. While I did, my mind ran in circles. I suddenly wondered when last I'd had my period. I'd been having so much fun with Trent, I hadn't thought about my cycle and that I might have to worry about something like that popping up.

I closed my eyes and tried to figure out how long it had been... three weeks? No, that didn't seem right. Four, five...?

Shit.

It had been more than six weeks. I was almost sure of that.

Oh, my God.

I couldn't be pregnant, could I? We always used condoms. Always. If Trent was anything, he was careful. No matter what, he always had a condom on hand. Not that they were foolproof, though. Condoms could still fail.

But I was on birth control, too. I never took chances.

This was crazy. I wasn't supposed to get knocked up with two forms of contraceptive, for God's sake.

I had to find out for sure. I couldn't be pregnant with Trent's baby. After everything we were going through, throwing a baby into the mix...

I pushed the thought out of my mind, pulled on clothes and grabbed my car keys. I ran to the store and bought two pregnancy tests.

When I got back home, Angie was awake.

"Oh, you're up early," she said, yawning.

"Yeah, I wanted to get a head start. Mind if use the shower first?"

"Go ahead. I need coffee."

With shaking hands, I locked myself in the bathroom. I turned on the shower, but instead of stepping under the water, I ripped open the tests and peed on one stick, then the other.

I set them on the counter and hopped under the spray while I waited for the tests to do their thing. My stomach twisted and turned again, but this time it was nerves.

I can't be pregnant.

I was on birth control. Didn't that mean anything?

After a quick wash, I got out and wrapped a towel around myself. Drawing a deep breath, I walked to the counter.

My fingers trembled as I reached for the first test. I bit my lip and squeezed my eyes shut, hoping to God that the tests would be negative.

Positive.

Both of them.

Fuck.

As if my body revolted, I threw up into the toilet again. I didn't have anything but water to vomit, but my body insisted that I deposit it all. When I was done, I pressed my hands to my cheeks.

What was I going to do?

"Bella?" Angie called on the other side of the door. "Are you okay?"

I rinsed my mouth out, threw the tests away, and opened the door, still just wearing my towel. "I'm fine. I think it's something I ate."

Angie looked worried. "Are you sure?"

I nodded. "I'll pick something up from the store after work if I don't feel better later."

"You don't want to call in sick?"

I shook my head. "I have a lot to get through today. I'll be fine, really."

Shit, shit, shit.

I couldn't even talk to Angie about what was going on. She didn't like Trent, she didn't approve of what we were doing, and if she found out I was pregnant with his baby...

I still had to wrap my mind around what was going on. I just wished I had someone I could talk to.

For a moment, Megan popped into my mind. Maybe I could talk to her; she was always understanding.

Then again, she was Trent's future sister-in-law. I couldn't tell her, not before I told Trent himself.

In my bedroom, I closed the door and sank onto the bed.

More than ever, I missed my mother. I wished I could talk to her, ask her advice.

What was I supposed to do now? Trent and I were sleeping together, but we weren't a couple.

He could still be an ass at times, even though I understood him better now. But I had no idea how he would react to this. I had no idea what to expect when I told him.

What if he lost his shit? God, he was bound to lose it.

Whatever the case, I had to talk to him, and no matter which way it went, I was in this alone without backup.

He didn't want a relationship with me.

Shit, I couldn't tell him. Not yet.

I took a deep breath and let it out with a shudder, wishing I could just make this all go away.

Finally, I got up and got dressed. I had to get ready for work and face Trent in the office, even if I didn't tell him yet. I had a job to do, a contract to live up to, a pseudo-relationship to figure out.

Could things get any more complicated?

18

TRENT

*S*he's not your girlfriend.

If I didn't remind myself of that every fucking time I thought about Bella, I was going to get my heart involved.

I couldn't afford to do that.

She *wasn't* my girlfriend.

Despite the fact that we were great together. Despite the fact that I had more fun with her than I'd ever had with anyone.

Never mind that I could actually see her as my girlfriend, which was something I'd sworn off after Waverly.

I didn't date, I didn't do love, I didn't put myself in a position where I could get my heart broken all over again.

I was just paying Bella to keep my parents off my case. That was all, there wasn't anything more to it.

No matter how much it felt like there was.

At least, that was how it had felt for a while.

The last two days, though, I had no idea what was going on.

It all started on Tuesday. Bella was still herself in the

office—on the ball all the time when it came to her job. She was professional, put-together, a *dream* to work with... and yet, something was different about her.

By Wednesday, it was as if the spark inside her had switched off. She didn't look at me with the same light in her eyes as she had a short while ago. Like she'd withdrawn from me.

Was it just me? Was I going crazy?

When she came in to work on Thursday, she was in a bad mood. Her mouth was turned down in a scowl, her hair was a little messier than usual, and when she came in with the coffee and my reports, she wasn't as chatty as usual.

"Is everything okay?" I asked.

"Of course," she said. "Why wouldn't it be?"

"You just don't look like everything is okay."

"What would that look like?" she challenged.

Yeah, she was *definitely* not in her usual mood.

I shook my head. "Let's go over those reports."

Bella sighed and flipped the folder open, running through the numbers. I listened, but I couldn't concentrate. I watched her, instead.

She had always been a vision to behold. But lately, the more she opened up to me about who she was, the more beautiful she became.

Today, though, I couldn't reach her at all.

"Do you need me to go through the stocks as well?" Bella asked, glancing up at me.

"No," I said. She'd never asked me that before—she usually just launched into them. "I can take care of that myself."

There seemed to be a question on her lips, but she didn't ask. Instead, she nodded curtly.

Didn't she want to be in the same room as me?

Maybe she was struggling with the same thing I was—we were so good together, we were always happy and having fun. It was tough not to see this as the relationship we kept portraying to everyone else. The relationship we both agreed we couldn't have for real. I was grumpy as fuck about the whole thing, too.

When she walked to the door, I had this sudden urge to not let her go. It was ridiculous, of course. She had work to take care of, and so did I. I wanted to spend more time with her, though.

"Bella," I said. "Have dinner with me tonight."

"Okay," she said, pausing at the door. Her voice was neutral. "Where? I can meet you."

"At my place," I said.

Bella hesitated. When we went out to dinner, I usually took her to a fancy restaurant where I could spoil her, but tonight, I wanted to be alone with her.

"Be there at eight," I added.

She nodded and shut the door behind her.

What the fuck was I thinking? I never invited women to my place to make dinner for them. It gave them the wrong idea, that I wanted more.

The thing was, we were already blurring all the lines between us, so I might as well go all out. I didn't like it when she was so withdrawn from me. I wanted to pull her back.

I wasn't sure why—I was playing with fire, but I wasn't going to back out now. We were flying to Colorado this weekend for my sister's wedding, anyway. I needed to spend some time alone with her first.

I left the office early and ordered groceries to be delivered to my house. When they were delivered, I got to work.

Chicken parmesan with roasted vegetables and a Greek salad were on the menu for tonight. I made jasmine rice with it, and chose a bottle of wine that would pair well with the chicken.

Bella arrived while I was cooking the chicken.

I opened the front door to let her in and kissed her on the cheek.

"Come in, make yourself at home," I said as she followed me to the kitchen.

"Mmm, it smells delicious. What are you cooking?" she asked with a small smile.

"Chicken parmesan."

"Fancy."

"It's a special occasion," I said with a grin.

"Yeah? What's the occasion?"

"Us, spending time together."

Bella only looked at me, and I struggled to read her expression.

"What can I help with?" she asked, not responding to what I'd said.

"You can make the salad, if you want," I said.

Bella nodded and I guided her around the kitchen as she gathered her tools and the ingredients from the fridge. She sat at the counter island and started chopping while I checked on the chicken and the rice.

I was very aware of her in my kitchen. She fit so well into my house.

She fit so well into my *life*.

"Did you have a good day at the office?" I asked.

Bella stopped chopping. "We work in the same office."

"I know," I said. "But we do different things. And I realized today I don't know if you have a good or a bad day, I don't know if your job is more challenging at some times than others. You just take it in your stride and make it work for me."

"That's my job," Bella said.

"I know, I know. But I still want to know if you had a good day."

Bella thought about it. "It was a better day than usual. Sometimes, the fires I have to put out are challenging, but today was pretty chill."

"I'm glad," I said. "It looked like you'd had a rough week when you came in this morning."

"You could say that," Bella said with a sigh.

I glanced at her. "Is there any way I can make it better?"

Bella shook her head immediately. "It's not your job to make my job better. Besides, it's just a... bad patch. I'll figure it out."

I realized I didn't want her to just *figure it out*. I wanted to be the one to help her with that. I wanted to be her hero. I wanted to take care of her—not that she needed it.

Bella was a strong woman who'd always stood on her own two feet. I'd seen it when I hired her, and I'd started to understand just how independent she was as I got to know her better. Like how she became friends with my family. It rubbed me the wrong way at first, and I still wasn't totally comfortable with it.

But I had to hand it to her. The girl had guts.

When the food was ready, we each dished ourselves a plate.

"I got us this," I said, holding up the bottle of wine. "It's a pretty good vintage for such short notice, and I think you'll love it."

"I'm sorry to be a pain, but... is it okay if I just drink water?" Bella asked.

I frowned. "Water?"

"Yeah. I... have a really bad headache. If I drink wine now, it will only make it worse."

"Oh, of course," I said. "Can I bring you headache tablets? I'm sure I have something in my medicine cabinet..."

She shook her head. "I took something before I came. I just don't want to take chances."

I nodded. "Okay, sure." I poured her water from the pitcher in my fridge and poured myself a glass of wine.

We carried our plates to the dining room. I'd set the table and lit candles, and a vase of fresh roses stood in the center.

Everything was perfect and romantic.

"This is gorgeous," Bella said.

"I don't usually eat in here, but I thought it would be a nice change."

"Where do you usually eat?"

I laughed. "In front of the television, like a real bachelor."

"It's the only way to do it," Bella said, a smile playing around her mouth. But the smile never reached her eyes.

"Listen," I said, clearing my throat. "I want to talk to you."

She lowered her fork with a frown. "About what?"

"Us," I said and glanced at her. "This thing we have going... it isn't working for me."

Bella pursed her lips.

"Oh," she said, her face falling. She put her fork down and rested her hands on either side of her plate before she reached for her water glass and took a big gulp. "I didn't realize you weren't happy."

She thought I was ending things between us.

I guess I *was* ending what we had, but not in the way she thought.

"I want to give a real relationship a try," I said.

"What?" Bella asked, blinking at me.

"I want to do this for real with you, Bella," I said. "Not just pretend. Not just no-strings-attached sex whenever we feel like it. I want you to be my girlfriend and go all out with this, no holds barred."

Bella stared at me, shaking her head almost imperceptibly. "I don't understand." Her voice had become thin. "Why?"

"Because I like you," I said. "I mean... I really *like* you."

God, I sounded like a teenager who didn't know how to express his feelings. But the problem was, I didn't know how to say it. I wanted to tell her I was falling for her, but putting it into words still scared me. Taking this step was already a big deal.

Bella hesitated.

"Will you be my girlfriend?" I asked.

Bella looked at me, and her hazel eyes were serious. She opened her mouth like she was going to say something, but she stopped herself. What did she want to tell me? What was up with her?

Finally, she smiled, and the tension melted from her shoulders.

"Yeah," she said. "I'd like that."

I stared at her, letting the words sink in, before I got up and walked around the table. I grabbed her and kissed her.

She moaned softly. I pulled her up to her feet and wrapped my arms around her. Burying my face in her neck, I started unbuttoning her shirt.

"What about the food?" she asked, giggling between kisses as I unzipped her skirt and pushed it down her thighs.

"The food can wait."

"It will go cold."

"I'll reheat it. I have to make you mine."

"I'm already yours," she said.

"I know," I murmured as I dove between her legs.

I pulled her panties down and breathed in her scent, then began to lap between her legs as she spread them open for me.

She buried her hands in my hair and threw her head back, losing herself in pleasure.

Now that she'd agreed to be mine for real, I wanted to show her my appreciation.

19

BELLA

When I left Trent's house, my body hummed with the aftermath of our sex.

My fingers tingled as I started my car. I paused to run my hands through my hair, trying to untangle it and look a little less like I'd just been fucked.

A smile played over my lips as I pulled out of Trent's driveway.

Trent hadn't held back tonight. He'd fucked me like there was no tomorrow. Then again, it hadn't just been fucking. The way he kissed me, touched me, the way he claimed my body had been so sensual, so emotional.

If I hadn't known better, I would have thought he'd made love to me.

I still had to wrap my mind around the fact that we were dating. He said he wanted to make it *real*.

How was that possible? How had the aloof, unreachable Trent Dillon fallen for me hard enough that he'd been willing to push his reservations aside and date me?

I had no idea, but I wasn't going to question it too much.

I felt a whole lot for him, too. I just wasn't able to put it to words yet. Not until I got my footing.

There were too many complications.

Like the fact that I was pregnant and I hadn't told him yet.

Shit.

Trent had asked me to stay the night, and I'd been tempted to stay and fall asleep in his arms. I couldn't, though.

I'd told him I still needed to pack for Colorado, which was true. Our flight was tomorrow.

But I also had to think.

How was I going to do this? I couldn't hide the fact that I was pregnant from him forever—at some point he was bound to notice. A pregnant belly wasn't exactly the same as a new haircut.

I drove home, parked and sat in my car for a moment while the engine ticked over. The darkness wrapped around me, shielding me from the reality that I had to face soon.

I couldn't sit here forever, though.

When I went into the apartment, Angie was on the couch with a blanket, watching television.

"Oh, you're here," she said. "I thought you were going to stay the night."

I shook my head. "I have to pack for tomorrow."

"You could have packed in the morning," Angie pointed out. "I would have stayed after hot sex. If you could count sex with Diablo as hot." She made a gagging face.

I shook my head, frustrated with Angie. She was so against me spending time with Trent. She was still convinced that he had no redeeming qualities, and she gave me shit about being with him. I'd tried to tell her he wasn't that bad, but she wouldn't listen.

If she found out we were really dating now, she would have a field day.

In my room, I shut the door and started laying out the clothes I'd need for the trip on my bed.

While I packed, my mind ran in circles.

Trent had sprung this relationship thing on me out of the blue. I'd never guessed he wanted a real relationship.

In fact, for a moment, I'd been sure he was breaking everything off.

A relationship with Trent—a real one—was very different from what we'd been doing until now.

The past three days, I'd withdrawn. I had to figure out how I was going to tell him about the baby.

I'd gotten more and more nervous by the day, working myself up into a lather.

At times, I thought it best to tell him in the office because he wouldn't make a scene with people around.

Other times, I figured it would be easier to tell him when we were alone.

I'd gotten my nerve up several times. Every time I told myself I would do it, I'd chickened out.

I was terrified of what he would think. Of what his reaction would be. We'd come to an understanding, but things were still raw between us. It was a delicate balance.

And now, we were dating.

He'd thrown me for a complete loop, and instead of telling him my news, I'd agreed to be his girlfriend for real.

Why?

Because I wanted it. I'd wanted to date Trent since the moment we first slept together, even if I hadn't been willing to admit to it—not even to myself.

Being with him was a dream come true.

Now, I was even more worried to tell him that I was pregnant with his baby. Until now, he'd been so adamant this whole thing between us was just physical that telling him had seemed wrong. Maybe he would think I was trapping him into something long-term.

Now, everything had changed. We were closer, sure. But not close enough to be talking about a future with kids.

Let alone actually having them.

Shit.

I didn't know what to do.

I knew he would support the baby. Financially, he would do the right thing. Trent was a good man.

Would he stick around and be a part of my life, a part of the baby's life? That part I didn't know.

What if he just ended the relationship? It had only just started, but maybe it would all be over as soon as it even began.

None of this was supposed to happen. I wasn't supposed to fall in love with my boss and I sure as shit wasn't supposed to get pregnant with his baby.

I'd have to wait until after the next wedding.

His sister was getting married. I couldn't break this news to him yet. This weekend was about Anya, not any drama that might come up if I told Trent his life was about to change.

We still had a contract, an image to uphold in front of his family. Even though the image had become very real tonight.

I zipped up my suitcase, suddenly determined. It was the only way I could deal with this—one day at a time.

I woke up early the next day to shower and get ready to leave. We didn't go into the office today—Trent had arranged for us to leave early so we could spend some time alone together, and I was excited about that.

When he sent a fancy black car to pick me up, Angie helped me carry my suitcase to the curb. She whistled through her teeth when she saw the car.

"He's pulling out all the stops to sell this, huh?" she said. "I really thought this whole thing was a mistake, but I have to admit, I'm jealous of the perks."

"The car?" I asked.

"The car, the clothes..."

"Yeah, the perks aren't bad," I said with a shrug. The driver took the luggage from me and put it in the trunk.

"Have fun," Angie said.

"Thanks," I said.

"Just remember who he is, okay?" Angie added.

"Trent?"

"*Diablo,*" Angie said with emphasis. "Just because he looks good in a suit doesn't mean he's not the devil under all that."

"Thanks," I said. "I know what I'm doing."

Angie sighed. "You keep saying that."

"I'll text you when I get there." I gave her a quick hug and got in the car when the driver opened the door for me.

The car took me to the airfield, where Trent was waiting. The driver took my luggage to the jet while Trent embraced me and planted a kiss on my lips.

"Ready for round two?" he asked.

"You bet," I said.

"It's getting easier and easier to pretend we're together," Trent said with a twinkle in his eye.

"We *are* together!" I cried out.

Trent chuckled. "That's my point."

I giggled and butterflies erupted in my stomach when Trent took my hand and led me to the plane. He'd taken my hand so many times before, but this time, it meant so much more.

We were together, a couple. And it was real.

We strapped ourselves into the seats, and soon, the plane rolled onto the runway. My stomach twisted and turned as we took off.

"Oh, God," I said, my throat tightening.

"What is it?" Trent asked.

"I think I'm going to be sick."

"What's wrong?"

I couldn't answer him. I grabbed the paper bag they always put in planes and threw up into it, my body doubling over as I retched.

Trent put his hand on my back and rubbed it in circles, which only made me vomit more.

When I'd deposited every bit of breakfast I'd had this morning, I sat back in the seat and let out a breath, squeezing my eyes shut. My breathing came in ragged gasps.

"Are you okay?" Trent asked.

"Fine," I said. "It's just..."

Morning sickness.

"I'm airsick is all," I said.

"We have something for that on board," Trent said. The moment we were able to undo our seat belts, he waved at the attendant to bring me nausea pills. I swallowed one down with a gulp of water from the bottle she'd also provided.

I sat back and took a shaky breath.

"Give it about half an hour, and you'll be fine," Trent said.

I nodded, but before I could say anything, my stomach twisted again.

The hostess had a bucket on hand—it might have been

an ice bucket, quickly repurposed—and I threw up into that. I got rid of all the water and the nausea pill.

"Shit," I said, my throat still tight. "Sorry. This is really embarrassing." The pill wouldn't do much if I couldn't keep it down.

Trent frowned. "Maybe you should eat something."

They brought me crackers and cheese, and I ate some of it and drank some more water... only to throw that up, too.

Trent looked at me as I sat back, exhausted after throwing up so much.

"What's going on with you?" Trent asked. "Are you sick?"

"I don't think so," I said. "It's just the turbulence."

"We haven't had any," Trent said.

"You know what I mean." I waved my hand around. "It's just the... air."

"You didn't have a problem with flying before," Trent said. He looked worried.

What if he put two and two together? What if he figured it out?

"When we arrive in Denver, you should see a doctor," Trent said.

I shook my head. "I don't think that will be necessary. It's just the flying today. Really, I'm fine. I don't want to make a fuss and draw attention away from the wedding weekend."

Trent studied me, concerned, but he finally nodded.

"Okay, but if you start to feel worse, I'm making an appointment."

I nodded. I could only hope that I wouldn't throw up during any of the important events. I had no idea if I could control it that way, but I had to try.

For a moment, I considered telling Trent and getting it over with. He deserved to know. And right now, I felt miserable.

But I stopped myself. If I told him now, I was going to screw up the whole trip. I would fuck things up between us, I would make it strained for everyone else, and if Trent didn't want to be with me anymore, the next two weddings were going to be a nightmare.

I just had to ride it out, try to keep it in, and stick to the plan of telling him when the weekend was all over.

My stomach rolled again, and I prayed I could make it through this weekend before it all blew up in my face.

Despite my determination, I was pretty sure that was the way it would go.

20

BELLA

J'd never been more relieved to touch ground and get off an aircraft.

When we landed, I felt transparent after throwing up so much. I hadn't had a chance to eat or drink anything—everything had come back up.

"How are you feeling?" Trent asked when we climbed into a sleek black car that waited for us at the airfield.

"Better," I said with a smile. It was only partially true—my stomach still twisted and turned, but not as violently as when we were in the air.

"Good," Trent said and he took my hand and squeezed it warmly.

I felt a pang of guilt. I wasn't being totally honest, and I hated it. I just couldn't tell him the truth. Not yet.

The car drove through the city, then into the mountains. I looked out of the window at the landscape stretching as far as the eye could see. Denver was so different from LA. After we climbed in elevation and drove through a vast forest, we finally came to a large, open area. We passed several small towns and ranches.

I was feeling much better now, and I listened as Trent told me stories of growing up with his siblings. Anya had been the rebellious one, and she'd moved to Colorado years ago to work on a ranch, where she met Kevin. It was a sweet story, and I smiled as Trent talked.

"This is the beginning of his property," Trent said as we drove along a wooden fence that encompassed Kevin's ranch.

"It's huge," I commented after a while. It felt like we'd been driving along his land forever.

"It's a pretty big parcel," Trent said, nodding. "You'd never think Kevin is worth millions from looking at him."

"He's very down-to-earth," I agreed.

"I like him for Anya," Trent said, nodding. "He's good for her. She can get so caught up in her head sometimes. She gets anxious and stressed, and I think he mellows her out. It's just what she needs."

It was sweet hearing Trent talk about his sister that way. He was so distant from his family, keeping them all at arm's length, but he really cared. Anyone who spent a bit of time in his company could see that.

Then again, not a lot of people spent time in his company—he didn't keep only his family at arm's length, he was distant from *everyone*.

The car turned through two stone posts and entered the ranch. We wove through pastures where cows grazed and passed a picturesque lake. The main house—a spectacular, enormous wooden lodge—came into view after another set of gates.

It was breathtaking.

We stopped in front of three handsome buildings that were arranged in the shape of a horseshoe, and Joni came out from one to meet us.

"Just in time," she said with a smile before she hugged me and then Trent. "Everyone arrived just before you, so the party is complete!" She looked at me warmly. "I'm so happy you're here!"

"Thank you, Joni. This place is amazing," I said.

Megan came through the door that led to the reception hall and squealed when she saw me. Running over, she pulled me into a tight hug.

"I was waiting for you to arrive!"

Trent only watched our gleeful greeting. He didn't understand why I was becoming friends with his family.

I especially liked Megan. I could relate to her, and we clicked. She was marrying into the family, coming from a modest background like me, and I felt like if anyone understood what it was like to be on the outside looking in, it was her.

"Come have a look at this place," Megan said, looping her arm through mine. "It's *divine*. Your room is close to ours. This weekend is going to be great!"

Megan pulled me away from Trent and Joni. I glanced over my shoulder at him, and he waved me off with a smile.

My stomach twisted dangerously, but I decided not to panic over the complication that this pregnancy had created. I would just live in the moment and enjoy myself for the weekend.

I only wished I could tell someone what was going on.

The rooms were incredible. We had a full suite to ourselves, with two large bedrooms and a private patio that looked over a small, landscaped yard. Bees flitted around rosemary and lavender bushes outside.

Trent and I were sharing a bedroom this time, and I was happy about it. We brought our luggage into the larger of the two rooms, leaving the smaller one unused.

"This isn't half bad," Trent said with a sniff. "It's peaceful out here."

"It's nice to get away from the city for a change," I said.

"Maybe we should do something like this again in a couple of months," Trent said. "Take a break from the hustle and bustle and unwind. What do you think?"

In a couple of months, I might be showing. Either way, Trent would know I was pregnant by that time.

Would we still be together by then?

"That sounds amazing," I said. And the idea of getting away with Trent on an adventure, just the two of us, did sound amazing.

We got ready for dinner with the family. I had packed a peach-colored dress with an empire waist and rhinestones along the bodice. I pulled my hair into a half-up bun and curled the hair that fell down my back. Stepping into sparkling flats the same color as the rhinestones on my dress, I completed the look with a small clutch.

When I came out of the room, Trent's eyes slid down my body, sending a chill down my spine. His gaze was hot, his eyes filled with hunger.

"You look amazing," Trent breathed.

"You look pretty good, too," I smiled at him, fighting the blush that crept onto our cheeks.

We'd slept together so many times, I should have been used to the way he looked at me by now. I shouldn't have blushed so heavily at his compliments, but I couldn't help it. When Trent looked at me like that, I felt like a goddess.

He wore a dark gray suit with a black shirt. With his dark brown hair combed to the side and his blue eyes intense, he looked suave and delicious. A part of me wanted to drag him back into the room so we could peel each other's outfits off.

But we had a dinner to attend.

I swallowed hard, and Trent held out his arm to escort me. I smiled at him.

The whole family was gathered in the dining room and my heart warmed as everyone greeted us.

The conversation came easily now. I joked and laughed along, comfortable with their banter. Trying to be discreet, I waved away the wine that the servers offered.

"Are you sure you're okay?" Trent asked with a concerned frown when he noticed me drinking only water.

"I still feel a bit queasy," I said. "I don't want to tempt fate."

"Ah," Trent said, nodding. "Better to steer clear, then."

It hadn't been a lie—I still felt sick. Not so bad that I would throw up, thank God, but the excuse had been perfect to avoid drinking alcohol. It was going to be hard to avoid drinking at the wedding this weekend, but I could figure something out.

"Everyone," Anya said, holding up her glass and tapping it lightly with her fork. The table fell quiet. "Kevin and I have an announcement to make."

"You're already getting married, and we all flew in for the wedding," Isaac called out. "Not enough attention yet?"

"Stop it," Claire cut her brother off. "You're just jealous they're not paying attention to you."

"Gotta get married for that, little bro," Grant called.

Isaac rolled his eyes and laughed.

"Like I was saying," Anya said, giving her brothers a pointed look. "We have an announcement. Kevin and I thought it best to tell you now that we have everyone together." She looked at her husband-to-be, who nodded his encouragement. "We're expecting a baby."

The table fell quiet for a second before it erupted in cheers and congratulations.

My stomach rolled.

"I can't believe it!" Joni cried out. "A grandchild at last!"

"Mom was scared it would never happen," Isaac laughed.

They chattered over each other, offering the happy couple congratulations and gushing about the baby. The women wanted to know what her due date was. The men clapped Kevin on the back, telling him what a good dad he would be.

When I glanced at Trent, he didn't look as excited as everyone else. He was smiling, but it seemed forced, and he only congratulated them once before he fell silent.

I reached for him and squeezed his hand. He offered me a smile, but it didn't reach his eyes.

Something was wrong. Was it because his sister was pregnant? Maybe Trent didn't like kids.

What if Trent didn't want children of his own at all?

"I want a lot of grandkids, you hear?" Joni spoke up. "That goes for all of you kids."

"Oh, don't worry," Anya said with a giggle. "We got a head start."

Trent spoke up. "With five kids, I don't think you have to worry about that, Mom. You won't need any from me to add to the pile."

My stomach dropped as everyone else bantered on. Trent didn't want children. This was exactly what I'd been afraid of.

He wouldn't want the child I was carrying.

A lump rose in my throat, and my eyes burned with tears. I struggled to bite them back—my emotions were all over the place these days.

Damn it!

"Excuse me," I said and got up from the table.

I fled to the bathroom, barely out of sight before I burst into tears.

I could already predict the disaster in store for me. When Trent found out I was pregnant, he'd want nothing more to do with me.

The more I thought about it, the harder I cried. I wipe angrily at the tears that spilled onto my cheeks, trying to do damage control on my makeup that was starting to smudge.

The door to the bathroom opened, and I froze.

"Bella?" Megan asked, stepping in. "Are you okay?"

I tried to swallow my sobs. I sniveled, mopping at my cheeks with a paper towel.

"I'm fine," I said, but the tears kept rolling and I hiccupped before they started pouring again. "I'm perfectly fine," I added, still crying.

Megan came to me, concerned. "I came to check on you. What's going on?"

I looked at my friend in the mirror.

"I'm pregnant," I blurted out, and cried harder.

"Oh, honey," Megan said softly. "Trent doesn't know?"

I shook my head. "I didn't want to tell him just yet, and now... Did you hear what he said? What if he never wants kids? What if, now that I'm pregnant, he never wants *me*?"

"I'm sure that's not how it will be," Megan said, but she didn't sound totally convinced. "Anyway, Trent is a good guy. He'll do the right thing."

"Yeah, he might do the right thing, but not because he wants to be a father. He'll look after us, I guess, but I don't know if we'll ever be a family the way this baby deserves." I cried harder again, unable to talk.

"Maybe you should just talk to him," Megan suggested.

"You heard him in there," I countered.

"Yeah, but making a quip at dinner is different from

when it's actually happening. I don't think you should take it to heart. Grant told me that when Trent is around his family, he says a lot of things that he doesn't really mean."

I tried to wipe the dark circles of makeup from underneath my eyes.

"You should just talk to him," Megan said.

"Do you think so?"

"I do. The most important thing in a relationship is communication. It also happens to be the toughest. You can get through this, but it will be so much better if you can do it together."

I nodded. Megan was right—I couldn't keep it from Trent forever. Maybe the sooner I told him, the better things would be. Maybe Trent would act differently than I feared.

Hell, maybe he'd surprise me and end up excited to have a baby.

It didn't sound like him, but how would I know if I didn't try?

Still, the idea of telling him made me feel sick to my stomach. I was terrified of what he would say.

"Okay," I agreed. "I'll tell him, but not now. After the wedding. I don't want to steal Anya and Kevin's thunder."

"That's a good idea," Megan said. She turned my shoulders to face her, helping me wipe off my smudged makeup. "This wedding should be... special for them."

But her face and her voice betrayed her as she spoke the last part. She suddenly didn't sound enthusiastic. Something was up with her, too.

Before I could ask, the door opened again and I heard Joni's and Enid's voices as they stepped in.

Shit.

Quickly, I ducked into a stall and locked myself in before they saw that I'd been crying. I didn't mind Megan knowing

—she would keep my secret—but the others didn't need to know yet.

I took a deep breath and let it out with a shudder.

It's going to be okay.

I just wished I could believe it.

21

BELLA

*B*y the next morning, I realized I'd have to abstain from more than just drinking.

For Anya and Kevin's ranch wedding, the weekend was filled with outdoor activities. At breakfast, I found out that one of the options was horseback riding.

I *loved* riding horses. I'd had a couple of lessons as a kid, when everything was still okay at home, and I'd loved it.

I was just about to say that when I remembered...

I was pregnant.

I couldn't ride horses.

Shit. It was so disappointing!

Anya explained that the pregnancy made her fatigued, so she was staying at the lodge to rest during the morning activity. When the other women decided on horseback riding, my heart sank. I wished I could join them, but I had to decline. I told them I had a bad headache and I needed to take it easy.

"Are you sure?" Joni asked. "We have a whole day of fun planned."

"I can't stand headaches like that," Megan spoke up and

gave me a knowing look. "I think it's better if you rest. Otherwise, it might get worse and you won't be able to enjoy the wedding."

"Oh, you have to feel better for the wedding!" Anya cried out. "If you have to rest now, that's totally okay."

I smiled and mouthed a thank you to Megan before everyone dispersed to go to their activities.

As I walked to the room, Trent caught up with me.

"What are you doing here?" I asked. "Aren't you going to the rodeo with the guys?"

Trent scoffed. "I don't know about you, but getting on a wild bull doesn't sound fun. It sounds kind of insane."

I giggled. "Yeah, it's a little crazy."

"I don't know why Kevin would want to risk getting injured before his wedding day, but he grew up like this. He's just... different."

I laughed. "He's a good guy."

"One of the best," Trent agreed. "But I'd rather do something else. When I heard you weren't going to join the girls, I figured we could do something together."

"Like what?" I asked. My stomach erupted in butterflies that Trent wanted to spend the day with me.

"If you're up for it, the ranch has really great hiking trails," Trent said. "I read it in the brochure."

"I didn't know you liked hiking," I said.

Trent pulled me closer against him and planted a kiss on my temple that sent a rush of warmth through my body. "There's a lot of things you don't know about me."

We got to the room and got ready for our hike. I dressed in leggings, trainers, and a tank top. Trent put on jeans and a T-shirt that showed off his muscles perfectly. I had to tear my eyes away from him as he packed a backpack for our hike.

We left our suite and found the hiking trail that began in a forested area just past the lodge. Trees bowed over the trail, the sunlight falling through the canopy of leaves in dapples on the floor, shading us from the heat. Birds chirped overhead, and it was incredibly peaceful and beautiful.

"I used to hate hiking as a kid," Trent said while we walked.

"Yeah?"

"Yeah, I always figured we have planes and cars, so why bother walking so far? My dad insisted we go on hikes during the summer holidays, and I would complain all the way. I didn't get it at all. But now, I appreciate it."

"A lot of things change when we get older," I agreed. "We see things differently than when we were kids."

"Yeah, the world changes, too. It can be such a terrible place, but we become more equipped to deal with it."

I nodded, but his words haunted me. Did Trent think the world was so awful that he didn't want to bring children into it?

Ugh, I was reading hidden meaning into his words. I had to stop before I worked myself into a panic.

After a couple hours, we found a beautiful, secluded meadow. It was surrounded by trees, tucked away from the rest of the world. A small stream trickled through one corner.

"This is a good place to rest," Trent said.

"Perfect."

He took a blanket out of his backpack, spreading it on the grass.

I sat down next to him, letting out a sigh as I stretched my legs.

"I haven't done this much exercise in a long time," I said. "How far do you think we walked?"

"I have no idea," Trent said with a chuckle. "Out here, with the clean air and great scenery, I feel like I can go on forever."

"Same."

We fell silent for a moment.

Trent turned to me, his blue eyes sparkling. He reached up and tucked a strand of hair behind my ear.

"I'm sure I'm a mess," I said. I was flushed from the exercise, and my ponytail was half falling out.

"You're a beautiful mess," Trent said.

He looked me in the eye, and his gaze was piercing.

Slowly, he leaned in and kissed me. It was gentle at first, his lips just brushing against mine. Electricity ran through my body, carrying a searing heat with it.

I was turned on and getting wet in no time at all.

The pregnancy hormones riled me up at his slightest touch.

Trent kissed me harder, his tongue slipping into my mouth, and I moaned in response. I melted against him, and he tangled his fingers in my hair as he pulled me closer to him.

Every nerve ending was alive, and my skin was on fire. I moved a hand over his hard chest.

I wanted him inside me.

Right now, none of my concerns mattered. We were alone, removed from the world in this secluded area, and I ached for him. The pregnancy hormones had a lot to do with it, but so did everything I felt for Trent.

No matter what happened in the future, no matter how this relationship had started out, I couldn't deny the fact that I was falling for him.

Carefully, Trent pulled me against him as we lay on the blanket. The thick grass was soft underneath the fabric, and Trent's body pressed against mine.

He rolled halfway onto me, his body muscular and taut as he loomed over me.

His cock was hard in his jeans, and when he thrust himself against me, my body tightened in response. I whimpered into his mouth.

Trent tugged at my clothes, peeling my tank top up. I did the same with his T-shirt, working it over his torso. We wriggled out of our clothes, breaking our kiss only to get rid of our shirts before he dove in and kissed me again. This time, his kiss was urgent, demanding, and I melted.

Trent moved away from my mouth and planted kisses down my neck. My skin broke out in goosebumps when he scraped his teeth against my shoulder. The skin on my chest tingled in anticipation as he worked his way toward my breasts, and I moaned when he licked a line along the cup of my bra.

When he pulled it down, the cool breeze made my nipple tighten even more than it already was.

Trent sucked my breast into his mouth, making wetness flood between my legs. He licked and sucked my nipple as I bucked my hips against him. My body was like a tuning fork, humming as he worked me into a frenzy.

Every part of my body tingled, the erotic feel of his mouth on my nipple translating to other parts of my body until I cried out and my toes curled. I pushed my hands into Trent's dark hair and tugged lightly at it.

He moaned deeply when I did. The sound he made against my breast was such a turn on, the feel of his voice delicious.

He ran his hands around my waist and I lifted my torso

so he could unclasp my bra. There was no one around for miles and with the trees shielding us, no one could see us getting naked. Not that I would have cared—I was so hot for Trent, nothing else mattered right now.

He pulled my bra off and tossed it to the side before diving back in with renewed hunger, kissing the bare flesh of my belly.

He set me on fire, planting kisses on my hips and stomach. Licking a line down the delicate skin next to my hip bone, he hooked his fingers into the waistband of my pants.

Slowly, teasingly, Trent peeled my leggings and panties down my body. He unwrapped me like I was a gift, like I was precious to him.

When he was finished, Trent stared at my naked body.

"You are so fucking beautiful," he said in a hoarse voice.

I smiled as I lay there, completely naked, and I didn't feel self-conscious in front of him at all. Trent stared at me with a look of pure adoration. There was nothing I could feel shy about when he looked at me like that.

Trent lowered his head and kissed the top of my mound. He spread my legs with his hands on my thighs and licked a line from my entrance to my clit. I cried out as heat washed through my body and threatened to consume me. He blew on me, my wetness turning cool as his breath hit my skin. Shivers raced over my body.

"Trent," I gasped.

He offered a throaty chuckle as he smiled at me before he closed his mouth around my pussy. When he flicked his tongue over my clit, my breath caught in my throat.

I arched my back, pressing the crown of my head into the ground. I gave myself over to the sensation of Trent's tongue flicking over my clit, drawing lazy circles, turning the fire inside me into a roaring furnace.

I bucked my hips against him as he licked, and an orgasm started to grow at my core. I pushed my hand into his hair, the other curling around the blanket I lay on.

My breathing became shallow and erratic and I teetered on the edge of pure pleasure, the orgasm threatening to break and shatter all over me. Trent kept me on the edge, somehow knowing how to keep me there without letting me topple over into the abyss of pure pleasure.

"Trent, please," I gasped.

"Come for me, babe," he moaned against my flesh.

He pushed his fingers into me just as he said it, and pumped them in and out while he licked my clit again.

I cried out as the orgasm peaked and washed through me. My core contracted and tightened. Heat consumed me, pouring through my body. I cried out, and then I didn't breathe at all as I let the pleasure take over.

When I finally came down from my sexual high, Trent's eyes were filled with satisfaction.

"You're so fucking hot when you do that," he said. He lifted his head, his lips slick with my sex.

"You did that to me," I gasped, gulping for air.

Trent grinned at me, and stood, pulling down his pants.

When he dropped them, I could only stare. His cock was delicious to look at no matter how many times I'd seen it.

He found a condom in his pocket and tore it open, wrapping himself up. I wanted to tell him not to bother—it was too late. But I didn't exactly want to ruin the mood by breaking my news now.

Trent kneeled between my legs and crawled over me as I trailed my hands over his chiseled shoulders.

He kissed me, his cock hard on my stomach, and my body tensed in anticipation of what was to come.

He tilted his hips and his cock pressed against my

entrance. I held my breath, and when he pushed into me, I let out a long, low moan.

My body opened to receive him, and I shivered as an echo of my orgasm ran through my body.

When he was buried to the hilt, he paused above me. His breathing trembled, and his eyes locked on mine.

Something passed between us that was brand new. Uncharted territory.

This wasn't just sex the way we'd had it countless times.

The way he looked at me now was with so much affection, it made my stomach tighten and my heart skip a beat. We weren't just fucking.

We were making love.

This isn't that, I told myself.

I couldn't let myself get attached to him. If I did, I wouldn't survive the heartbreak when things fell apart. I had to keep my head straight.

But it was impossible not to see a future with Trent when he looked at me like that.

He kissed me again and slowly slid out, pulling his length out to the head. When he pushed back in, my eyes opened wide. He filled me completely.

I wrapped my legs around his hips, pulling him in closer. I wanted as much of him as I could get.

Trent cradled my head in both his hands as he thrust. His eyes remained locked on mine. We were together, melded into one as he moved inside me.

Heat spread through my body, setting me alight inch by inch. Soon, a second orgasm grew at my center.

I wrapped my arms around his neck and held onto him as he drove into me. He bent down to kiss me.

Trent pumped into me harder, and my body grew weak, numb with pleasure. When my orgasm blossomed, I curled my body against his. My muscles clamped down around his cock.

He slowed his motion, pulling back to watch the climax play out on my face. I was in heaven.

When the feeling faded, he held onto me tightly and rolled us both over. I yelped as he pulled me with him, and then I was on top.

I giggled. He'd done this before, but I was never completely ready for it.

"You're incredible," I breathed, looking down at him.

"On top of every great man is a good woman," Trent said, his eyes gleaming.

Bracing my hands on his chest, I gyrated my hips around his cock as he held my breasts in his palms.

Trent's face changed. He clenched his jaw, and his brows knitted together. He looked at me with a fierce hunger.

He pushed up and kissed me, steadying my body with his strong arms around my back. He sat up, adjusting me in his lap, and tilted his lips to mine. His tongue slid into my mouth, and he grasped my ass, moving my body up and down along his length.

"Fuck, that feels so good," I moaned against his mouth. His hands on my ass pulled me tighter against him, and my breasts bounced against his chest.

My clit rubbed against his pubic bone and the sensation of pure pleasure rocked through my body with every thrust. I was getting closer.

Judging from Trent's breathing, he was getting closer, too. His cock hardened inside me, growing bigger still.

I cried out a moment later and let myself come again, trembling against his body.

Finally, he barked out a sharp cry and I felt him orgasm,

too. His cock throbbed inside me, and the feeling was incredible.

He held me in place, pressing his face against my chest. My arms wrapped around his shoulders, and time stretched out forever.

I never felt closer to Trent than in moments like this. I loved the way we were reduced to the most raw, vulnerable forms of ourselves. Only the pleasure in our bodies, and how perfectly we fit together, mattered.

Nothing could get to me. In these moments, Trent was my security, shielding me from the rest of the world.

It was when we were like this that I saw a side of Trent that no one else saw—a side that wasn't closed off, but open and loving and caring.

We gradually came back to Earth, our hearts hammering against each other.

Slowly, I got off his lap. I didn't want to break the spell, but we couldn't stay here forever.

We collapsed onto the blanket together, trying to catch our breath.

Trent looked at me. Even though he didn't say the words, I felt his affection. It mirrored my own.

I wanted to tell him about the baby. Everything was so perfect between us, and we were so close right now, how could it go wrong?

"Trent, I want to talk to you about something," I said.

"Yeah?" he asked, his eyes studying my face.

I nodded and rolled onto my side, resting my head on my arm.

This was it. This was the moment I told him.

"I..." The words died in my throat.

I couldn't do it. How could I ruin it all right now?

He was going to lose his shit, and all this would disappear. I wasn't ready to let go yet.

"What is it?" Trent asked.

I hesitated. "Did you mean it when you said you didn't want kids?" I asked instead.

Trent was silent for a moment.

"I don't need a brood like my parents to feel fulfilled," he finally said. "I'm happy with the way things are. I don't need to change anything, to bring a life into this world to complete me."

I swallowed hard. That seemed like a pretty definitive answer. My stomach twisted, and I felt sick.

I couldn't tell him about the baby now. Why go there when it was clear it wasn't what he wanted?

I would have to tell him soon, but the moment was perfect, and I didn't want to ruin it. I wanted to enjoy our time together while this lasted.

Before he found out the truth and it was all over.

22

TRENT

*a*t the rehearsal dinner, everyone was dressed to the nines, including Bella. She wore a black cocktail dress with a slit that ran up her thigh. That dress made me want to tear it right off her.

After our romp in the meadow, I felt like we were closer than ever before. I couldn't get enough of her. I'd wanted another round before we came to the rehearsal dinner, but time wasn't on our side.

I could stay in bed with her forever, fucking, talking, laughing, and fucking again.

Bella was different than any other woman I'd had in my life before. I'd always been attracted to her—what man wouldn't be? She was smoking hot.

And *really* good in bed, as it turned out.

Since the wedding in Vegas, my attraction to her had changed. It was more than physical lust. The more I got to know her, the more I realized how beautiful she was on the inside.

She was stronger than any woman I knew.

During the dinner, Bella and I stole secret glances at

each other. I put my hand on her thigh under the table, then later held her hand on the table, touching her whenever I could. She leaned into me when she laughed at a stupid joke I made, and whenever our eyes locked, shivers ran down my spine.

Even though we were getting closer, I still felt like she was holding back. Even if it was just a little bit.

Something was bothering her. Did she think this wouldn't work out between us?

I couldn't blame her for that. We'd started this whole thing as a fake relationship, and I'd made it very clear it wouldn't go anywhere. Not only that, I'd been a grumpy son of a bitch for a long time with her. No wonder she was uncertain about me.

I would just have to show her that things were different. Prove her wrong.

"Trent, honey," Mom said when everyone stood in groups after dinner, drinking and talking. Bella, Megan, Anya, and two of Anya's bridesmaids stood huddled in a cluster, chatting excitedly. "Can I talk to you?"

"Sure," I said, though I didn't really want to talk to her at all.

When Mom came to me wanting to *talk* like this, it was always something serious. Tonight had been so great—I wasn't in the mood for anything to ruin that for me.

"I want to talk to you about what you said last night."

I frowned. "Which part?"

"The part where you said I shouldn't expect grandchildren from you."

I sighed and threw back the whiskey I'd been drinking, waving at a server to come top me up. Couldn't we just celebrate Anya's wedding without getting so serious about what came next for me?

When Bella asked me about it, she hadn't been invasive. She'd been polite, simply asking my opinion, but I couldn't help but feel that she'd been disappointed by my answer.

What if I didn't want kids? Would that be a deal-breaker for her?

"What about it?" I asked. "It's true, isn't it? You have more than enough kids to give you grandchildren without counting on me."

Mom narrowed her eyes at me. "I wish you wouldn't make it sound so *clinical.*"

I shrugged. "How else am I supposed to make it sound? You want grandkids, you're going to get them."

The server arrived with my drink and Mom kept quiet until he left.

"I don't like the way you're talking about it," Mom said. "I don't understand why you're so set on not having children. It's natural to want your legacy to continue, sweetheart."

"That's *your* opinion, Mom," I said. "I don't feel that way. A lot of people don't feel that way. I'm glad you had so many kids and that it made you happy, but that doesn't apply to all of us."

Mom pursed her lips and sipped her glass of wine.

"So, you're serious, then?" Mom asked.

"Positive," I said.

"And what about Bella?"

I narrowed my eyes at my mom. "What about Bella?"

"How does she feel about you not wanting children?"

Well, that wasn't something I could know without asking her, was it? We were still in the early stages of our relationship, though. I'd only just recently asked her to be my girlfriend. Not that my family knew that, of course, but still.

It wasn't the time to talk about things like expanding the family.

What Mom didn't know was that I wasn't necessarily *against* having kids. My comment was just a knee-jerk reaction. I always pushed against my family's controlling behavior. It was the only way to have independence with them—to say I wanted exactly the opposite of what they did.

"I think that's between me and Bella, don't you?" I asked tightly.

Mom wanted to say something, but I cut her off.

"Look, Mom, I get what you're saying, but it's none of your business and the last thing we need is for you to interfere in our relationship. Bella and I are both adults and more than capable of making these decisions on our own."

Mom looked visibly hurt. "I just want you to be happy," she said.

"Thank you," I offered.

Mom turned away from me to join the rest of the party. I'd been hard on her, I knew that. Maybe I shouldn't have been so harsh. A pang of guilt shot into my chest. I hated it when I hurt my mom's feelings.

The thing was... she'd done it, too, hadn't she?

She'd refused to believe Waverly cheated on me, and that had been a hell of a lot worse than this.

That only made me feel marginally better.

But the truth was, I had to protect myself.

~

The next day, we sat under the shade of large trees, where chairs had been arranged. Bella wore an olive-green dress, and I wore a tie to match. She clutched her hands in her lap while we waited, glancing around.

"This is so sweet," she said, looking around at the outdoor chapel the decorators had created. A wooden arch wrapped in vines had been set up in front of a large tree, under which the ceremony would take place. From our seats, we had a prime view of the rolling pastures, all the way to the mountains on the horizon. "I love outdoor weddings."

"It's beautiful," I agreed. "I think my sister planned this for months. Maybe even years. Don't girls dream about this day since they were kids?"

Bella giggled and nudged me. "Yeah, well, we're all waiting for our Prince Charming, you know?"

I smiled. For a moment, I wondered what Bella's ideal wedding would look like.

I pushed the thought away—I wasn't going to think about getting married right now.

I glanced at Kevin who stood at the front, looking confident and excited about what was to come. My family was thrilled to have Kevin joining them.

Them, not *us*, I thought. I'd stopped thinking of myself as integrated into my family years ago.

Once upon a time, I'd wanted their approval, I'd cared what they thought, but all that had changed. I did what I wanted now.

The last thing I needed was their meddling, pushing me to do what they wanted, and not just letting me live the life I wanted for myself.

It left a bitter taste in my mouth.

"Are you okay?" Bella asked. She could pick up on my moods, and I forced a smile.

"Perfect," I said.

Before she could press, the music started from the string quartet seated off to the side, and we all turned to watch the wedding party proceed down the aisle. Claire and Anya's two best friends were the bridesmaids, and Kevin's little nephew was the ring bearer. Then we stood as my dad escorted Anya down the aisle. She was beaming, clearly excited to step into this new chapter.

I was happy for her.

The reception was held in one of the barns. The large space had been decorated to the nines. Chandeliers hung from the beamed ceiling, white linens adorned the tables, and a backdrop of fairy lights hung behind the bride and groom's table. The food was top notch, the live music from the country-rock band they hired was good, and the alcohol was free flowing.

Maybe a little too free flowing, in my case.

My head spun after I'd thrown back one too many drinks while talking to my brothers and Kevin. I walked up to Bella, where she sat talking with Megan.

"Dance with me," I said.

"Oh, I'm not a great dancer—"

I grabbed her hand and pulled her onto the dance floor, despite her protests.

"It's okay, I can dance for both of us," I said. "I'll lead. You just follow."

She nodded, and I moved us both to the music, sending her out for spins and bringing her back in close again. Her body felt incredible pressed up against mine, and she laughed when I spun her around.

"See?" I said. "You *can* dance."

"All thanks to you," Bella said with a smile.

For a second, I wondered what it would be like if this were *our* wedding. If I was spinning her around in our first dance as husband and wife.

I stopped that train of thought right there.

I couldn't let my mind go to places like that.

I had no intention of marrying anyone, ever. Getting

married would make my family happy. I wasn't living for their happiness.

I wanted to live my own life, whatever that looked like.

As the music changed to a slow song, Bella came in closer, and we swayed to the music. I breathed in her floral scent, relishing the feel of her arms around my neck.

It felt amazing.

But the thoughts about marriage bothered me more and more.

We'd been all over each other the past few days, and things had gone fabulously with us. But if I kept it up, creating expectations I couldn't fulfill, it would only lead to heartache and disappointment. I couldn't do that to either of us.

After the slow song, I excused myself, and Bella returned to sit with Megan. I'd lost my buzz, and it was time for another drink.

I got a whiskey at the bar and took my drink outside to look at the stars. I didn't want to get trapped in another conversation with a family member. After a while, I returned to the reception, but I tried to avoid everyone as much as possible.

Even Bella.

I wasn't trying to hurt her, but I needed space. I loved being with her, but was I getting in over my head?

I'd insisted we not get emotionally attached. And that was exactly what I was doing.

What if she wanted marriage and kids?

What if I was never able to give that to her?

By the end of the night, I was grumpy and sullen. Not to mention irritated with myself for being like this in the first place, for letting my thoughts get the better of me.

When we got to the suite, Bella was quiet, too. She

looked like she wanted to say something, but she stopped herself.

"Well, goodnight," I said to her, standing in the common area between the two bedrooms.

It was awkward as fuck, and she looked at me quizzically. But I couldn't share a bed with her tonight. I couldn't get so close to her.

"I think I'll sleep on my own tonight." I drove a hand through my hair. "I... need some space right now."

She shifted her weight from one foot to the other. "Yeah, I guess we should try to get a good night's sleep for a change. We didn't get much sleep last night."

"Right. We have to fly back to LA tomorrow."

I couldn't sleep with her tonight, no matter how much I wanted it. I had to get my head straight.

"So... I'll take the other room tonight," she said, her voice rising at the end, almost like a question.

"No, I'll take it. All your stuff's in the main bedroom."

"Oh, all right," she said.

A part of me sank in disappointment, but I held firm. It was better this way.

"Goodnight," she said as she turned away from me. I didn't call her back, although I wanted to.

Pushing her away wasn't fair. I knew that. Should I try to fix it? Did I want to?

Where would this go if I kept her close and we continued in the same direction?

I hadn't thought that far ahead when I asked her to be with me for real. Maybe I should have considered what would happen. I'd been so caught up in my own emotions that I hadn't been logical about it.

Now, I didn't know which way to go. Would breaking things off with her be better?

I tried to imagine what it would be like if I told her I wanted to end it.

The idea made me feel sick. I couldn't imagine losing her. I couldn't imagine pushing her away so far that I could never get her back.

In the empty bedroom, I slowly removed my clothes until I stood in only my boxers. I headed toward the bed, but my steps faltered until I came to a stop.

After a long moment, I turned around and went to Bella's room.

When I pushed open the door, she was already in bed, her hair fanned over the pillow.

Without a word, I walked to the bed and climbed in beside her, sliding in between the sheets until I felt her warm body against mine.

She was still as I pulled her against me, rigid, but just for a moment. Then she melted against me.

I didn't want to fall asleep without her. I didn't want to wake up without her in my arms in the morning. Whatever was happening between us, this felt right.

I could argue with myself about it all day long, but in the end, all I wanted was to be with her.

What the hell had I been thinking, withdrawing from her like that? What was I doing?

Whatever it was, it wasn't going to happen again. This was where I was supposed to be—by her side.

No more pulling away.

23

BELLA

*T*he wedding was over, along with the roller coaster of emotions.

As Trent's driver took us from the airfield in LA back to my apartment the next day, I panicked.

I had to tell Trent about the baby. I'd told myself—and Megan—I was going to do it as soon as the wedding was over, but now that we'd come this far, I was terrified.

I couldn't keep it from him. He deserved to know as soon as possible. And I deserved to know what his response would be. Would he accept me and the baby, or would he tell me he didn't want us in his life at all?

Trent was so hard to read. It was always up and down with him. One moment, we'd been having a great time dancing last night. The next, he was pulling away. One second, he took the spare bedroom. The next, he climbed in next to me.

My head was spinning, and I hadn't even thrown the baby into the mix yet.

Roller coaster or not, I couldn't hide it from him any longer.

He's going to be furious. He's going to dump me. Maybe fire me. He's going to tell me he never wants to see me again.

That was the worst-case scenario, and it was the one I was preparing myself for. Even though I hoped for a different outcome.

I twisted my hands together in my lap as the car entered my neighborhood. I hadn't thrown up in the plane on the way back, which had been a welcome surprise, but now my stomach was lurching all over again. I'd texted Angie when we landed, and she'd messaged that she was just about to leave for a date. Which meant I could talk to Trent alone at my apartment.

No more excuses.

Trent was lost in his own thoughts, too. Something was going on with him, but I knew better than to pry. That only made him withdraw more.

When the car stopped in front of my apartment, I turned to him.

"Will you come in?" I asked. "I know you need to get home and unpack, but I'd like to talk for a bit."

"Sure."

We got out, and Trent helped the driver carry the luggage to my door. I unlocked the apartment as Trent asked him to give us a few minutes alone, and the driver returned to his car.

In the living room, Trent sat on the couch and watched me pace back and forth. I fidgeted, trying to figure out the best way to start the conversation.

"Is everything okay?" he asked. "What's wrong?"

I opened my mouth to speak, then clamped it shut again. How to begin? What was the best way to drop this bomb-shell on him?

"Talk to me," Trent said. He was getting worried now. I was already screwing this up.

"I'm pregnant," I blurted out. "I—I'm going to have a baby."

Trent stared at me, frozen. His expression was impossible to read.

When he didn't say anything, the silence became unbearable.

I started talking.

"I don't know when it happened. Maybe our first night together... I was on birth control, though. I'm always good about taking the pills. And you were safe, too. I don't know how it happened."

He only stared at me, sitting there like a statue.

I couldn't tell what he was thinking, and the silence made my anxiety worse. I'd prepared myself for an outburst, but this weird silent treatment was killing me.

"We're both responsible for it, though," I added, not wanting to position myself as the guilty party somehow. "I mean, we both took precautions, and neither of us meant for this to happen."

I chewed my bottom lip, willing him to say something. *Anything.*

"You're right," he finally said. He swallowed hard and rubbed the back of his neck. He'd become pale.

"What?" I asked, blinking at him. "Did you just say I'm right?"

"We did take every precaution," he said. He shuffled his weight on the couch and looked down.

"You're not... mad?" I asked in a small voice.

"Why would I be angry?" Trent asked with a frown. "I'm just stunned. This is the last thing I expected." He licked his bottom lip and leaned forward with his elbows on his knees, his chin resting on his clasped hands. His expression was worried.

I didn't know how to react to that. I'd expected the worst. I'd prepared myself for an outburst. He wasn't happy by any means, but he wasn't telling me it was over between us, either.

I didn't know what to say. Trent didn't say anything, either. He sat there quietly, and I had no idea what was going on in his head.

I knew he needed a moment to think—I'd had a while to get used to the idea, but this was news to him. Hot off the press with all the emotions that came with it.

The air in the room felt stifling. The longer the silence stretched out, the more anxious I felt. I leaned against the wall and shut my eyes, hoping everything would somehow work out.

"Okay," Trent finally said, blowing out a long breath.

I looked at him. "Okay?"

"We'll deal with this."

"We will?" I asked.

Trent nodded. "Yeah. Don't worry about anything financial. I won't leave you hanging. I'll support you and the baby."

To my horror, the front door opened just as he said the last part.

Angie stood in the door, her eyes wide. She glanced at me, then at Trent, obviously in shock. She cleared her throat and fidgeted with her purse strap.

"Don't mind me," she said quickly. Angie hurried past us and headed toward her room.

Trent closed his eyes and pinched the bridge of his nose between his thumb and forefinger.

Great. Now Angie knew.

I sighed. She'd find out eventually. Might as well get it all out in the open.

I waited until I heard her door shut before I spoke.

"Is financial support all you want to provide in this... situation?" I asked carefully. Trent had said he wouldn't leave me hanging *financially*.

Trent clenched his jaw. "You know I don't want kids."

I blinked at him, stunned.

"Yeah, I know," I finally snapped, anger flaring in my chest. "You made that abundantly clear this weekend."

He was quiet, thinking back to his words at the rehearsal dinner, no doubt. "Yeah, I'm sure that was hard to hear, but I didn't know any of this was going on. But, you know, just because this is not what I would have chosen, it doesn't mean I won't do the right thing now."

He was painstakingly calm, but inside, I was freaking out. He didn't want kids, but did *doing the right thing* mean he was going to propose?

If he did, I'd have to say no. The last thing I wanted him to do was marry me because I was pregnant.

I wanted him to marry me because he was in love with me as much as...

As much as I was with him.

When that thought crossed my mind, I felt lightheaded. I walked to the couch and sank onto the armrest, pressing my hand against my forehead.

"Are you okay?" Trent asked, standing and taking a step toward me so he was by my side. "The pregnancy must be making you lightheaded. That's a thing, right?"

Right. I would let him think it was the pregnancy making me swoon and not the idea that I was madly in love with him.

"I read something about that, yeah," I said dully.

"We have to get you to a doctor," Trent said firmly.

"I'm fine, I don't need a doctor right now."

"Well, you need a prenatal appointment, then. We need to make sure you and the baby are healthy."

At least he cared about our well-being—mine and the baby's. That was something.

"I already made an appointment for next week," I said. "Do you want to come with me?"

I asked the question without thinking, and I immediately regretted it. He hesitated, and I wondered if he wanted to be involved at all.

"Okay," he finally said.

"You sure?"

He nodded. "Just let me know when and where, and I'll be there."

"Okay," I said.

Trent stepped away from me. I felt the distance he put between us acutely.

"I have to get going," Trent said.

"Sure," I answered.

He had to go home to process the news. I didn't want him to feel pressured to stay, so I didn't ask him to. We said goodbye awkwardly, and he left.

I closed the door behind him and leaned against it, letting out a long breath.

Angie appeared in the doorway of her bedroom.

"Hey," she said.

"Hi," I said.

"Good weekend?"

I raised an eyebrow. "I guess so." After my conversation with Trent, the Colorado wedding already felt like a lifetime ago.

Angie leaned against the wall.

"My date was a disaster, so I left early." She looked at me with a mixture of curiosity and something else... maybe amusement. "I couldn't help but overhear..."

"Yeah," I said with a sigh. "Want some tea? I could use a cup."

"Sure."

I walked to the kitchen, and she followed me.

"So, you're really pregnant?" she asked. "And Trent is the father?"

"Yes, as crazy as it is. I guess you can get pregnant even on birth control *and* with condoms. Who knew."

Angie sucked in air through her teeth. "Wow."

I filled the tea kettle with water and set it on the stove. I really wanted a cup of coffee, but now that I was pregnant, I'd have to learn to like herbal tea.

"And you're keeping it?" Angie asked.

I nodded. "Of course." I put a hand to my abdomen. I was already feeling attached to this baby.

Angie shook her head. "I can't believe this. Diablo's baby?" She shuddered. "I can't imagine sleeping with him, let alone bringing his offspring into the world. Gross."

I looked sharply at her.

She tried to backtrack. "I mean, of course it's a happy thing. Congratulations are totally in order." She offered me a smile.

"Thanks," I said, though I could tell she wasn't being genuine. The tension grew thicker in the room as we listened to the water heating up on the stove.

I grabbed two mugs and a tea box from the cupboard. "It's not how I would have chosen for it to happen," I finally said as I plunked a tea bag into each cup. "But I am starting to get excited about becoming a mother."

Angie nodded, then moved on to her next concern. "Do

you think the baby will cry all the time? I mean, as grumpy and demanding as the father is, maybe the kid will be a hellion. Kids do take after their parents."

"I'm sure the baby will be fine."

"It's different sharing a home with a baby, though," Angie said. "All that crying in the middle of the night... You're going to have to make a lot of changes."

"I'm aware of that," I said.

It dawned on me what Angie was trying to say. She didn't want to be my housemate now that I was having a baby. The realization hit me like a ton of bricks. Would Angie really just want me gone?

"He said he'll take care of you financially, so that's something," Angie said. "Money is no object to him, of course. Hey," she said, her face brightening. "Maybe he'll buy you and the baby a place of your own. Then you won't have to worry about sharing a space with anyone... or how much of that space the baby takes up."

Angie looked at me with an expectant expression.

Yeah, her point was coming across loud and clear.

I stared at her. Unbelievable.

I thought we were better friends than this. I thought she'd be more supportive, but then, she hadn't really been very supportive of any of my choices lately. She'd been more mocking than anything.

The water started to boil, and I shut the heat off and poured the water into the mugs.

"I'll be out by the end of the month," I said. "You don't have to worry."

"Oh, you don't need to move out *that* soon. I just meant you might want to find a new place before the baby comes. You'll want that extra space, you know?"

"Sure," I said and picked up my cup of tea, adding a

spoonful of sugar. The lump in my throat grew. "I'm going to my room."

"Okay."

I left the kitchen and my would-be friend behind. So much for having a support system.

Alone in my room, I wanted to cry. Angie hadn't even said I could stay until the baby was born.

I guess I'd hoped there was more between us than that.

I'd been wrong, but I'd been wrong about a lot of things lately. Some good, some bad.

I set the cup of tea on my nightstand and collapsed on the bed, exhausted.

I had a hard couple of months ahead of me, and the baby wasn't the only thing I had to worry about.

Somehow, I would figure it out. I'd made it this far in my life, despite all the obstacles I'd had to overcome. I could survive this.

I began to unpack my suitcase, but soon ran out of energy. It had been a long day, physically and emotionally, and all I wanted to do was sleep.

Tomorrow would be another day.

Hopefully, it would bring answers about what to expect from Trent.

24

TRENT

I couldn't sleep. Every time I closed my eyes, I heard Bella's voice again.

I'm pregnant.

How the fuck did this happen? We'd been so careful, and she'd still gotten pregnant.

It wasn't supposed to be like this. I wasn't ready to be a father. Just the thought of a baby on the way made my stomach twist into a ball.

I rolled over onto my stomach and closed my eyes again. Being a father had *not* been on the agenda. At least not now.

Especially not after what Waverly did to me. She ripped me apart, and I'd told myself I would never get into a position where someone could do that to me again.

Having children with someone was a lot more involved than anything I'd been prepared for.

And yet...

I told my mom I didn't want kids, but that had been to get her off my case. To be honest, I hadn't really thought much about children. I'd just wanted to push my family away.

The more I thought about it now—being a father—the more I got used to the idea.

Bella was a wonderful person, and there was no doubt she'd make a good mother.

Maybe it could even be fun raising a kid with her.

I found myself wondering what our kid would look like. Bella was beautiful—our baby would be the cutest thing ever.

I realized with a shock I was actually sort of excited about this.

I fell asleep soon after that dawned on me. It was pointless fighting it. The truth was, this was happening.

The next morning I got into the office earlier than usual. Only the secretary at reception was on duty. Bella hadn't even come in yet. Usually, she brought me my coffee, but I made it myself so that she didn't have to worry.

In my office, instead of going straight to my email inbox, I opened the browser and searched for local preschools. What kind of schools were in the area? Were they good enough for our baby?

I got lost in the search, and when someone knocked on my door, I was yanked back to reality. Bella opened the door with a cup of coffee and looked at me.

"Oh, you beat me to it," she said. "You must have gotten here early."

"I did." I frowned, studying her. "Are you okay?" She looked rundown, with circles under her eyes like she hadn't slept well.

"I'm okay," she said.

I didn't believe her. "Tell me what's wrong. Is it the baby? Are you feeling sick?"

Bella shook her head and sighed. "It's not the baby. Well, not directly." She hesitated.

I held out my hand, beckoning for her to come to me, and she walked around my desk. I swiveled my chair to her and pulled her closer so that she sat on my lap. The smell of her filled my nostrils and I breathed in deeply—I would never get enough of her. It wasn't even sexual. It was just Bella.

"I just realized I don't have as many people in my corner as I thought I did. Angie..." She swallowed hard, and she looked stricken. "She's not as supportive as I thought she'd be."

"What happened?" I asked. I took Bella's hand and stroked my thumb over her knuckles while she talked, telling me what her friend had said.

"I told her I'd leave by the end of the month," Bella concluded. "I don't need that pressure on top of everything else. If she can't be supportive at all, I'd rather not live with her."

I nodded. "It's a good call. I'm sorry it turned out that way."

Bella shook her head. "It's fine."

I frowned, a thought occurring to me.

"Will she say anything now?" I asked.

"About what?"

"About us. The baby, all of it. She knows it all, and she's an employee here."

Bella shook her head. "We're not hostile to each other. Things are just strained. I'm sure she has enough sense to keep quiet about it to the others in the office. She's selfish, but she wouldn't go out of her way to hurt me."

I nodded. If Bella trusted her, that was enough for me.

"So you're planning to move by the end of the month? It's already the fifteenth."

"I guess so," she said with a sigh. "I'd rather get it over with sooner than later."

That didn't leave her much time to find a new place.

"Where will you go?" I asked.

Bella shrugged. "I'll have to start looking for a new place. Or a new shared place. I might not be able to afford a place of my own."

"Move in with me," I said.

Bella blinked at me, surprised by my offer.

Hell, I was surprised, too. I'd said the words without thinking.

It would mean giving up the last bit of my resolve to be a lone wolf. Would it feel like another surrender?

But having Bella with me every night was an idea I could get my head around. Waking up to her every morning sounded amazing.

Shit, I was getting attached to her. It had happened so fast.

"I'll think about it," Bella finally said.

I stiffened. Why didn't she want to jump on my offer and move in with me?

I realized that I'd wanted her to say yes. Fuck if I was going to admit that to her, though.

I'd had way too many vulnerable moments the last couple of days, so I acted nonchalant.

"Let me know what you decide," I said.

She nodded and I squeezed her, holding tightly onto her on my lap. She glanced at my screen.

"Are you... looking at preschools?"

I shrugged. "Never hurts to get a jump on things, right?"

She giggled. "The baby is a bit young to worry about that."

"Well, they do say a child's future is built on the right preschool."

Bella laughed. "Where did you hear that?"

"I read it. This morning."

Her eyes danced with laughter when she looked at me.

"You're getting all mushy on me, Dillon. I don't know this side of you at all."

I shrugged, still trying to keep up my nonchalant act, but Bella was already in a better mood, and that made me happy. I hated it when she wasn't okay.

My heart rate increased, and my throat swelled shut. Part of me was still uncomfortable with getting attached to her.

If I got this close, it would hurt like hell to lose her.

For a moment, Waverly and the heartache she'd brought slammed into my chest.

But Bella wasn't Waverly.

Besides, what was the alternative? Pulling away from her, keeping her at a distance, running away from what was happening?

I didn't want that. I wanted to be there for her and the baby.

Yeah, I had to conquer these stupid fears and man the fuck up. Bella was the one I wanted, and that was all that mattered right now.

The rest would follow, we just had to figure it out one day at a time.

"Thank you," Bella said and dropped a quick kiss on my lips. It was the first time she'd done anything so affectionate in the office, but I was holding onto her on my lap. I guess we were both changing.

"For what?" I asked.

"Being there for me," she said. "You have no idea how much it means."

"Of course," I said.

She stood to go back to her duties for the day, and I turned to my computer to do actual work. Preschools could wait for now.

~

Three days later, Bella had her first prenatal appointment.

I was a lot more nervous than I thought I would be. We sat in the waiting room together, and I felt almost sick with nerves. Would the baby be okay?

I glanced at a heavily pregnant woman who sat back in a deep armchair, flipping through a magazine. She seemed so calm about the baby she was having. How could she, though, when a million things could go wrong?

"Ms. Williams?" the nurse called and we stood, walking to the office.

She smiled brightly at us as we got settled.

"Let's get a couple of facts down first, shall we?" She began to ask Bella all kinds of questions about her cycle, the date of her last period, and other things I knew nothing about.

When she was done, she nodded at Bella.

"Right, let's get you checked out." She sent her to the exam room to get undressed while I waited in the office. A moment later, the nurse led me to join Bella, who lay on the exam bed wearing one of the paper gowns they offered in these places.

"That's a good look for you," I said when we were alone in the room, waiting for the doctor. Bella laughed.

Soon, the obstetrician, a Dr. Browning, entered the room and introduced herself to us both.

"Ready to see the baby?" the doctor asked.

Bella nodded excitedly, and the doctor squirted jelly on Bella's stomach before sliding a wand over it.

Gray shapes appeared on the black screen until she focused on a small kidney-shaped blob.

"There we go," she said with a smile. "That's your baby." She pressed another button or two, and then the sound of a very fast heartbeat filled the room.

"Oh, my God," Bella said, and her eyes welled with tears.

I stared at the small blob that would slowly turn into a tiny human, and the sound of that heartbeat reverberated through my very being.

This was it. The baby. Until now, the idea of having a baby had been abstract, nothing more than a concept. But seeing the baby on the screen made everything real. I'd *known* it was real, but still—this changed everything.

The doctor checked for a few other things before Bella could get dressed again. After having blood drawn for a few tests and getting some dietary advice from the doctor, we left the office.

"Oh, my God," I breathed when we stepped outside. "That was incredible." I didn't have the adequate words.

"Magical," Bella offered.

I pulled her against me into a tight embrace. "How are you feeling?"

"Stunned," Bella admitted. "And... excited."

That made me happy. "Let's go out to dinner. We should celebrate."

"You think so?" Bella asked with a smile.

I nodded. I'd tried to be nonchalant before, but I didn't

bother hiding my excitement now. Seeing that baby had changed everything.

It was my baby. *Our* baby.

"Good. Because I'm starving," she said. "And this area has a ton of new places to eat I'd love to try."

We walked down the sidewalk in the trendy neighborhood, looking for a restaurant, when I spotted a baby store.

"Let's go in," I said.

"We don't need any baby clothes yet," Bella laughed. "I'm only seven weeks along."

"But look at that," I said, pointing at the window display. There were lots of little baby clothes, stuffed toys, a crib, and a colorful mobile hanging overhead. Never before in my life had I given a rat's ass about anything like this, but suddenly I thought it was... cute.

"We can just browse," I said.

Bella grinned. "Okay. Why not?"

I took her hand and we walked into the store, looking around. The baby stuff was adorable. And there was so much of it.

"I'm gonna be honest," I said as we looked at the changing stations, blankets, and all sorts of tools to change diapers. "Some of this brings back memories from when my siblings were babies, but I had no idea most of this stuff existed."

She nodded. "I guess babies need a lot of stuff. We both have a lot to learn."

Finally, we stopped in front of the onesies.

"Let's get one," I said.

Bella laughed. "We don't even know what the sex is."

"Then we'll pick something gender neutral. Look." I picked up a light green onesie with *Mommy Loves Me* printed on it. Another had *Daddy Loves Me* on it.

"I think we should get both," I said, holding them up. "What do you think?"

Bella smiled, reaching for one and feeling the material.

"I think they're perfect," she said.

I beamed at her.

"But we should wait until the second trimester before we buy anything else, okay?" Bella said.

"When's that?"

"In six weeks," she said.

"I can deal with that," I said with a grin. "Six weeks, and then we're cleaning out these shelves, babe."

Bella and I laughed, and we took the clothes to the front to pay. I couldn't help my excitement when the clerk handed us the bag.

We were going to be parents!

Now I just had to figure out where things stood with Bella.

25

BELLA

*I*t had been more than a week since Trent asked me to move in with him. I still hadn't decided what to do.

But the fact that he hadn't mentioned it again made me concerned.

I wanted to live with Trent. More so now that he'd shown so much enthusiasm about the baby. His reaction after the OB appointment, buying baby clothes and celebrating at dinner, had set me at ease.

He was excited to be a father.

It was a big leap from my initial fear that he'd get furious and dump me because he didn't want kids.

A small part of me still wasn't sure, though. As much as I wanted to do this with Trent and live with him so that he could be a part of the journey, he didn't seem super eager about having me move in with him.

He was casual about it, treating the idea almost like a business contract that could go either way.

His businesslike manner had been fine when we were just *pretending* to date. But now that things were serious and we were going to have a family together, I didn't want him to be businesslike about it.

I wanted to know what he was thinking, what he was *feeling*. But figuring Trent out on an emotional level was next to impossible.

He played his cards so damn close to his chest, I never knew if he was bluffing.

The idea that he might not want to be with me made me queasy. What if I took the leap, moved in with him... and this wasn't the happily ever after I was hoping for?

What if he was sticking with me just for the sake of the baby? He might grow to resent being tied down.

I was driving myself crazy with worry.

On our one-month anniversary since we started officially dating, I decided to do something special for Trent. I wanted us to have a fun evening without worrying about the future for once.

I asked him if I could cook us dinner at his place, and he happily agreed.

After work, I stopped for groceries and got the ingredients for my mom's basil pesto pasta dish, which I'd grown up with. It had been the first thing she taught me to make, and she'd always said it was a crowd pleaser.

At his house, Trent opened the front door and greeted me with a kiss.

"Perfect timing. I just got here myself. Let me carry that for you."

He took the grocery bags from my hands and led me to the kitchen. As he started to unpack the ingredients, I washed my hands.

"What can I do to help?" he asked.

"Nothing. Relax. Or check your email, which I know

you're dying to do after your meeting with the investors. I got this."

"You sure?"

"Uh-huh. Now shoo."

He grinned and did as I asked, taking his laptop into the living room. I set about chopping vegetables and boiling water, smiling as I worked.

It was kind of fun playing house with Trent. Maybe it could be this fun all the time if we lived together.

A short while later, he came up behind me, kissing my neck, and warmth flushed through my body. He always knew how to make me feel amazing. "Something smells incredible."

"I think you'll like what I'm making you," I said with a smile. "How was the meeting, by the way?" Trent had been in a meeting with his investors when I left the office earlier.

"Great," Trent said, nodding. "It's always good, though. They have a lot to show for their investment, so there aren't any complaints." Trent rubbed his hands together before he undid his sleeves and rolled them up.

"You always have a lot to offer," I said sweetly.

Trent chuckled and planted a kiss on my cheek. "Not as much as you do, babe. Sure you don't need any help?"

"You can get yourself something to drink, and pour me a glass of sparkling water," I suggested.

Trent reached for a glass while I dished the pasta onto our plates. We carried everything to the dining room table.

"This looks delicious," Trent said as we sat down at the table. I'd put white roses in a vase and lit candles all around the dining room, switching off the lights so that the room had a romantic feel to it. "And romantic."

"I wanted to spoil you," I said. "Happy anniversary."

"Happy anniversary." He lifted his glass.

"To our future," Trent said, nodding toward my stomach. We clinked our glasses together and took a sip before we dug in.

"This reminds me of my childhood so much," I said, twirling pasta around my fork. "It's my mom's recipe."

"It's so good," Trent said, talking around a big bite.

"I wonder what she would say about the baby. It's a shame she's not here to be a grandmother—she always wanted that so much." I was suddenly emotional.

Trent reached for me and squeezed my hand. "I know she'd be proud of you."

"Really?" I asked. "I don't know... None of this was planned and I've always been such a planner. This is way out of my comfort zone, and not how I envisioned this happening at all. I always thought I'd have my life figured out first."

"You're not in a bad space, babe," Trent said. "I've got you. Sometimes, life happens. There's nothing wrong with that, we just have to adjust our course a little and keep going. I know she'd be proud of you because you're responsible and strong. And you care so much about everyone around you."

"Thanks, Trent," I said. "I wish you could have met her, too. And my dad. They were both such incredible people."

"They had to be if they produced you," Trent said with a warm smile. "I feel like in a way, I do know them because a bit of them always lives in you and the way they raised you."

I smiled at Trent, warmed by his words. He was right—my parents would always be with me in one way or another in the life lessons they taught and the person I'd become. It was nice to think about it that way.

"It's a sweet thought to imagine that our traits will carry on through our baby, too," I said.

"Yeah, I've been thinking about that," Trent said. "I want to give him or her the kinds of things I didn't get from my parents."

"Like what?" I asked. Trent had grown up in a rich household and he'd never wanted for anything.

"I want to offer unconditional support, no matter what. It's so much bigger than anyone realizes. Money can't buy support and love in the way that we really deserve as humans."

I took Trent's hand and we interlinked our fingers. That was exactly why he would be a good father. He would be there for our child.

My own childhood hadn't been full of fancy vacations or restaurants, and my parents couldn't buy me everything I wanted. But I'd always had their love and support, and that was what really mattered.

It was so good to know that Trent and I were on the same page.

After we ate, Trent cleared the table, telling me to relax while he cleaned up. A few minutes later, he joined me on the couch in the living room. He wrapped his arm around my shoulders and pulled me closer, kissing me.

"Happy anniversary, babe," he said.

I smiled and kissed him back. "It's been a wild ride so far, huh?"

"It's only starting," he said with a grin and kissed me again.

He slid his tongue into my mouth and I sighed, melting against him. Trent was everything. I was wrapped up in not only the feel of him, the heat that rolled off his body, but the way he cared for me.

Who knew Diablo could have such a soft side?

Trent cupped my cheek, his hand slowly trailing down

my neck, and the warmth between us turned into something hotter, something more urgent.

I looked at him, seeing the need in his eyes as he moved his hands over my back, stopping at my hip. Pulling me closer, he unbuttoned my blouse and lifted it over my head, then pulled the cups of my bra down.

My breasts sprang free, and he massaged one as he moved the nipple of the other to his mouth. The sensation ignited a spark inside me, and I grabbed at his chest, fumbling with the buttons on his shirt.

"Allow me," he said with a grin as he finished the job, removing the shirt and undershirt to reveal his muscled chest.

I caressed his broad shoulders as he undid my bra, then the pants I wore. I wiggled out of the clothes as he unbuckled his belt and pushed his pants and boxers down.

He stood before me where I sat on the couch, his erection bobbing in my face. A drop of precum collected on the tip. Keeping my eyes locked on his, I bent forward and licked the drop, gathering it on my tongue.

He growled, lunging at me.

I giggled, lying back on the couch where he positioned me.

"I need you, Bella," he gasped.

"I'm all yours," I whispered as he rolled my panties down my legs.

Opening my thighs, he moved two fingers along my slick lips, tickling the delicate flesh.

"You're so fucking wet, Bella."

"That's what you do to me." I gasped as he pushed one finger inside, then the other.

Trent pressed his mouth against mine, kissing me

deeply. I bent my knees on each side of his hips and bucked up against his erection.

"I need you inside me now," I whispered.

He broke apart to look at me, his eyes dark and intense. Keeping his gaze on mine, he moved his cock to my entrance.

Slowly, he pushed inside me. The feeling of his bare cock inside me was exquisite, and we moaned in unison.

"Fuck, you're so tight," he said.

I wrapped my legs around his hips and my arms around his shoulders, clinging to him.

He began to stroke inside me, slowly at first, kissing me on the lips. His hands moved over my breasts, rolling each nipple between his thumb and finger. It only turned me on more, and I pressed my heels against him, driving him in deeper.

"You like that?" he asked, looking at me. "You like me fucking you?"

I bit my lip and nodded. "I love it."

That only made him drive into me faster, and I gyrated against him. He reached down to rub circles over my clit, and I gasped in pleasure, my mouth falling open as he pumped into me.

"Yes, Trent, right there."

I dug my nails into his skin, arching my back against him. A warm, sweet feeling rushed through me.

"That's right," he whispered, watching me as I began to climax. "Come for me."

"Oh, fuck," I gasped.

I couldn't hold on any longer. Trent's fingers pushed me over the edge, and my muscles contracted around his cock.

As I cried out in ecstasy, he thrust into me more quickly. He grunted and pushed in all the way, then stayed still.

His cock shot his warm release deep inside me, pumping me full of his cum.

Breathless, he kissed me with his cock buried in my walls and my limbs wrapped around him. We couldn't get any closer. He made a few more slow strokes inside me, then stilled.

He rested his head lightly on my chest. I closed my eyes as I ran my fingers through his hair, smiling to myself.

This was perfect.

He lifted up to kiss me again, then pulled back to look at my face.

"I'll never get over how good you feel without a condom on," he murmured.

I smiled. "It's amazing."

He pulled out of me and reached for his undershirt to wipe me, then himself, clean. Lying back down on the couch beside me, he snaked his arm underneath my neck and pulled me against his gorgeous body.

I lay on his chest, listening to his heartbeat as it slowed. My body still buzzed with the afterglow of our sex, and his fingers tickled a little as he ran them slowly up and down my arm where he held me close to him.

"Tonight was incredible," I said.

"You're incredible," Trent mumbled. I could hear the smile in his voice without looking at him.

"I..."

I clamped my mouth shut, cutting myself off.

I'd nearly blurted out that I loved him.

I hadn't even realized it until now, but I *did* love him.

Somewhere along the way, between pretending for his family, getting closer to him, and now carrying his baby, I'd fallen in love with Trent Dillon.

I just didn't know how to tell him that. Or if I *should* tell him.

He was invested in the baby, but a part of me was still scared he would pull away from *me*.

I couldn't tell him I loved him only for him to shut me down. I was too vulnerable, too raw.

"Yeah?" Trent asked.

"I... think it's a good idea to move in together," I said, changing direction. It wasn't that I didn't mean what I said. I really did want to live with him. "If you're okay with that, of course," I added.

"Sure," Trent said. "I was the one who suggested it, after all. I'm okay with it."

I nodded, my heart sinking a little.

I'd hoped for a bit more enthusiasm. Not being just *okay* with it.

He was still on the fence about me moving in. It sounded like he didn't mind either way. I wanted him to be happy about it. This sounded like he was doing me a favor.

"I do have another possible living situation to explore, if we decide not to do it," I tacked on. Maybe if he knew I had other options, he'd be more reassuring. Maybe he'd insist I move in.

"Oh, okay," Trent said without emotion. "Just keep me posted, and we'll take it from there."

I blinked at him. Why was he so neutral about it?

I wanted him to tell me there was no need for another apartment. If he really wanted me to live with him, he would insist I do so. I wanted him to be more excited, more emotionally invested in the idea of us living together. It was a big deal. But he was acting like he could take it or leave it.

"I will," I finally said, not knowing which way to go with the conversation after that reply.

Not long after, Trent's breathing evened out, getting deeper as he drifted off to sleep.

Suddenly, I felt all alone again.

~

*M*y mind was still full of Trent's noncommittal answer when I met with Megan for lunch a few days later. I tried to push my worries aside, though, as we talked about her upcoming wedding.

"I'm *so* excited!" I said. "I just know it's going to be beautiful."

The wedding was going to take place in a Napa Valley vineyard. I was looking forward to seeing Megan find her happily ever after.

"I got the flowers taken care of, so that's one thing done," Megan said. "After days of bickering, we finally settled on the bouquets for the bridesmaids." She laughed. "But there are still so many last-minute details to take care of."

Despite the wedding talk being a welcome distraction, my mind kept drifting back to Trent.

"Are you okay?" Megan asked as she finished her sandwich. "You seem distracted."

"Sorry," I said. "I promise I'm listening."

"Oh, I'm not worried about that. I'm worried about *you*. Are you doing okay? Coping with everything?"

I let out a heavy sigh. "Not really." I hesitated before I pushed on. Megan had become a close friend in the past two months, and I knew I could talk to her. "I have to move out of the apartment I share with Angie soon."

"Why?" Megan asked, frowning.

"Angie doesn't want me to live there with a baby on the

way." I bristled just thinking about how unsupportive my supposed best friend had been.

"Oh, my God. Really?" Megan asked, shocked.

"Yeah, it's complicated, I guess. I just..." I glanced at Megan. Trent and I hadn't talked about revealing the pregnancy to his family yet. Megan already knew, of course, but no one else did. "We're not planning to tell the rest of his family yet, okay?"

"I won't say anything. Don't worry," Megan said. "You can trust me."

I nodded. I felt like I really *could* trust Megan. It meant so much to me that she was such a good friend.

I'd already told her about Trent's excitement over becoming a father, and she was happy for me. She still didn't know how our relationship had started out—I knew Trent wouldn't want her to know. She assumed I wasn't moving in with Trent because of the short time we'd been dating.

"Hey, I have an idea," Megan said, her face lighting up. "Why don't you move into my apartment?"

"What?" I asked, confused. "You're getting married. I can't possibly do that."

"No, I mean *my* apartment, the one I live in alone. I'm moving in with Grant after the wedding. I was planning to take the four months' rent still left on my lease as a loss. But you could move in and take over the lease. It would be a win-win! What do you think?"

"I think..." I tried to wrap my mind around it. Megan didn't live too far from Dillon Tech, and it wasn't a bad idea. "I think it might actually work."

"Let me show the apartment to you," Megan said, waving her hand so the server could bring us the check.

"Right now?"

"Why not? If you love it, then it's settled. We'll just get the lease transferred to you. If you don't, no worries. There's really no pressure at all."

I nodded. The more I thought about it, the more I liked it.

We left the restaurant and drove to Megan's apartment in a small community surrounded by greenery.

When we stepped inside the first-story home, I immediately loved it. Megan took me on a tour of the place—an open-plan kitchen-living area, two bedrooms, and a small, enclosed yard.

"It's great," I breathed.

"Think about it, and let me know," Megan said with an excited smile. "I think it would work really well. And there are other young families who live in the building."

I nodded. "Thanks so much for showing me. And offering."

"Of course."

I sighed. "Can I use your bathroom? I have to pee. Again. It seems like that's all I do these days."

Megan giggled and showed me to the bathroom, which was spacious with a nice bathtub and a window that let in sunlight.

As I finished and opened the door, I heard Megan talking in the living room. She was on the phone, and she didn't sound happy at all.

"Well, if that's how you do business, don't count on me for a good review," Megan ended the call sharply, hanging up. She huffed.

"Is everything okay?" I asked.

Megan turned around, frustration etched on her face.

"The caterer just canceled on me. I had him booked months ago!"

I raised my eyebrows. "That's awful, Megan. But you still have time to find someone else, right?" The wedding was still a few weeks away and finding a new caterer didn't seem impossible.

Megan was close to tears, and I gave her a hug.

"Thanks," Megan said. "I guess it's not too late to find someone else."

I nodded. "It's going to be okay."

"Will it, though?" Megan let out a shuddering breath, sinking onto her couch. "I feel like this whole wedding is doomed."

"What?" I asked. "Why?"

"Shelby backed out of being my bridesmaid, so the wedding party number is off. Grant will have more guys than I'll have bridesmaids, and the photos will look off-balance. The caterer just canceled after making me change the menu twice, and the singer of the group we originally booked canceled last week, too. He needs throat surgery, Bella. What are the odds?"

"Oh," I said. A lot more had gone wrong than I'd realized.

"Yeah. It's rough. What if it's a sign?"

"What do you mean?" I asked.

"I'm terrified that it's the universe telling me I shouldn't get married."

"That's not true," I said and took Megan's hand, squeezing it. "You and Grant are perfect together. All these issues can be fixed. Just because you have a few obstacles in your path doesn't mean things are doomed."

Megan nodded, but she didn't look convinced.

"Are you getting cold feet?" I asked carefully.

"I don't know," Megan said. "I don't know if any of this is a good idea anymore."

She covered her face with her hands. I moved closer to her and put a hand on her shoulder and squeezed. She was quiet, trying to pull herself together.

I searched for something more to say that would make her feel better, but I came up with nothing. I wished I knew how to help.

Not that I was very good at that. I couldn't even help myself right now. It seemed that no one was sure where they stood anymore—not Megan about her wedding, and not Trent about me.

"I'm sorry, Megan," I said. I didn't know exactly what she was going through, but I knew how she felt.

I wanted something concrete to hold onto, but everything in my life had become a big question mark. The very foundation I stood on was shaky.

That scared me more than anything.

26

TRENT

I tossed the key in the air and caught it in my fist. Entering my house from the garage door, I walked with a spring in my step.

I'd had a new house key made for Bella.

It took me longer than it should have, but I was ready to ask her to move in with me—in earnest this time.

I just had to be delicate about it—without making her feel pressured.

When she told me she was exploring other options, my heart sank.

I wanted her to move in with me, but I'd read that putting too much stress on a pregnant woman wasn't a good idea, so I'd tried to play it cool and let her decide for herself.

But maybe I'd come across too laid-back, like I didn't care.

I cared.

A lot.

The truth was, I was a little spooked by how fast things were changing. I'd be damned if I would admit it to her, but I didn't like change.

I didn't like stepping out of my comfort zone. I was a creature of habit, and I'd worked long and hard to get where I was. To step out of that mold was... hard.

But I was ready to take this step. I wanted this to work.

I'd invited her over. Tonight, I'd be honest about my feelings. I'd give her the key and book a moving company to help her move in.

I wanted Bella here.

She belonged with me.

A knock sounded on the front door. I crossed the space to open it, whistling.

Bella stood on the front step looking drained.

"Hi," she said, giving me a tired smile.

"Hi. Are you okay?" I kissed her on the cheek, and she nodded.

"Yeah, I'm fine. It was just a long day."

I shut the door behind her, and we walked to the living room. It was Sunday, and I hadn't seen her yet today.

"Want anything to drink?" I asked.

"No, I just want to sit down. Being pregnant is exhausting."

We settled on the couch, and she kicked off her shoes. She leaned her head against the couch and closed her eyes.

She was clearly not in a good frame of mind.

I still held the key in my fist, and I shoved it in my pocket. It wasn't a good time to talk to her about her moving in. I'd wanted it to be a surprise, a joyous thing, not something that came on the back of a difficult mood.

I pulled her legs into my lap and began to massage her feet.

She smiled at me. "That feels good."

"Isn't this like catnip to pregnant women?"

She laughed, but the smile didn't reach her eyes. "Something like that."

I rubbed her feet for a while, then she curled up next to me on the couch. I put my arm around her and tugged her closer—it was so good to be able to do this, to have her this close to me.

"Better?" I asked.

"Yeah," she said.

She still sounded dejected.

"Is everything okay?"

Bella hesitated before she answered. "I saw Megan today."

"Oh, that's nice," I said. "You two have really been hitting it off."

Bella nodded. "She suggested that I take over her apartment lease when she moves in with Grant."

I blinked at her. "What?"

"If I moved in, she wouldn't have to put up a huge amount for breaking the lease. I went to see the place. It's really nice. It has enough space for the baby and even a small yard, which isn't something I counted on. The area is pretty good, too. I mean, you know Megan. She has great taste."

I nodded, my heart sinking again. Did she really want to live on her own?

When she said it the first time, I thought she was just considering it as a passing thought. I hadn't realized she was serious enough to go look at another place.

"Can you keep a secret?" Bella asked.

I frowned. "A secret?"

"From Grant, I mean," Bella said.

I hesitated. I didn't like keeping secrets, and I wasn't a

fan of drama. But Bella looked like she needed to talk. I wanted to be there for her.

"Yeah, I can keep a secret."

Bella sighed. "Megan is freaking out. The wedding planning isn't going well. A lot of things are falling apart. A few people she was counting on are canceling. She thinks it might be a sign she shouldn't get married."

"Really?" I asked, stunned. "Are you sure about this?"

"Yeah, she basically said as much," Bella said.

I shook my head in amazement.

That seemed like a huge overreaction on Megan's part. So, a few things went wrong. It didn't mean she should just give up.

"Well, let's not get carried away here. Maybe Megan just has a lot on her plate and she's stressed out. Getting married is a big deal. Maybe she was just venting, but she didn't really mean it."

"Yeah, maybe," Bella said, nodding slowly.

She didn't sound like she believed me, so I pushed on.

"I'm sure it will work out before the wedding. These things usually turn out fine in the end."

Bella glanced up at me, and I locked eyes with her. I meant every word I said—my brother was madly in love with Megan. From what I'd seen of them together, the feeling was mutual. They were perfect for each other, and they deserved to be happy. I doubted something as small as few cancellations would ruin everything.

"Actually, I was thinking about that," Bella said. "The part about it working out, I mean."

"Yeah?" I asked.

She nodded and offered a small smile.

"I want to find a caterer who can replace the one who

canceled. Also, Megan's musical act canceled, and I have a few bands in mind to suggest. Once Megan has a couple of solutions, she won't feel so overwhelmed by it all. I want to ease some of the pressure by taking over some of her responsibility."

That raised my hackles, and I sat up straight.

"Bella, I don't think that's a good idea," I said.

She frowned. "Why not?"

My mouth turned dry as I searched for the right words.

"Because it's their wedding. It's not your problem," I said flatly.

"I know it's not my problem. I just want to help."

"But it wouldn't be helping to get involved," I said tightly.

This didn't sit right with me at all, her wanting to take over part of the wedding. The more I thought about it, the more riled up I felt.

"You should just mind your own business," I said.

She pulled back a little and looked at me.

"Megan is my friend. That's what friends do. They help each other out."

"How is that helpful?" I insisted. "You don't know what's best for Megan. It's... overbearing."

"Trent, I don't think I'm being overbearing by finding a caterer to show Megan she has options. I just want to show her it's not some sign from the universe she shouldn't get married."

"Frankly, it's not your job to show her anything."

Bella's jaw dropped and she looked at me, stunned. She shifted away from me, putting distance between us.

"I just want Megan to realize it's not so bad," Bella said. "In the grand scheme of things, she's silly to think it means more than a few inconveniences."

I looked at her. She wasn't backing down.

But the more her words sank in, the less I wanted to back down, either. I hated when people thought they could control others' lives.

"Maybe Megan knows her own mind, and you should back off," I snapped. I was suddenly upset that she wanted to make a big deal of this. "It's not your place to try to control this."

Bella laughed bitterly.

"I can't believe what I'm hearing," she said. "I'm trying to help Megan and you're telling me I'm wrong. I'm not trying to control anything."

"That's exactly what you're doing. You're getting involved in her life. You think you know what's best for her and Grant. What is that if not controlling and overbearing?"

She gasped. "You're being an insulting jerk, Trent."

"If that's what you want to think, go ahead," I said, my jaw clenched. "You take from it what you want if that's how you want to play this."

"I'm not playing anything!" Bella cried out.

I shook my head and stood from the couch, walking to the bar on the other side of the living room. I poured myself a stiff drink and took a gulp.

"Trent, why are you telling me that I'm wrong for caring?"

"Don't throw this back on me," I said hotly. "I'm telling you the best way to handle this. I'm not going to let you try to control my brother's wedding."

"Excuse me? You're not *letting me* do anything. I'm my own person, and I sure as hell don't need your permission if I want to do something. I can't believe you're being so harsh about something *nice*. It's not a crime to want to help someone out, you know."

I scoffed, shaking my head before I took another gulp of my whiskey.

"You're acting just like them," I said under my breath.

"Excuse me?" Bella asked. "What did you just say?"

"I said," raising my voice so she could hear me clearly, "you're acting *just like* my family."

"Is that a bad thing? From what I've seen of your family, they're pretty great people."

"You think they're great because you're on the outside, looking in. You haven't seen what they can be because around you, they're all wearing a mask. They're trying to impress you. But I know who they really are. And I'm starting to realize you're a lot more like them than I thought."

"Please, enlighten me, since apparently I know nothing," Bella said sarcastically.

"You think you know what's best for someone else, taking over where it's not necessary, butting in when you should butt *out*. You're meddling in people's lives. It's fucking manipulative, Bella."

She stared at me.

And then I added one last thing before I could stop myself.

"I can't imagine living with someone who has so much in common with my family."

The words fell out of my mouth, and they were angrier than I meant them to be. But I was too riled up to take them back. Too upset to change course.

The air around us grew thick with tension.

Bella was quiet for a moment, studying me.

"I understand," she said.

I opened my mouth to keep arguing, but that didn't work when it was one-sided.

Bella collected her things, walked to the door, and let herself out without another word.

I looked at the door, hoping she'd come back. Outside, her car started and she drove off.

Fuck.

What had I done?

I threw back the rest of my drink, and reached for the bottle.

27

BELLA

The next two days, I called in sick to work.

And I did feel sick. My emotions were a mess, a big cluster of confusion and heartache.

I had to sift through the fog of my feelings to figure out what to deal with first.

I was furious with Trent for insulting me, for comparing me to the bad part of his family, the part he kept trying to avoid. I was upset that he said I couldn't see it, that none of them had been genuine with me.

And when he said he didn't want to live with me, my heart broke.

We were over.

I could hardly believe it. I thought I meant more to him than this. But he'd thrown me away at the first sign of trouble.

And to think, I'd fallen in love with the guy.

I paced through my bedroom, alone in the apartment. A pang of sadness tugged at my gut.

Not only was I missing Trent, but I wouldn't get to see

Megan's wedding. After what happened between Trent and me, I couldn't imagine pretending to be with him for the third wedding.

By the angry way he looked at me that night in his house, I knew he wouldn't want me there, either.

I collapsed on my bed and curled into a ball, letting myself cry. Again. It seemed like all I'd done the past two days.

What we had together had been so good. I knew he felt it, too. How could he end it over something like this?

After I cried all the tears I had left, I pushed myself back up. I dried my eyes and blew my nose.

I couldn't afford more time to be upset. Things with Angie were tense, and I had to move out of my apartment soon. I hadn't heard from Megan again, and I didn't know where I was going to live.

When I dialed Megan's number, Trent's voice played in my head again.

You need to butt out. She knows her own mind.

I shook my head. I couldn't believe he'd called me manipulative for wanting to help my friend.

"Hey, Megan," I said when she answered, trying not to sound as bad as I felt. "How are you?"

"I'm doing much better, Bella. And I've been meaning to call you. Sorry I freaked out on you the other day. I was in a bad space."

"Oh, I'm so glad you're doing better."

"Thank you so much for listening to me vent. It helped a lot."

"Anytime." I took a breath. "Listen, I was wondering if you're still moving out of your apartment. I need to make a decision about where I'm going next."

"Oh, of course! I'm still moving out, definitely. So the apartment is yours if you want it. I'll send you the contact info for the property manager."

"Okay, great. I'd appreciate that. So everything's still on for the wedding?"

"Yes. I realized I was being silly. I love Grant way too much to let little inconveniences like that interrupt our wedding. He's the guy for me, and this is our big day. The caterer canceling isn't going to change that." She laughed.

"I'm happy you're feeling better about it."

"Yeah, I was under so much stress, I wasn't thinking straight," Megan said. "When I talked to Grant, he offered to jump in and take over some of the planning. That helps so much. It was overwhelming doing it all on my own."

"I understand," I agreed. "Wedding planning is no joke."

"If I'd known from the beginning, I might have suggested we elope!" Megan said with a laugh.

I laughed too, but my mind drifted to Trent. He'd been right that Megan was overwhelmed and freaking out because of stress. She and Grant had figured it out.

Megan had been the one to work it out for herself, and I hadn't even said or done anything.

But he was wrong to accuse me of meddling. I'd just wanted to help my friend.

I could imagine why he thought I was trying to take over, though, if that was all he ever knew from his family. I hadn't really seen that behavior from them, but I *was* on the outside, looking in.

Still, Trent had been hurtful to me.

"Can I ask you a question?" I asked Megan.

"Of course."

"Do you and Grant have good communication? I mean,

when you get stuck about something... is it simple to sort out?"

"God, no," Megan said with a snort. "Men are weird. They don't know how to express their feelings, so they blow up. Or go all mute like a statue. That's Grant's go-to."

I sighed. "That sounds about right." Trent had used both tactics at different times. At least this time, he'd shown how he felt, which was more than he'd ever done before.

"Why?" Megan asked.

"Oh, it's nothing," I said. "I was just thinking out loud."

"Well, now I have something to ask you," Megan said.

"Yeah?"

"Will you be a bridesmaid in my wedding?"

I was speechless. "Me?"

"Yes, you. And it's not just because you can fit in Shelby's dress, either," she said with a laugh. "I consider you a true friend, and I'd be honored if you would be a part of my wedding."

"Are you sure, Megan?"

"Absolutely. I want to see your smiling face in my wedding photos. Will you do it?"

I beamed. If we were together in person, I'd throw my arms around her and hug her.

"I'd love to," I said.

Megan had become a true friend to me, too. I wanted to be there for her, however she needed it. I was glad that this way, I'd get to see her wedding.

It was going to be awkward to see Trent at the event. Now I wouldn't be there as his date or even his pseudo-girlfriend. I'd be there as part of the wedding party, and I was sure he wouldn't be happy about that.

Too bad, though. We would have to deal with it when the time came.

After I ended the call with Megan, I called her property management company to iron out the details. Once that was taken care of and I knew I had somewhere to live, I opened my laptop and started looking for a new job.

I couldn't work with Trent now. Not after what had happened between us and how we'd fallen apart.

I couldn't work with him knowing that I was carrying his baby. It would hurt way too much to be his assistant and pretend nothing had happened. Hell, he might even fire me.

I had to find a new job. I couldn't avoid him forever.

Finally, after calling around, I found a company that desperately needed a temporary office manager since theirs was going on maternity leave.

The irony wasn't lost on me.

They were desperate enough that they offered a decent salary, even though it was a reduction from what I made at Dillon Tech. Luckily, I still had the money Trent paid me for attending the three weddings.

With a shock, I realized the third wedding wouldn't count if I didn't go with him. I'd have to return a third of his check. The rest of it, I was keeping since I'd done the job. I'd been at his side and I'd sold the relationship.

For a while, I'd even sold it to myself.

I wrote a check to Trent for one third of the amount he'd paid me. I put it in the mail along with my resignation letter. I'd return to Dillon Tech over the weekend to collect the things I had at my desk. I couldn't risk running into Trent again.

When I dropped the letter in the mail, it felt so final. I felt sick all over again.

My heart ached. I was losing Trent. It was over, when I'd hoped this would last forever.

Nothing good lasted forever, though. I'd learned that the

hard way, time and again in my life. What I knew about myself was that I'd always bounced back before, so I could do it again.

I had to do what was best for me and the baby, and Trent made it clear he didn't want to be with me.

28

TRENT

*I*t was three days after Bella stormed out. I woke up feeling like shit, but what else was new?

Maybe it had to do with the fact that I'd finished a fucking bottle of whiskey. Again. Or maybe it was that Bella hadn't bothered coming to the office since our fight.

How long was she going to stay away? She couldn't avoid me forever, could she?

She was carrying my baby, for fuck's sake! And she worked for me. If she wanted to keep making a living, she had to show her face in the office at some point... I just hoped today would be the day. I just wanted to see her.

Not that it would change how I felt about it all.

I was too fucking proud to reach out to her because that would make it look like I was wrong. I wasn't.

I got up and made a cup of coffee, hoping it would help the pounding in my head. I was already late to the office, and I needed to get moving.

When I heard someone outside, my heart leaped. Could it be her? Had she come to see me?

It won't change things if she did, I told myself. I had to stick to my guns.

I opened the door, but it was the mailman dropping the mail in my box.

"Have a nice day, sir," he said with a smile.

"Thanks."

I trudged out to get the mail as he walked off, whistling.

There was only one piece of mail. A letter from Bella.

I carried it inside and shut the door again. My heart pounded as I tore it open. Was it going to be a letter? Would she say she wanted to work things out?

But there was no personal letter. Only a check and a formal letter of resignation.

Fuck.

The resignation letter was professional and to the point. She was no longer working at Dillon Tech, effective immediately.

As my throat closed up, I looked at the amount on the check—a third of what I'd paid her for the weddings. Obviously, she was done attending them with me.

She was done with me, period.

I sank into the couch, staring at the slips of paper.

How had this happened?

I knew exactly how it had happened. I'd been a dick to her.

What could I expect after I'd blown up at her like that the other night?

I was on such a hair trigger about anything connected to my family. It was a bad idea to get Bella mixed up in my family in the first place. Now, she was involved with them, and I couldn't fucking deal.

Not that I thought I was wrong—I had a right to feel the

way I did. Interfering with my brother's wedding wasn't her place, and someone had to tell her.

I just wished I could have done it in a way that didn't fuck everything up.

This was it. Bella wouldn't be in my life. I'd screwed up my relationship with her.

I scoffed. Why had I ever thought things could work out between us? That had been my first mistake.

I'd fallen for her, and now there was a gaping hole in the center of my chest.

Fuck.

I stuffed the check and letter back in the envelope and tossed it on the coffee table. Shoving down my heartbreak, I headed toward the bathroom to shower and get dressed for another shitty day at work.

Of course, the office had fallen into chaos without her there. This was exactly what I'd wanted to avoid in the first place—losing her as an employee by dating her.

Guess I'd fucked up there, too.

While I showered, I played the argument back in my mind, and thought about what Bella had said about Megan's meltdown.

Had she pulled out of our agreement only because she was pissed at me, or had she also canceled because there wasn't a wedding to attend anymore? I'd heard nothing from Grant that would indicate the wedding was off, but that didn't mean it wasn't. Maybe he just hadn't let me know yet.

On the drive to my office, I called Grant and arranged to meet over dinner tonight. I had to know what was going on, even if it was only for curiosity's sake.

"Let's meet up at eight at Antoine's," I suggested, trying to keep the grief out of my voice.

"Yeah, sounds good," Grant said. His voice betrayed no

emotion, either. I couldn't get a read on him. "It'll be nice seeing you."

"Yeah, you too."

I didn't explicitly invite Megan, but I didn't *not* invite her either. Whatever happened, tonight I would find out what was going on with them. And hopefully, I could get some intel on Bella.

~

When I arrived at the restaurant, Grant sat at the table alone.

"Hey, bro," he said, standing to shake my hand and clap me on the back.

"Where's Megan?" I asked.

"She'll be here. She's running a bit late," Grant said.

Ah. So they were still together, then.

"She's signing some paperwork with her property management company. She'll join us as soon as she's done," Grant added as we sat down.

"Sounds like you guys are moving forward fast now that the wedding is creeping up," I said. "Giving up her apartment is a big deal, huh?"

"Yeah, it's the next step," Grant said and rubbed his hands together. "I can't wait to spend the rest of my life with her, man."

I laughed. "You're so whipped it's not even funny. You used to complain about high-maintenance women all the time, saying that you'd never settle down."

Grant nodded, chuckling. "It all changes when you meet the right one."

"So how are things with you guys?" I asked. "Must be tough now that the pressure is on with last-minute details for the wedding."

"We have our moments," Grant said. "The wedding planning is tough on her. Actually, she had a bit of a meltdown last week." Grant laughed, shaking his head. "Megan has that thing where even when she's angry, she's cute."

"You thought she was cute when she had a meltdown?" I asked, surprised.

"Well, obviously not *while* she was having it. When she told me she'd nearly canceled the wedding, that threw me for a loop. The cute part came afterward. Everything looks different in hindsight. Now when we look back, we can laugh about it."

"She almost canceled the wedding?" I asked.

"Yeah, she was really freaking out about everything. The stress just got to her. But we worked it out. I took over finding a band and a caterer, and that made all the difference."

"So, still going strong, then," I said.

Grant grinned. "You know it. She's really great. I wouldn't ever risk losing her."

I nodded.

They were together, and they'd figured it out for themselves. Good. That was exactly what I'd figured they would do—what I'd told Bella. Turned out I was right.

"I'm glad you guys are okay," I said. "I was worried."

"You were?" Grant asked. "You knew about this?"

I nodded. "Yeah, I heard a little. Bella and Megan talk. You know how women are. Bella was saying she wanted to take over organizing the caterer and the band." I shook my head. "She wanted to manipulate Megan into doing what she wanted."

Grant frowned. "Whoa. Manipulate? That's a strong word. Is everything okay between you two?"

Before I could answer, Megan arrived, joining us at the table. She kissed Grant before she sat down.

"Sorry I'm late," she said. "I ran into your parents on the way here, and I asked them to join us."

"What?" I asked, but before anyone could say anything else, my mom and dad walked in the entrance of the restaurant.

Great. Fucking great.

"Hi," Mom said as they arrived at the table. "Great minds think alike. Your father and I wanted to eat here tonight, and then we ran into Megan out on the sidewalk."

"You boys don't mind if we join you, do you?" Dad asked.

"I'm not doing this," I said, not even trying to be polite. I wasn't in the mood. This wasn't supposed to be a big family dinner. "I'm out."

"What?" Grant asked.

"Oh, honey, no," Mom said. "That's not what we were trying to do. You should stay. If you don't want us here, we'll go." She looked at Dad.

"Come on, man," Grant said, irritated.

Fuck, I was being a dick.

"It's fine," I said, swallowing down my anger. "Sorry. I'm just in a shitty mood tonight. You should stay. We'll all stay. Okay?" I let out a breath, trying not to sound exasperated.

Mom and Dad hesitated, but then they nodded and sat down. We were one big happy fucking family.

When everyone was settled and the server appeared to take the drink order for the table, Grant turned his attention back to me.

"What's going on with you and Bella?" he asked. "It seems like things aren't exactly how they should be."

Megan glanced at me, her face carefully expressionless. What did she know?

"We broke up," I said. There was no point hiding it.

"What?" Mom and Dad cried out in unison. Grant looked troubled, too, but I watched Megan. She didn't look shocked or surprised at all to hear the news.

"You knew, didn't you?" I challenged Megan.

"Yes, I knew," she said. "Bella is taking over my lease, and I just saw her at the management company where we signed the papers. She was upset, and she told me you guys split up."

A pang shot into my chest. So, it really was final, then.

She was moving into an apartment on her own, and I didn't fit in her life anymore.

"Honey, why?" Mom asked.

I sighed. "I'm not going into it."

"But she was so great for you," Mom pushed. "We all thought she was the one who could turn things around for you."

"She's a great girl, Trent," Dad added.

That did it.

"I'm sorry I disappointed you again," I said sarcastically. "That's just classic Trent, right? Letting all of you down again by breaking some girl's heart."

Mom frowned, confused. "What are you talking about? Letting us down?"

I'd already been close to the boiling point, and now that she'd asked, the dam broke.

"You can't for one second be sorry for *me*, that I'm the one going through something painful. You're all so worried about Bella, just like you were worried about Waverly. That woman couldn't make a wrong move in your eyes, and you refused to believe me when I told you she cheated on me. What will your blame be this time? What accusation will you cook up to make it look like I fucked up again?"

Mom and Dad both looked horrified.

"Trent, now you listen to me," Dad started, his voice hard. "I can see you're upset, but that's not the way things happened."

"No?" I asked. "Your exact words to me were that you didn't believe she cheated on me. You said it over and over. All of you. None of you took my side. You pushed me to just work things out with her. As if Waverly had been a part of this family, and not me."

I was seething. I probably should have left before I made a scene, but two years of anger and resentment were coming to the surface now.

"No, honey, that's not what it was at all," Mom said.

"We never said we didn't believe you," Dad continued. "We said we *couldn't believe* she would do something like that. We were shocked Waverly wasn't the person we thought she was. It wasn't that we didn't believe you, we were just surprised by it all."

I stared at my dad. Mom and Grant nodded along.

I wasn't sure if I could believe them.

"Is that what's been going on?" Mom asked. "The past couple of years, you've been so withdrawn from us. Is this why?"

"I'm just so *sick* of not being good enough," I admitted. "I'm the one who fucked it up with Waverly, because there was no way she could have made a mistake, right? It felt like it was all on me."

"Trent, none of us thought you were to blame for things falling apart with Waverly," Grant said.

"But you all encouraged me to work things out with her," I insisted.

"Yes, we did," Mom admitted. "I see now that was the wrong thing. I... I just thought maybe she was unhappy, and that had driven her to cheat. I thought maybe therapy might help. I shouldn't have tried to get involved, but I just wanted to see you happy."

So they *had* believed me?

Had I really misunderstood all this time?

I shook my head. That wasn't all, though. They'd tried to control me, and I was fed up.

"But you guys were all up in my business. I didn't need you trying to control everything when I'd just lost my girl-friend. After a while, I just wanted you to butt out. But instead, you set me up with one blind date after another, thinking you could push me past the hell I was in. As if it were that easy."

Mom and Dad both looked upset. Mom's eyes shimmered with unshed tears.

"We were never trying to make you feel like you weren't good enough. We were just trying to help. I didn't realize it was so bad..." She closed her eyes, pulling herself together. "I should have asked you if that was what you wanted." She looked at me again. "I should have asked you if you were okay. Honey, getting your heart broken is a big deal. We knew you were hurt. We were just trying to help in the only way we knew how."

Dad nodded in agreement with her.

I blinked, letting it sink in.

They had done all that... because they cared? It was a hard concept to wrap my head around.

"I think we should order something to chew on while we process this," Grant cut in.

I nodded, shifting in my seat, my mind spinning.

After our drinks and food arrived, the conversation started up again and turned to lighter things. The tension was still thick in the air, but as the night went on and we talked, spending time as a family, things got a little better.

I was still upset, and I needed time to let the news sink in. Mom and Dad both looked kind of shocked by everything they'd heard.

But there had been a shift. I wasn't sure how it would play out, but I had a little hope that things with my family could improve.

Grant and Megan did their best to carry the conversation, and I was grateful for them.

Finally, the meal was over and we paid the check. As Dad said goodbye to Grant and Megan, Mom turned to me and put her hands on my cheeks.

"You're one of the best things I've ever done, sweetheart," she said. "I didn't want to see you hurt. But most of all, I never wanted to hurt you. I love you, honey. I always will, no matter what."

Dad shook my hand. He said nothing, but his eyes were filled with emotion.

I sighed when they left.

"Well, that was more emotionally draining than I expected," Grant said.

I nodded. "Sorry to make a scene."

"It's good. And it was about time you told us what was going on in that head of yours." Grant chuckled. "I had no idea. None of us did."

I nodded. Maybe I'd held things in a bit too much.

"I'm just running to the ladies' room," Megan said. She grabbed her purse and walked away from us, leaving us alone.

Grant looked at me.

"What are you going to do about Bella?" he asked.

"Nothing," I grumbled.

"Look, I know you don't want us getting in your private life, but I have to say this."

I looked at him.

"I think you need to fix things with Bella," he said. "If you don't, you'll be sorry. She's a good woman. People like her don't come along every day."

I shook my head, unwilling to face the pain of losing Bella. Not now. "I'm not going there. I can't be with someone manipulative and controlling. I've been trying to get *away* from that."

"Look, bro, I love you, but you're being a jackass."

"What?" I asked, surprised.

"Bella isn't manipulative. She wanted to help us because she cares, not because she had an agenda."

I clenched my jaw, and Grant pressed on.

"You're so stuck in your beliefs that you let them color your perception of everything around you. It's not fair to write off Bella because you were hurt by Waverly... or because you're so jaded by life that you *think* everyone's trying to control you."

I wanted to say something, but Megan returned and Grant smiled at her.

"Ready to go?" he asked.

Megan nodded and they both said their goodbyes before leaving the restaurant.

I left in a huff, irritated when I got in my car. Who did Grant think he was, telling me he knew where I'd gone wrong? He was overstepping.

Except... what if he had a point? What if Grant was right about Bella, and I'd been wrong?

I'd already realized I was wrong about my family. They were only trying to help. Maybe I'd misjudged Bella's intentions, too.

To anyone else, to someone who wasn't paranoid about being manipulated like I was, Bella's efforts would come across as perfectly reasonable.

Fuck.

She *was* telling the truth. She was only trying to help.

Bella never had some malicious agenda to meddle in Grant's and Megan's lives.

She was just being kind, trying to lift some of the weight off her friend's shoulders. She was just being herself.

Feeling like the biggest idiot on the planet, I let out a heavy breath. I really *was* a jackass.

I had to talk to Bella.

I loved this woman, yet I'd been a dick to her.

I only hoped it wasn't too late to undo the damage I'd done.

29

BELLA

I taped up a box with blankets and wrote the contents on the side with a marker.

With a sigh, I carried it out of the apartment and down the stairs to load it into my car.

I'd spent the past few days moving my things bit by bit to Megan's apartment. Tomorrow was the day the movers would come to pick up my furniture. It had been a lot of hard work, and I was exhausted. I got tired so much faster these days—pregnancy wasn't a joke.

When I brought the box out to the street, I froze.

Trent was standing on the curb, leaning against his car.

I swallowed. He was the last person I expected to see.

"Hi, Bella. Can we talk?" he asked.

"Yeah," I said and loaded the box in my trunk. "There's a café down the street from here."

I didn't want to invite him into the apartment. I knew we'd need to have a conversation about the baby. Might as well get it over with, though it would be painful.

"Okay."

I slammed the trunk closed. Without looking at him, I

started walking, and he fell into step next to me. We got a table outside the small café, and only after the server left with our drink orders did he say something.

"Bella, I'm so sorry," Trent said. "I really fucked up. I was wrong to think you were trying to manipulate Megan."

I shook my head. I wasn't ready to hear that he was sorry. He'd hurt me. I was holding onto that anger. I could deal with anger—it was much easier than dealing with heartache.

"I can't just forgive and forget, Trent," I said.

"Why not?"

"You hurt me," I said bluntly. "And I realize there's just going to be more of that if we stick together. We can't make this work. Some people just aren't right for each other. There's no need to try to figure out what went wrong. We just have to accept that so we can co-parent this child." Trent didn't answer me, so I added, "That is, if you're still interested in being in the baby's life."

"Of course I am," Trent said immediately, and I believed him. It was one thing he'd been sincere about since the start.

The server arrived with our coffees, and we kept quiet until she left. The tension in the air was thick.

"I want to be with you, Bella. I want you to move in with me."

I shook my head. I hated that he was pushing this.

"We're not compatible, Trent. I can't rearrange my life to do what you want."

Trent frowned, upset with my words, but I didn't care. I knew what I wanted, what I *needed*, and that was to move on. It was difficult, but I had to do it.

"Bella," Trent started, but I cut him off.

"You can send me paperwork with a tentative co-parenting arrangement, and I'll have an attorney look it over."

I was strictly business, keeping my emotions far, far away from this conversation. If I let myself feel anything at all, I was going to lose it and start crying, and I couldn't afford that. I had to protect myself.

"Bella, this isn't what I want, and I'm not convinced it's what *you* really want either," Trent said. "I told you I was wrong, and I'm sorry about how I acted. I was a total dick to you—"

"There's no need to keep apologizing, Trent," I said calmly. "This is over, and it sucks, but we both know it won't work." I fished in my handbag and found some cash to pay for my drink. "I think I should leave."

I got up and walked away, leaving him behind.

I should have felt relieved it was over. I should have been glad he didn't follow me.

But there was a part that wanted him to follow, that wanted him to fight for me.

I squashed that part down. I couldn't harbor hope for what was over between us.

It hurt way too much to keep hope alive.

It was settled. He'd taken me at my word that we were over, and we had a plan in place to discuss how we would parent our child.

This is for the best, I told myself. Anything else would have made it harder.

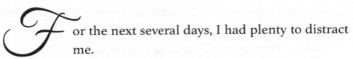

For the next several days, I had plenty to distract me.

I moved into my new apartment. The place was

gorgeous, and I was comfortable. Though I was sad to lose my friendship with Angie, I was relieved to be in my own space where I didn't have to share a common area with someone who didn't want me around.

The next day, I started my new job.

It was nowhere near as exciting or taxing as my old job at Dillon Tech. The office was a tight ship, and I didn't need to put out any fires. I was just here to keep the ball rolling. It wasn't exactly challenging work, but it paid the bills.

I could pretty much do it in a stupor, which was good, because my mind was filled with what could have been with Trent.

I couldn't stop thinking about him.

Damn it, I loved him.

Despite everything that had happened between us, I loved Trent. Getting over him proved to be not just difficult, it was impossible.

Sometimes, I found myself reaching for my phone to call him. I stopped myself each time, though, before I dialed his number.

I kept reminding myself why I'd left in the first place. Trent had hurt me. He'd been hurt, too, by his ex-girlfriend and by his family. It was sad, but he didn't seem capable of opening up in a new relationship.

A leopard didn't change his spots, right? And Diablo didn't just stop being a devil.

I just had to keep focusing on what had gone wrong... even though my dreams at night were filled with all the good times between us. Every morning when I woke up, I had an ache in my chest, a void that only Trent had been able to fill.

Damn it, why was this so incredibly hard? I had to stay strong.

Trent obviously was.

He hadn't bothered to contact me again. His attorney had reached out to me to say a co-parenting agreement was being written. But there'd been nothing from Trent directly.

If he had really changed, if he really wanted to be with me, he would have tried harder. But he obviously didn't care all that much.

With Megan's wedding just days away, I'd have to face him again. I could avoid him in every other instance in my life, but he would be there.

I couldn't help wondering if he'd moved on enough to bring a date to the wedding. Would she be fake... or real?

The very thought of him dating again so soon was enough to tear me up completely.

I loved Trent. Too bad love wasn't enough to make our relationship work.

30

TRENT

I fucked up.

Not just a little. Not just in one area of my life.

There were so many ways I'd fucked up, and to such epic proportions, it made my head spin.

Bella had been the best thing to ever happen to me. And I'd pushed her away. I'd let my own stupid hang-ups about my family get between us, and I'd driven her off.

I loved her, and my life was empty without her. But she wanted nothing more to do with me.

She'd made that pretty damn clear, and there wasn't much I could do about it.

I'd tried to get her back, and she told me she wanted me out of her life. I'd completely ruined all chances of making it work with her, and I couldn't keep bothering her.

Bella was pregnant with our baby, for fuck's sake. She didn't need the stress I'd bring into her life.

So I did what she asked. I left her alone.

And I tried to move on, but that was impossible.

I just fucked up other parts of my life. I couldn't hold onto any new executive assistant the agency sent me even if

I tried. I was in the worst mood I'd ever been in, and they were all terrified of me at the office.

The replacement EA I hired last week had quit after I made her cry.

Well, fuck. I knew I was hard to work with and I could be a total pain in the ass, but what was I supposed to do? I'd lost Bella. Not only as an EA who ran this office with deceptive ease, but as a partner, the woman I loved, the mother of my child.

It hurt like a bitch and I didn't know how to make things better.

But I couldn't take out my shit on my employees. Being with Bella had made me realize many things. For starters, I'd been a dick to my employees.

The next EA the agency sent, I did better. She of course couldn't compare to Bella, but I did my best to be patient and not say stupid, mean shit to her.

And amazingly, she did a better job when I wasn't a fucking asshole.

The whole thing made me realize how much I'd screwed up everything. I'd let my bitterness dictate my life.

Worst of all, I'd let it push Bella away until she was gone for good.

The night before Grant's wedding, I flew to Napa Valley to attend the bachelor party.

The event was scheduled to be another weekend of festivities, just like the first two had been, but I wasn't in the mood to fuck around. I would be here for my brother, and I would attend the wedding. But tomorrow, as soon as they said their vows, I would return to LA.

I'd expected to be here with Bella. And now I'd have to go through this without her.

The chateau on the vineyard was stunning, with rolling

hills of grapevines all around it framing a spectacular sunset. The men were all gathered in the bar when I arrived, and they seemed excited to see me.

Maybe word hadn't traveled about how I'd blown up at my parents. Or maybe it had, and my family was more forgiving than I'd expected they would be.

"Glad you're here, man," Grant said, clapping me on the back. He looked like he'd had a few drinks already. "I thought you might not come."

"I wouldn't miss your wedding, Grant," I admitted. I didn't add how hard it was to be here alone, but there wasn't much I could do about it, anyway.

"Come on, have a drink," Grant said. He poured me a glass of whiskey.

I drank a sip, swallowing past the lump in my throat. Bella should be here with me. It was wrong that she wasn't. Somehow, showing up here just brought all the pain of losing her to the surface.

But I had to keep it together. This weekend wasn't about me, it was about Grant and Megan. I just had to keep my head down until I could get out of here and retreat to my routine in LA.

The drink helped make things tolerable, and I quickly asked for another.

Halfway through my second, Grant pulled me aside.

"Can you do me a favor?" he asked. "I need a few more bottles of red. The wine's running out quicker than I thought, and I don't want to leave the party."

"Yeah, sure," I said.

"It's in the cellar just through there," Grant said, pointing at the stone steps that led down from the back of the bar area.

I nodded. "I'll be right back."

I descended the stone steps and walked through a wooden door to the cellar. When I got there, I froze.

Bella stood in the cellar.

I hadn't expected her to be here, and I had to fight the urge to rush to her and scoop her in my arms.

She blinked at me like a deer in headlights, two bottles of white wine in her hand.

"Hi," I said, not knowing what else to say. "You're... here."

She looked incredible in a pair of jeans and a loose, flowing blouse that flattered her figure. Under her clothes, I was sure she was starting to show, but it was hard to tell with what she wore. Her blonde hair hung in waves down her back.

"Yeah," she said and cleared her throat. "I'm one of Megan's bridesmaids, since Shelby pulled out."

"Oh." I hadn't known about it. I hadn't expected to see her at all, but now that I did, my eyes took in the sight of her greedily.

But I could tell she didn't feel the same way. Her body language was closed off, and she looked at me with disdain.

"I better get this up there," Bella said tightly. The atmosphere was so fucking strained, and a lump pressed against my throat.

"Yeah," I said.

The door behind us slammed shut and I heard the lock turn.

"What the fuck?" I muttered and walked to the door, trying to open it. "Hey!" It was impossible to open. I hammered my fist against the door. "Is this some kind of joke?"

"Are we locked in?" Bella asked.

"Yeah." I heard movement on the other side of the door.

Someone had shut us in here. "This isn't funny. Let us out!" I shouted and banged on the door again.

"We're not letting you out yet," Grant said on the other side.

"What the fuck is going on?" I demanded.

"We're leaving you in there until you two talk," Megan said. They were both in on this.

My anger flared.

"Grant, what the fuck? You can't force us to do anything," I answered, trying the door again, but the old door was sturdy, and there was no way I could get it open without them unlocking it. "Open the damn door. I'm not in the mood for games."

"It's not a game," Grant answered. "We know that we're... *meddling and manipulating*, but we're leaving you in there until you settle whatever's going on between you. Whether you decide to call it off for good or get back together is your call, but you have to actually talk."

I shook my head. "This is fucked up. Come on, bro." I leaned my forehead against the door.

"We'll be back to check on you later," Grant said.

"Or you can unlock this right now and I won't kick your ass, Grant," I threatened, but there was no answer.

Had they left?

I heard their footsteps on the stairs leading to the ground floor outside.

Unbelievable.

"Oh, God," Bella said. She looked around the room and sank onto a wooden bench that stood in the middle of the cellar. "They really locked us in here."

"Yeah," I said grimly. "They want us to *talk*."

"I don't have much to say," Bella said.

I heaved a sigh. I was going to fucking kill Grant when I got out of here.

Silence stretched out between us for several moments. It was strained and painful to be in the cellar, locked together when she clearly didn't want anything to do with me. I slid down against the door and sat with my back to it.

"How are things?" I asked. "With the baby, I mean."

"Oh, they're going okay," Bella answered. "The last prenatal appointment went well."

"You've been to another appointment?" I asked, failing to keep the disappointment out of my voice. I'd thought she would invite me to join her for that, at least.

"It was just a routine exam," Bella said. "Blood test and boring stuff. No ultrasound, so you didn't miss anything."

"Okay."

"I'm still waiting on the co-parenting paperwork from your attorney," Bella said. "You can stipulate that you want to be a part of the appointments too, if that's what you want."

I started to agree to that, but I stopped myself.

Maybe I *should* use this opportunity to talk to Bella. If I didn't tell her how I really felt, when would I get the chance?

If I didn't fucking fight for her, what kind of a man was I?

"I'm not going to do that," I said. "I don't want to co-parent."

"What?" Bella asked, confused. "I... I thought that's what you wanted. You don't want to be a part of the baby's life?" Her face fell.

"No," I said. "I want to *parent*. Not co-parent. I want to raise this baby with you, Bella. I don't want to be the dad who gets visitation. I want to be a partner to you and a real dad to the baby. Bella, I love you."

Bella stared at me, her face cracking. Her brows knitted together and her eyes welled with tears.

"You can't do this to me," she said in a whisper. "I can't play games anymore."

"I'm not playing games," I said. "I've never been more serious about anything in my life."

"You don't want marriage and kids. You've hated all of this," she waved around her, indicating the wedding, "since day one. You're clearly not the marrying type, or the type to want kids."

"Yeah, I did hate the idea of marriage and kids... *until* I met you. I want to be with you, Bella. Marriage, kids, happily ever after."

Bella shook her head, so I kept going.

"I was a fool. I had a lot of misconceptions because of my family, because of what happened with my ex. It turned out that was a mistake, too." I explained to her what had happened between me and my parents at the restaurant. "The thing is, I saw you through the same lens. I was so sure everyone wanted to control my life that I didn't even give you a chance. That was wrong of me. I'm trying to work on that. I want to be a better man for you."

She looked at me, her eyes watery.

"That night you left my house, I was going to ask you to move in. I'd already had a key made." I ran a hand through my hair, my nerves on edge. "But I screwed it all up by flipping out over the thing with Megan's wedding. I know you were just trying to help, Bella. Because that's who you are. You're not my ex, or my parents. You're the woman I love. And I was such a fucking asshole to you. I'm so sorry."

Tears rolled over Bella's cheeks and I stood. I walked to the bench, sitting down next to her, and pulled a tissue out of my pocket. She took it from me.

"These stupid hormones make me cry about everything."

"It's okay," I said. "You're allowed to cry."

"I love you, too," Bella said softly.

I stared at her. Had she just said what I thought she'd said?

"I want to be with you, too," she said. "I missed you so much."

I wrapped my arms around her and pulled her closer. She melted against me.

"Are you sure you want to do this?" she asked. "Raise the baby together? Be with me?"

"Absolutely positive. If you can trust me again and give me another shot at this."

She looked up at my eyes, searching for something. Then she smiled. "I trust you, Trent."

"Will you move in with me, then?" I asked. "Give us another chance?"

Bella gazed at me, a smile playing on her lips. "Not so fast, Trent. You forced my hand in taking Megan's lease. I'm not sure I'm up for moving again so soon."

I laughed. "How about I pack and move all your stuff myself—and pay off the lease—as penance?"

She grinned. "Deal."

I tilted her chin up and wiped the tears off her cheeks before I closed the distance between us and kissed her.

She sighed against me and I held onto her, kissing her, vowing that I would never let her go again.

I held her for a long time, rocking her in my arms.

Finally, I heard footsteps on the stairs outside. Someone unlocked the cellar door, and it swung open.

Megan and Grant stood before us. Grant had a grin on

his face and Megan beamed as they saw us sitting cuddled up on the bench.

"I figured from the silence, you were either so mad you weren't speaking, or you'd worked things out," Megan said. She clasped her hands together happily. "But it's obvious our little scheme worked. I'm so happy to see you like this."

"We figured out our shit all right," I said. "But what the fuck, man?" I glared at Grant.

"I know, I know," Grant said. Clearly, he'd expected me to be pissed. "What can I say? You're my brother, but you're a stubborn piece of work."

"I know," I admitted with a smile. "Thank you for meddling."

Grant looked at me. "So, you finally got your head out of your ass?"

I took Bella's hand and intertwined our fingers. "Yes. I get it now. There's a difference between getting involved out of love and manipulating for the sake of control."

Grant nodded, looking relieved. "Yeah. You finally got the memo."

"I'm so glad you guys worked it out," Megan gushed. "I know it's been a rough road, but you deserve to be happy. You both do." She stepped forward and hugged Bella. "This is the best wedding gift ever!"

Bella giggled and looked at me with stars in her eyes. I hadn't ever been this fucking happy. Grant clapped me on the back.

"Come on, have a drink with us. We should celebrate."

"I'll be there later," I said, glancing at Bella. "We have some more talking to do."

"We do?" Bella asked.

"We do," I said with a smile.

Megan nodded. "We'll be upstairs."

Grant and Megan walked away, joining their respective parties.

"What do we need to talk about?" Bella asked.

"I don't want to talk," I said and grabbed Bella, kissing her again. "Right now, I want to get you naked and *not* talk."

Bella giggled, blushing hard again. I fucking loved it when her cheeks grew pink like that. I loved everything about her.

I pulled her tightly against me so she could feel my need for her. I ached to be inside of her, to have her legs wrapped around me so I could claim her as mine and show her exactly how important she was to me.

I took Bella's hand and led her out of the cellar and through the chateau to my room. I didn't know where she was staying, but she would stay with me now. Something told me I wasn't going to get any resistance.

"I love you," I murmured when we stepped into my room as I brushed my thumb over her cheek.

"I love you, too," she said, clasping her arms around my neck and pushing her soft body against mine.

And then there was no more time for talking.

~

The next day, everything was perfect. I woke up with Bella in my arms, her head on my chest, and this was exactly where she belonged.

I studied her face, her long lashes brushing her cheeks and her blonde hair fanned over my shoulder. I was pretty damn sure I'd died and gone to heaven.

How was it possible that someone like me—a grumpy, jaded man—could have such a happy ending? I knew the answer to that.

It was all Bella.

She was a wonderful woman and she brought out the best in me, even when I didn't think there was anything left worth salvaging. She made me want to be a better man, not just for her, but for the baby we were going to have, too.

When she woke up, I planted kisses all over her face.

"Morning," she giggled and stretched against me. Her naked body against mine made my cock punch up against the sheets, but we had to get ready for the ceremony. We could do more of what we'd done last night later.

And I planned to.

After she showered and dressed, Bella left the room to get ready with the other bridesmaids and the bride while I got dressed in the room. Then I made my way to the small chapel that overlooked the vineyard, with stained glass windows and upright wooden seats. It was like something out of a fairytale, almost more so than the other two weddings we'd attended.

When the music started, Bella was the second woman to walk out, carrying her small bouquet, her hair and makeup immaculate. She looked like a vision, and when she caught my eye in the crowd, she smiled brilliantly at me.

One day soon, she would walk down an aisle again, but I wouldn't be in the seats. I would be up there where my brother stood now, and Bella would be wearing a white dress. It was too soon to propose right now—although it was what I wanted. I still had to fully earn her trust.

We'd been through an ordeal the past couple of months, and we had to find each other again—with our new direction in mind.

That was fine. I would give her the time she needed because I knew which way this was going to go. I loved her and I was going to be the man she deserved. We were having a baby together, and it was just a matter of time before I made her my wife.

I could wait until the time was right. In the meantime, she would move in with me, and no matter what happened, we were in this together.

31

BELLA

Six months later

"*J*ust breathe," Trent said. "Breathe through the pain."

"That's easy for you to say," I groaned when another contraction ripped through my body, locking my belly in a vise. I cried out and curled around my stomach in the car as Trent sped through LA to the hospital. "Just get us there alive!"

"Don't you worry about my driving, just worry about keeping that baby in until we get there," Trent said.

I nodded, trying to ignore the fact that he was breaking every traffic rule in the county. But it was easy to forget about his driving when yet another contraction wound me up so tight I felt I was going to burst.

The contractions had come on hard and fast. I'd been at home, reading a book. Trent had been at the office. My water broke, and I'd barely called Trent when the contractions started getting serious. This baby made it clear he or she wanted out.

We'd told the doctor we didn't want to know the baby's gender until the birth. We'd decided we wanted it to be a surprise.

"Here we are," Trent said and skidded into the ambulance bay in front of the ER. "I need a wheelchair out here!" he shouted. "She's in labor and the baby's coming fast!"

The nurses jumped into action right away, getting me out of the car and into the wheelchair.

"I'll park, and then I'm right behind you," Trent said and hopped in behind the wheel again while the nurses escorted me through the hospital. They set me up in a room in the maternity ward.

"Oh, wow," our doctor said when she walked into the room and saw me curling on the bed. "Looks like things are moving fast. The baby must be almost ready to meet you."

"I'm ready to get this pain over with," I gasped.

The last month had been tough, and I was ready to evict this child. I'd felt like an elephant, my ankles had been swollen, I hadn't been comfortable in anything, and the California heat hadn't helped.

"Let's see what we've got," Dr. Browning said and pulled a stool up to the edge of the bed. She looked between my legs. "Oh, yeah, we're ready for this one. You're already ten centimeters dilated. Got the party started without me, huh?" She grinned at me, but I was in too much pain to laugh at her joke when another contraction coiled my stomach tight like a drum.

"Okay, you're going to wait for the next one, and then I want you to push," the doctor said, getting into gear to deliver the baby. The nurses flitted around the room, making preparations.

This was happening too fast.

"I can't do it without Trent," I gasped.

"He'll have to hurry up if he wants to be here for this. This baby isn't going to wait on anyone."

I cried out when another contraction started.

"Push!" the doctor encouraged, and I did as she ordered.

The door crashed open and Trent ran in, a cap askew on his head and his gown flapping behind him like a cape.

"Just in time, Dad," Dr. Browning said.

I cried out and grabbed Trent's hand in a death grip when I pushed.

"One more," the doctor said. "We've got the head." I did as she asked and Trent leaned in.

"You've got this, babe," he said. "I'm right here."

Trent had been by my side through it all—every appointment and ultrasound, every backache and food craving, every mood swing and shower of tears. I believed him when he said he was here with me now—he wouldn't go anywhere.

"Okay, I need you to breathe through the next one," the doctor said. "Don't push on this round."

I let my head fall back on the pillow as I tried to catch my breath.

"You're doing great," Trent said. He looked at me with warmth in his eyes. "You're perfect, and the baby's going to be perfect."

"Okay, ready for the next one?" the doctor asked when I breathed through another intense surge of pain.

I nodded, and when the next wave came, I pushed. I shut my eyes, and time seemed to stand still.

A moment later, the sound of a tiny cry filled the room.

Tears ran over my cheeks and Trent's eyes misted over, too.

"What is it?" Trent asked.

"It's a boy," Dr. Browning beamed. "Ten fingers, ten toes, and perfectly healthy."

"Oh, God," I cried, tears staining my cheeks as I let it all go.

"A boy," Trent breathed.

He had to be the proudest father on earth.

A nurse brought our baby to us. He was red and wrinkled, but he was the most beautiful little creature I'd ever seen.

I moved my fingers over his face, taking in every detail.

"Hello, little baby," I whispered. "Hello, Henry."

We'd agreed on the name if it was a boy a couple of weeks ago, and it fit perfectly. Henry Dillon, the little boy who was already so incredibly loved.

"He's perfect," Trent breathed. "He's got your nose."

"He has your eyes," I said.

Trent laughed through tears and pressed his lips against my forehead.

"Well done, Bella. I'm so proud of you. He's everything."

Trent squeezed my hand and kissed the baby's head. We laughed as we held our little bundle of pure joy.

I barely noticed as the doctor and nurses finished with their tasks around the room, cleaning me up and making me comfortable. The moments with my new son—our new family—seemed to go on forever.

The nurse helped me with the very first breastfeeding session, and Henry latched on like a champ. He nursed, then fell back asleep.

Finally, Trent looked down at his phone. "I sent Grant a text that you were in labor and he did the rest," Trent said, looking sheepish. "They're here. Half the Dillon clan. And they're all dying to meet the new addition."

I laughed. "That's fine. Send them in."

"Be right back." Trent gave me and the baby a kiss, then left the room to meet his family. Moments later, the doors opened and Trent's family poured in.

Megan and Grant entered first, followed by Isaac and Claire. Anya and Kevin had flown in last week, just to be here to welcome the new baby. Kevin walked with his arm around Anya, who was eight months pregnant and sporting a round belly. Joni and Ray stepped in, followed by Enid.

The room was crowded, and I smiled at them all through my tears. They huddled around the bed, looking down at little Henry in awe.

"He's beautiful," Megan said.

Joni reached out to stroke his tiny little hands. "Welcome to the family, little guy," she said proudly as she looked at her first grandchild. She and Ray exchanged a smile. Enid grinned as she looked at her great-grandson.

"He's just perfect," Grant said. "Good job, you two."

"Was everything okay with the birth?" Anya asked, running her hand over her large belly. I could tell she was a little nervous with her own delivery coming up soon. "How did it go?"

I laughed. "It wasn't nearly as bad as I feared. Not with Trent here."

Anya smiled. "Now that I see Henry, I can't wait." Kevin squeezed her arm.

I smiled, my emotions welling up again. It was hard to bite back the tears.

Trent was at my side all the time, beaming proudly as he showed off his son.

He'd been so supportive every step of the way. Since the moment we got back together, Trent had gone above and beyond to prove to me that he was in it for the long haul.

Now that I saw the way he looked at his son, I didn't know how I could have ever worried he wouldn't want to be involved. He was so excited about the baby, so attentive and caring. He was going to make an excellent father, just as he'd turned out to be a wonderful partner to me.

It was going to work out just right. I could feel it in my bones.

"I have an announcement to make," Trent said, and everyone fell quiet. I frowned. I had no idea what he was talking about.

"Actually," Trent said, and glanced at me. "It's not an announcement. It's a question."

He reached into his pocket and pulled out a black velvet box.

Everyone in the room seemed to hold their breath, and all eyes turned to Trent.

"Bella, we've already walked a long road together," Trent said. "And I've loved every minute of it. I love you more than I can ever say, and doing this with you—being a parent and raising this beautiful boy—is the dream I never realized I had. The only thing missing is to make our relationship official. Bella, will you marry me?"

Tears poured down my cheeks. I was unable to hold them back, and I nodded.

"Of course," I said. "Yes, Trent, I'll marry you."

Trent took out the ring and slid it onto my finger. It fit perfectly. I had a feeling Megan had helped him with that, and judging by the way she beamed at me, I was right.

Trent kissed me.

"Congratulations, you two!" Joni cried out and the whole room erupted in cheers and applause.

I laughed, unable to contain my happiness.

EPILOGUE
TRENT

Eight months later

I stood at the mirror and straightened my tie.

"You look good, bro," Grant said.

I shook out my hands and brushed the shoulders of my suit jacket. Everything had to be perfect.

I turned to look at Grant, then the rest of the guys. Patrick, Kevin, and Isaac all looked just like Grant did, wearing the same color suit with red flowers on their lapels.

"It's going to be great," Patrick said, clapping me on the shoulder. "Married life is fantastic."

I chuckled. "I think I know what to expect." Bella and I might not have been married until now, but we'd been living together for the past year, and parenting baby Henry for eight months—we weren't strangers to playing house.

"The wedding night is the best," Grant said with a wink.

I laughed openly at that. Every night with Bella was amazing.

"Let's get this show on the road," Patrick said. "It's time."

I nodded and we left the groom's suite where we were getting ready. We walked through the hotel where the wedding would take place. My family had all opted for romantic destination weddings, but Bella and I had agreed to do it right here in LA, in a fancy hotel, and to save the destination for our honeymoon. Bella didn't know it yet, but I was taking her to the Maldives.

When we walked into the room where the ceremony would take place, it had been transformed with a cream carpet, rows of chairs covered in white with pink ribbons and white roses. Guests mingled with each other.

I walked in and greeted my friends and family, making the rounds, thanking them for coming.

When I reached my mom, she beamed at me, cupping my cheeks.

"My darling boy," she said. "You're all grown up now."

I laughed. "I've been grown up for a while now."

"I know, I know. But I'm just so proud of you today. A beautiful woman in your life and a perfect little boy..." As she said it, my grandma came to us with Henry in her arms. He wore a cute little suit, just as dressed up as the rest of us.

"Look at you, big guy," I said and cuddled him for a second when he reached his chubby little hands toward me. "You're a rock star."

"I've been waiting for this day to come. I couldn't have arranged it better myself," Mom continued.

"I'm glad you *didn't* arrange it," I said with a smile.

My family had finally backed off. Mom hadn't even put her two cents in with the wedding planning, leaving it entirely up to Bella and me. I took it as a sign things had changed.

"I'm so proud of you," Mom said.

"Thanks, Mom." I smiled and hugged her before I made my way to the front of the room where the guys were already lined up.

When the doors opened, everyone stood and turned, and I watched as first Anya, then Jessica, and then Megan walked through the doors. They all wore pink dresses. Megan smiled at me, and I chuckled. She and Bella were best friends now, and I loved that my soon-to-be wife had found a sister in Megan.

Finally, Bella came into the room. She walked alone, and she looked beautiful.

She wore a white ballgown with crystals all over the bodice, dripping down the skirt as if she'd stood in a shower of stars. Her blonde hair was curled and fell over her shoulders and her eyes filled with love when they locked on mine.

She came to me, and I reached out to her. When our hands touched, electricity ran through my body. Her touch would always make me feel alive.

"You look incredible," I whispered.

"I have so much hairspray in my hair, it's like a helmet," she said with laughter in her eyes. "You look so handsome."

I squeezed her hand and we turned to the priest. I didn't hear a word he said about marriage and what it meant. All I could think about was that Bella was mine, and in a few minutes she would be my wife.

When it was time to say our vows, I turned to her.

"Bella, my love," I started. "You have no idea how you changed my life. I was so set in my ways, sure that it was the only way forward, and you really rocked the boat. Not only did you show me what it means to reach out to others and open up to let them into my life, you showed me how to look at the world through different eyes. You taught me how to find the beauty in everything, and you've made me happier than I ever thought I deserved to be. I promise to do everything I can to make you as happy as you've made me, every day, for the rest of our lives. I promise to stand by your side forever, and to be a good husband and a good father. I love you."

Bella's eyes welled up with tears, and she blinked them away. She took a deep breath, then began to speak.

"Trent, when I met you, you were a difficult person to be around. Your hard shell was tough to break through, and there was a time when I wondered if anyone could. But when I got to know you, I realized that you have such a beautiful, gentle soul, and it was worth the effort to get through your tough exterior. I promise to keep fighting for you, and for our relationship, every day. I promise to be there for you, to support you as you've done for me. You're my everything. Fate brought us together, and we've had some bumps along the way. But you're my happy ending."

A lump rose in my throat and I swallowed hard.

"And now," the priest said, "by the power vested in me, I pronounce you husband and wife. You may kiss the bride."

I grabbed Bella and spun her around, dipping her low to the ground before I kissed her. Everyone applauded loudly, and when I planted Bella on her feet again, she laughed, her cheeks bright red.

I took her hand and we turned to face our family and friends, and the rest of our lives together.

After the photos, we moved to the reception area. The space was beautiful, and it was everything Bella had wanted for her special day. She stood with Henry in her arms, talking to my mom. Megan pulled me aside.

"It was a beautiful wedding," she said.

I smiled. "Thanks for your help in planning it. I know Bella appreciated it."

"Does she know where you're going yet?"

I shook my head. My mom was taking Henry for two weeks for us so we could break away and have our honeymoon, and I wanted to spoil Bella rotten every second we were away.

I also wanted to get around to making another baby.

In the meantime, until she became pregnant again, Bella worked with me in the office as my executive assistant as she had before. She was so fucking good at her job and without her, my whole office had fallen apart.

I'd implemented some of her changes in the office, though. When I started to get tense and grumpy, she openly called me Diablo to remind me I was being a bear. These days, though, I rarely heard the nickname.

Lately, there was nothing for me to be grumpy about—I was happier than I ever was, and it changed everything.

"She looks so happy," Megan said.

"I hope so," I said. "It's my goal in life to make sure that never changes."

"You're a good guy," Megan said.

I chuckled. "Hard to imagine that I could be, but she brings that out in me. I was the bad guy all this time, you know."

"You were just misunderstood," Megan said with a smile.

"Thanks for that," I laughed.

Megan patted my shoulder before she walked to Bella and they started talking. I watched as Bella mingled with my family. She fit in with them perfectly. She was close to my sisters, and to Jessica, too.

Thanks to Bella, I'd never been closer to my family. Since I learned they'd never meant to hurt me, a lot had changed in the way I approached them. But I was under no illusion that I was solely responsible for my being a part of the Dillon clan again.

It was all Bella, drawing me in, making me a part of everything.

God, I was so grateful for her.

When she came up to me, she was smiling. Henry tangled his hand into her curls and she laughed.

"Oh, hang on," I said. "That's not a toy, big guy." I carefully unwrapped Henry's hand from her hair. "Come here." She handed him to me and I bounced him in my hands.

He laughed as I gave him a kiss. He was our perfect son, and I loved him and Bella more than anything.

"What were you and Megan gossiping about?" Bella asked.

"You," I said simply.

"Good things, I hope?"

"Babe, I couldn't say something bad about you if I wanted to."

Bella laughed, and I kissed her.

I'd worked my whole life to have a successful company and a lot of money. I'd made it big, I'd had all the riches, my name meant something in the business world. It wasn't until now that I understood what it really meant to be rich.

I had something now that money could never buy.

And I was never letting her go again.

Want more spicy, feel-good romance?

Read The Wedding Hoax!

First rule of a pretend marriage?
Don't get knocked up.

Keep reading for your Sneak Peek!

SNEAK PEEK OF THE WEDDING HOAX!

About the Book

First rule of a marriage of convenience?
Don't get knocked up.

When I tell off my new boss after he cuts in line,
I think he's about to fire me.
Instead, CEO Harry O'Donnell proposes.

He wants me to marry him and move in for six months.
See, Harry needs a wife to inherit his family business.
I need a windfall to pay for my mom's medical bills.

How hard could playing wifey be?
Answer: very.
From Harry's touching vows at our sham wedding,
To the sly glances he sneaks when he thinks I'm not looking,
One thing's clear.
Our *no sex allowed* agreement won't last long.

Neither will the ten-foot wall I built around my heart.

Now, against all odds, I'm pregnant.
And I want Harry to love me—and our baby—for real.

Rule number two?
Never, ever, fall for your temporary husband.

Chapter 1: Simone

"Did you want your coffee black?" A bored barista was staring back at me, like she desperately wanted to roll her eyes.

"Could I get a splash of almond milk? Or maybe oat milk." I laughed nervously.

I was starting a new job as a staff writer at *LA Now.* I'd decided to check out the trendy coffee shop across the street from the building.

Which may have been a total mistake, judging by the barista's new, annoyed expression. "So, which is it? Almond or oat?"

I smiled. "You know what? I'll go with the—"

"Can I get the usual, Sandy?" A deep voice was suddenly booming next to me, a sense of command in the stranger's every word.

I looked over and saw a sharp vision in an even sharper suit. He was tall, with an angular jaw and intense eyes. His dark brown hair was slightly tousled on top in that perfect way guys like him always pulled off.

There was also the matter of just how well he was filling out his suit, his muscles leaving an imprint against the fabric—

Wait.

Did this asshole just cut in front of me?

"Hey!" I chimed into the conversation.

"Oh. Hey." The stranger seemed almost as annoyed as the barista. "Did you need something?"

"Yeah. I need you to get behind me."

It took everything in me not to let my cheeks flush at the thought of the stranger actually *getting behind me.*

"How about I pay for your drink instead?" he suggested with a shrug. "I've got places to be this morning, so I'd rather Sandy take care of me first if it's all the same to you."

"It's not all the same to me." I stood my ground. "The rules apply to everybody, buddy. If we all just start cutting in line because we're busy, society will break down within months."

"Really? Months?" He let out a tired sigh. "I was hoping it'd be weeks. Maybe even days."

And then a small grin crept across his face.

"Jerk." It was my turn to roll my eyes.

I looked back at Sandy across the counter. "Sandy, could you get that coffee going for me, please? I'll go with the oat milk."

"Got it. Coming right up." Sandy nodded as I tapped my card against the reader. "And don't call me Sandy. Only the people I like get to call me that."

"You're going to like me, Sandy! One day! I promise!" I called out after her as she went toward the back of the coffee shop. "I'm very likable!"

"Clearly." Mr. Big Shot laughed as he settled in line behind me.

It was the last thing he said to me before Sandy handed us our coffees at the same time. Her face was blank as she gave me my cup, even though she beamed when she handed Mr. Big his to-go coffee.

Of course, he was drowning in female attention.

Even though he was probably too *busy* to notice.

"Thank you," I said to Sandy as I took my cup. With slumped shoulders, I carried it to a booth at the back of the coffee shop, tucked away in the corner.

I stared in my cup for a long moment, trying to calm my nerves.

LA Now was one of the top magazines in Los Angeles, and this staff writer position could really change things for me.

There was a lot riding on my new job.

I hoped I wouldn't botch it like I did ordering coffee.

"Simone!"

The voice of my best friend made me look up, snapping me back to reality. Taylor grinned as she walked over to the booth, carrying her latte.

"Taylor! I didn't see you come in," I said.

Taylor was my best friend and the reason I'd been able to get a job at *LA Now* in the first place, since she was one of the best editors on their staff. She was also one of the best people I'd ever met, period, which is why I was already grinning like a maniac at the sight of her.

"Are you ready for your first day?" She took a seat across from me.

"Yes, I'm ready! Kind of. Well, maybe not." I nervously chuckled again. "What happens if I get fired on my first day? As in, how bad would that look on my resume?"

She laughed. "You're not going to get fired on your first day."

"You said the CEO can be moody." I fidgeted with my napkin.

"Harry might be a bit of an asshole, but he's not a *total*

asshole. He only fires people on day one if they piss him off beyond belief."

"What pisses him off beyond belief?"

"Nothing you'd ever do." She thoughtfully took a sip of her latte. "You're too nice of a person to piss anyone off."

"I pissed off Sandy."

"Sandy? The barista?" Taylor's mouth fell open. "Really? But she's so sweet to everyone! What'd you do?"

"Nothing! I just took a little too long to get my coffee order together. Then this guy came in, cut the line and tried to order ahead of me, and I let him know I wasn't having it. I might have called him a jerk."

"Shit." Taylor's eyes went wide.

"Shit?"

"Was he wearing a really nice suit? Handsome in a suspicious way? Like, almost impossibly handsome?"

"Yeah? How'd you know?"

"That's Harry. Our boss." She grimaced. "He has a habit of thinking the world revolves around him. Probably because it does. Anyway, he cut me in line when I first got here, too."

"And? What'd you do?"

"I let him do it because I knew he was the boss."

"Right. That's smart. Much smarter than calling him a jerk."

"You'll be fine. Don't let it get to you." Taylor shook her head. "When you see him in the office, just pretend it never happened, like you two never met before."

"Lying to my boss feels worse than not letting him cut in line—"

"And being unemployed feels worse than anything else," she interrupted. "Just promise me you'll do what I say. Okay?"

"I promise I'll think about it."

"Close enough."

∽

Two hours later, Taylor and I stood in the copy room in the offices of *LA Now*.

"Do you want me to show you how to work the copier again?" Taylor asked, playfully patting its side. "Don't be ashamed if it takes you a few tries to get it. It practically took me a month."

"How are you so bad with technology? Doesn't your family own a computer shop?"

"Rude. You're being so rude right now." Taylor scoffed playfully. "Seriously, though. Do you need anything else? This is the last thing to cover on your orientation."

I thought about the question for a minute. She'd been assigned to show me around the office and introduce me to the other writers and editors on staff.

Unfortunately, she'd also been responsible for helping me set up my laptop and email. She was clearly out of her league there, and I'd told her I could handle it on my own.

Or maybe I'd just leave a desperate SOS message on an IT guy's voicemail.

"I think I've got it." I smiled back at her. "But..."

"But?"

"But maybe you could show me to Harry's office? So I can apologize before he comes out here and fires me—"

"If you interrupt Harry while he's in a meeting, he'll *definitely* fire you." Taylor leaned against the copier. "Like I said, just pretend it never happened."

"Right."

I couldn't admit to Taylor the real reason why I wanted to be introduced to Harry.

A part of me just wanted to *see* him, to make sure my eyes hadn't been lying to me the first time.

Sure, he was an asshole, and sure, he was my boss, but that man was a work of art.

Or maybe I was just a little thirsty for male attention, especially since I hadn't been with anyone since my disaster of an ex—

"Are you still standing here?" Taylor interrupted my thoughts, her tone lined with disbelief. "Go! Get to work!"

"Sir, yes, sir." I saluted with a grin before I headed to my office.

I tried to push all thoughts of Harry away. But his perfect, annoying face keep popping up in my mind.

Working for him wasn't going to be easy.

Chapter 2: Harry

No one talked to me like that.

The woman at the coffee shop had completely thrown me off in the very best way, my whole morning gone out the window. I couldn't get her out of my head.

Not her deep hazel eyes, and not her auburn hair that cascaded down her shoulders.

Fuck.

I wanted to talk to her again. I wanted to brush my fingers across her cheek, run my hands through her hair, push her up against the counter and—

"Sir? Your father's here to see you." Paul, my executive assistant, was suddenly standing in front of my desk. "Do you want me to tell him you're busy?"

"No. Send him in." If I sent Dad away, he'd just pester

me until I talked to him. And I knew exactly what he wanted to talk about.

Paul nodded before leaving my office. A few seconds later, my dad stepped through the door. He was wearing a Hawaiian shirt, despite his usual gruff exterior. Retirement seemed to have that effect on people, softening them out over time. Even if it was just their clothing choices.

"Son."

"Dad."

"I just wanted to check up on you," he started. "You're always so busy nowadays. I figured finding you at the office would be a safe bet."

"That's what you want, isn't it? The kind of son who works hard. The kind of son who wants to take over the company someday—"

"The kind of son who's going to be married soon, I hope?" He interrupted. "You know the rules, Harry. If you're not married by your fortieth birthday, I won't be able to officially hand you the keys to the company."

"You hear how that sounds, right? Married by my fortieth birthday? It's like a fucked-up fairy tale."

"Language."

"Sorry. It's like a fucked-up fucking fairy tale—"

"That's always how it's been in our family, Harry. You've known that your whole life. We were never going to break tradition just because you don't respect it."

"So, what? All of my years running this place don't count for anything?"

"I'm proud of you for stepping up, Harry. More proud than I've ever been... but no. That doesn't change the tradition."

"If I'm not running the company, then your only other option is Sean." I scoffed. "I love my little brother, sure, but he doesn't have any experience in publishing, Dad. I don't even know if he likes it."

"He works for a magazine, same as you—"

"He works in the IT department! And he works at *Front Stoop*—our competition!" I scoffed again. "Dad, come on. You can't be serious with this."

"You're the one who needs to get serious, Harry," he replied. "When are you going to settle down? Find someone to build with? To share your life with?"

"I already have someone like that in my life. Her name is *LA Now.*"

"Funny." My dad wasn't smiling as he spoke. "Is that really all you want your legacy to be? Is that the kind of legacy you think our family name deserves?"

"Maybe I'm not the marrying type."

"If you're not the marrying type, then you're not fit to be CEO. You don't know how to commit to something bigger than financial spreadsheets and quarterly reports? Then you don't know how to commit to anything—"

"It's under control," I blurted out, cutting my father off.

"What?"

"It's under control," I repeated. "Just because I'm not the marrying type doesn't mean that I haven't met someone. I never said I was single."

"Are you serious?" My dad's face brightened. "You met someone?"

"Yes, and she's like you. Extremely ready for me to settle down, even if I think we need more time, even if I don't want to be forced into it because of *tradition*—"

"She sounds like a smart girl." He beamed. "When do your mother and I get to meet her?"

I huffed. "I need to get back to work. We can discuss all this later when I don't have back-to-back meetings."

"Sure, sure. Of course." He seemed relieved as he stood up. "We'll talk about it later, son. Good job. As always."

"Thanks, Dad."

I watched him walk out the door and swallowed.

What had I just done?

Was I really going to fake my own wedding just to keep the company?

It didn't have to be real. All I had to do was hire an actress or a model to pretend to be my fiancée, maybe hire some paparazzi to follow us around, maybe even have them meet my mom and dad—

No.

All of that felt so wrong. And yet, I was running out of options. I was turning forty in two months, and unless I came up with a better idea, all of my work at *LA Now* was about to go right down the drain.

I couldn't believe my parents would let my brother take over as CEO. I loved Sean, I really did, but he had no clue what he was doing when it came to running a magazine.

Computers were his scene, not running a magazine or managing people.

Which meant that if I wanted to keep the company, I had no choice but to get married.

Shit.

∾

"It's happy hour! Shouldn't you look, I don't know, happy?" Paul asked as he slid a shot glass toward me.

We were catching up after work over drinks, a ritual between us ever since I'd hired him as my assistant. Outside of work, Paul was the opposite of formal, with a laid-back vibe and perfectly messy hair. He also dropped the *sirs*, which was great since otherwise our whole friendship would've been super uncomfortable.

"I am happy, Paul. See? Don't I look happy?" I forced a smile. "I've never been happier."

"Liar." He laughed. "Seriously, man. What's up?"

"Nothing." I lied with a shrug. I didn't see the point in telling him the truth behind my father's visit. It wasn't going to change anything. "Just a rough day at work."

"As usual." Paul laughed again. "When are you going to start getting used to these rough days? Because I'm pretty sure those are the only kind of days that CEOs get to have."

"No, I'm pretty sure they get straight-up bad days, too. And vacation days, in their dreams."

"They also get the fun option of working through major holidays. I mean, who doesn't want to clock in on Christmas Day?"

"Sometimes, Paul, I feel like you're trying to talk me out of my job."

"Ha! No way. You think I want to be some other guy's assistant?" He quickly downed the shot in front of him. "I'm just messing with you, man. Sorry you had a rough day."

"Thanks."

"Drinking might help," he said as he nodded down toward my still untouched shot glass.

"I don't think drinking like a frat boy is going to help anything," I joked, motioning for the bartender to take my drink. "I'll have a whiskey, please. Neat."

"Can you make that two, actually? Both on that guy, right over there." Taylor pointed toward Paul as she spoke before she appeared between us at the bar.

"Taylor!" Paul happily wrapped his arms around her, then pulled her into a big hug. "Thanks for coming out!"

"Please. You know I'll always come out for you, Paul."

She beamed. "Although, I hope you don't mind. I invited a friend out with us tonight."

"Is she going to kill the vibe?"

"Not on purpose, no." A familiar voice answered the question with a laugh. "But if I somehow kill the vibe tonight, I accept full responsibility. All apologies in advance."

Holy shit.

It was her.

The woman from the coffee shop was standing right next to me.

When our eyes locked, she suddenly looked away like she was nervous. I was taken aback by her response.

After our run-in this morning, she didn't seem like the kind of person who'd ever back down first.

"Sorry," she started. "I didn't know you were going to— Taylor didn't tell me—"

"That we were having drinks with the boss? Absolutely not," Taylor replied. "If I did, you never would've agreed to come out with us."

"The boss?" My eyes went wide. "Wait. *You* work for *me*?"

"Yep. Simone Didier. New staff writer at *LA Now*. Pleasure to meet you." She awkwardly held out her hand.

And I completely ignored the gesture. "Why are you acting like this is our first time meeting each other?"

"Oh. Have we met before?"

"You weren't the crazy lady talking about the fall of society in the coffee shop this morning?"

"Doesn't sound like me." Her face was stone.

I couldn't help but laugh. "You really are something else, aren't you?"

"Something like that, yeah." She nodded along with her

words. "Anyway, I'm actually feeling really tired. Long first day, you know? I think I might head out—"

"Nope. Can't leave yet," Taylor interrupted. "Paul and I need to go say hi to a few of our other friends, and then we'll circle back."

"Gotta make the rounds," Paul added, falling in line behind Taylor as they headed away from the bar. "Especially if we're trying to firm up our team for bar trivia next weekend."

"You work the girls, I'll work the boys?" Taylor asked.

"Sounds like a plan," Paul said.

I watched as they both walked away, leaving me alone with her.

Simone.

I glanced at her out of the corner of my eye as she fidgeted with a napkin.

The awkward silence stretched out between us. I craned my neck to see Taylor and Paul working the room, toasting and living it up with various people in every corner of the bar. It was pretty impressive, even if it was also pretty annoying, watching them work their extrovert magic.

"I'm not sorry."

"What was that? I could barely hear you."

"I'm not sorry," Simone repeated, jutting her chin out. "About what happened at the coffee shop."

"Oh? So, now you remember meeting me back at the coffee shop?"

"It was Taylor's idea to pretend like it never happened," she confessed. "She was worried you were going to fire me."

"I don't fire people over such small slights."

"It wasn't a slight, though, was it? You were trying to cut in front of me. I was there first."

"Sure, but I offered to buy your drink. I had a morning meeting to get to—"

"You're not more important than other people."

"Are you always this self-righteous, Simone? Will your head explode if I tell you that life has a shit ton of gray areas?"

"Are you always this obnoxious? Why can't you just say sorry for doing something wrong?"

"How about we both apologize on the count of three?" I suggested.

"Not going to happen." She scoffed. "Only one of us owes the other an apology, and it's not me."

There she went again, talking to me in a way no one did.

It was such a turn-on.

In that moment, I wanted to kiss her, to crush my lips against hers, just to see if she'd push me away or kiss me back.

I couldn't deny that I was attracted to everything about her—her defiance, the way she stood her ground, even her self-righteousness, too.

There was something so raw about her. I wasn't used to people being that way around me, especially not as a CEO. People were either kissing my ass or trembling in fear.

But not Simone. Simone was refreshing, like a glass of ice water on a hot summer day.

"Can I buy you a drink?" I asked, my eyes raking up and down her delicious frame, spending a little too long on her chest.

"If that's your way of saying you're sorry, sure," she shot back.

I smirked as I once again called for the bartender's attention.

I wasn't sure what it was about this woman, but she drove me crazy.

In a very, very good way.

Chapter 3: Simone

"Tell me about your family."

"What?" I'd been sipping on a whiskey sour, half-distracted. I was keeping an eye on Taylor as she moved throughout the room, hoping that she'd *circle back* to the bar any second now and rescue me from this awkward situation.

I was having drinks with my boss.

Seriously?

I was dying on the inside. It didn't help that I'd decided to idiotically stick up for myself, either.

"Tell me about your family," he calmly repeated. "How's the drink, by the way?"

"Great. Really great, actually. And as for my family..."

"I get it. You don't want to go first." He chuckled. "Keeping your cards close to your chest."

He took a deep breath before he went on. "My family is ruining my life."

"Really?"

"Really. They're so obsessed with following tradition they can't see the forest for the trees." He pinched the bridge of his nose, frustration rolling off him. "I love them. I do. But they're so close to turning everything into shit and they don't even realize it."

"Sorry. I'm confused."

"Confused?"

"Didn't your family start this magazine years ago and basically give you your job?" I replied. "I mean, aren't they super influential or something?"

"Yes and yes."

"That's why I'm confused, then. That seems like the kind of thing to be thankful for," I said. "I'm sure a lot of people would love to have a leg up like that. It makes everything so much easier."

"Easy to say when you're standing outside of it all."

Easy to say when you were born rich, prick.

I briefly thought about my own family, my dad's funeral flashing through my mind. I took another sip of my drink, pushing away the memory.

"Your turn." He smirked. "What's your family like?"

"They're fine."

"Really? That's all? After I just spilled my guts?"

"It's just me and my mom." I shrugged. "There's not much to say."

"Fine, then. Change of topic. What's the craziest thing you've ever done?"

"Uh, pulled an all-nighter back in college. Ordered like twenty pizzas to the dorms. Caused complete chaos. Oh, and sometimes I'd sneak some vodka in a water bottle before going to class."

"Are you serious?" Harry slowly blinked. "Please tell me you're joking."

"What's wrong? Not crazy enough for you?"

He leaned toward me with a wicked grin. "I'm just surprised. A woman who looks like you... I just figured you'd be getting into all kinds of trouble."

His eyes stayed on me as he spoke, heat momentarily flashing in his gaze. My face started to burn in response, as I felt my cheeks flush a deep red. He was so close to me now that all he had to do was lean over a few more inches for our lips to touch, for us to be skin to skin.

God, I wanted him to lean over a few more inches.

It didn't help that he smelled like heaven—woodsy, clean, and expensive. The kind of man who went skiing in his free time and stayed in the most luxurious cabins.

Just then, he shifted back into place, moving away from me. "I think I'm starting to figure you out, Simone."

"Figure me out?"

"Yep. You're a Goody Two-Shoes." He chuckled. "That's why you're so self-righteous, right? You spend so much time following the rules, you think everyone else should, too."

"Are we still on this?" I chuckled, too, in disbelief. "I thought you apologized when you bought me a drink!"

"I never agreed to those terms."

"You're right. I should've read the fine print."

"You've always got to read the fine print, Simone. Always." He flashed a smile before downing the rest of his whiskey.

And I couldn't help the way my eyes lingered on his lips, wondering how they'd taste if I closed the gap between us at the bar.

$\sim$

"Mom! Did you want red sauce or white?"

Two hours later, I was in the kitchen at home, prepping a quick dinner of pasta. Taylor had taken mercy on me after an hour or so at the bar and thankfully dropped me off at the apartment I shared with my mother.

"I think red sauce sounds good for tonight," my mom replied, her motorized wheelchair buzzing its way into the kitchen, too. "But what are you in the mood for?"

"Whatever you're in the mood for, Mom."

"You know you don't have to do that." She sighed. "Cater to me like this because of... the accident. I'm still your mom.

I'm supposed to be taking care of you, not the other way around."

Because of the accident.

I winced away from the memory, even though it played as clear as day in my head.

Nine years ago, my parents had been in a horrific car wreck. My dad had been instantly killed by the impact, while my mom fought for her life at the hospital. A few weeks later, she was released, but she wasn't the same.

The accident had not only taken her husband, it'd taken the use of her legs, too. She'd been paralyzed from the waist down ever since, even though she pretended like nothing much had changed. She was keeping a brave face for me, despite all the pain.

And I tried to do the same. "I'm not catering to you because of the accident, Mom. I'm just not particular about my pasta sauces."

"Liar." She chuckled as she handed me a black pepper shaker. "Smells like it could use more seasoning."

"Hey! Back off, lady," I joked. "Two chefs is too many chefs in the kitchen."

"Uh-huh. Right." My mother squinted, like she was trying to get a better view of the pan. "How was your first day of work at your new job, Simi?"

"Good. Until Taylor bamboozled me into having drinks with the boss."

"Oh? Is your boss nice?"

"Nice?" I took the salt my mom was handing to me as I spoke. "I wouldn't say he's nice. He's maybe Jerk Lite? Still, he did buy me a drink. But he won't apologize for trying to cut in front of me for coffee this morning. And he doesn't seem to appreciate how lucky he is when it comes to being born rich, which is annoying for an entirely different reason—"

"Uh-oh."

"What? Did I put too much salt in the pan?" I panicked, moving my hand away from the stove.

"You're talking about him a lot. When all I asked was a simple question." My mom shook her head. "You know what that means, don't you?"

"That I'm giving him way too much of my headspace when I should be focused on making dinner?"

"That you like him."

"Absolutely not!" I shot back. "Mom, he's not my type. At all. He's basically a trust fund rich kid who lucked into running a company. And even if he was my type, Taylor says he's obsessed with *LA Now,* which means he wouldn't have time for a relationship, anyway—"

"Wow, you've really thought this through," my mom muttered.

"Go! Out of the kitchen!" Flustered, I motioned for her to leave. "I'll bring you dinner when it's all done!"

"It's okay for you to have fun sometimes, Simone." She smiled. "Things don't always have to be so serious."

I smiled back at her. "I know, Mom. Seriously, though. I need to finish up this pasta so we can actually eat something tonight."

"Or we can just order out..."

"Mom!" I pretended to be wildly upset, as I threw my hands up in the air. "Are you suggesting that I'm not the best cook in all of Los Angeles?!"

"You know what? You're right. I believe in you, Simi." My mom chuckled as she turned her wheelchair around, heading out of the kitchen. "Besides, all the good restaurants are closed by now, anyway."

Chapter 4: Harry

I'd been thinking about her all night.

I couldn't have stopped even if I tried. She was stuck in my head like a way-too-catchy song, despite my best efforts to get her out of my mind.

There was just something about how honest she was with me, how she was never afraid to tell me exactly what she was thinking.

And I couldn't lie, the fact that she never backed down was sexy as hell.

Shit. Was this the most honest connection I'd had with a woman in months? Years?

I knew that Simone wasn't after me for my money, at least, which was a pretty good start. Hell, she'd probably slap me in my face if I even suggested taking her out for dinner. It wouldn't be appropriate for a Goody Two-Shoes like her to go out with her boss, after all.

But what if I wasn't her boss? What if I was something more?

"Mr. O'Donnell?" Simone popped her head in my open door and interrupted my train of thought.

I gestured for her to sit down, and she took a seat across the desk from me. She was wearing a pencil skirt that hugged her round hips. Her sleeveless blouse skimmed over her perky tits. It was her second day of work, and she was already driving me crazy with that killer figure.

When I didn't say anything, lost in thought, she tilted her head.

"You called me into your office?" she asked. "You wanted something, I assume?"

"Right." I coughed to buy myself more time. What I was about to suggest was *insane*. I needed to be sure I pitched it perfectly. "It was fun hanging out at the bar last night, wasn't it?"

"Something like that. Sure."

"Do you think you could do more of that? For a few months, maybe?"

"Do what?"

"Hang out with me."

"Oh, God." She groaned. "Did Taylor sign us up for the same bar trivia team or something? I told her I'm not good under that kind of pressure—"

"Would you..." I cleared my throat. "...marry me?"

"I'm sorry? I think I misheard you." Simone slowly blinked. "Did you just ask me to—"

"Remember how I told you my family is so obsessed with tradition that they can't see the forest for the trees?" I shrugged. "This is what I was talking about. They want me married by my fortieth birthday or else I'm out as CEO."

"Wait. What?" Simone shook her head. "But you're good at this. That profile of you in *Forbes* said that you saved this place from bankruptcy a million times over."

"You read that profile of me in *Forbes*?" I smirked. "Ms. Didier, have you been cyberstalking me?"

"Don't let it go to your head. I was just doing research about my boss. It's not that weird."

"Whatever you say." I smirked even wider. "Still. If I don't get married soon, I'm out of the company. If I don't at least feign interest in carrying on the family line, they'll replace me with my brother." I winced. "Sean works in IT. He doesn't know how to run *LA Now* unless we're talking about running it into the ground."

"So, what? You want me to marry you just so you can keep your job?" She scoffed.

"It wouldn't be permanent. I think six months should

suffice. If you agree, I'd have us sign a contract. And I'd pay you for your time, of course. I was thinking something around half a million?"

"I have to go, actually. There's somewhere else I suddenly need to be." She abruptly stood up and turned away from me. "Thanks, but no thanks, Mr. O'Donnell."

"Wait! Just give me a chance to explain!"

But it was already too late. Simone was headed down the hall, her feet moving so fast it almost seemed like she was running for her life.

Look for The Wedding Hoax on Amazon!

Made in the USA
Monee, IL
01 February 2024

52726680R00173